SAVE ME

A CORRUPTED HEARTS NOVEL

TIFFANY
SNOW

 Montlake
Romance

Published by Montlake Romance, Seattle

www.apub.com

Amazon, the Amazon logo, and Montlake Romance are trademarks of Amazon.com, Inc., or its affiliates.

ISBN-13: 9781503900929
ISBN-10: 1503900924

Cover design by Eileen Carey

Printed in the United States of America

For Melody Guy. You make me a better author.

We were a strange love
Her and I
Too wild to last
Too rare to die.

—*Atticus*

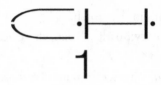

1

The bullet hit with enough force to make me stumble back. I glanced down at the spreading red stain on my chest, utterly dismayed.

"Take cover!"

A hail of bullets had me ducking behind the door of the shack. *So much for escaping through the front door.*

"They're advancing!" someone yelled, and a thrill of fear went through me.

I checked my ammo. Only one magazine left. *Damn it.* This had gone from bad to worse pretty darn quick. Time was running out. And it hurt to breathe.

There was a shout from outside. More bullets. But not directed at my team, holed up inside the musty shack. I heard a yell and dared to peek outside. The attackers were falling, cut down with deadly accuracy by someone I couldn't see.

It happened so fast, then there was silence. Tentatively, I stepped outside and lifted my mask.

"Your team sucks."

Clark was leaning casually against the wall, not a mark on him.

I tossed my paint gun down in exasperation. "It's not my fault. Yari had an asthma attack. Cindy tripped and sprained her ankle. Bint had a text from work and had to remote in from his phone."

"What about Georgie?"

I sighed. "He tried to bravely sacrifice himself so we could escape."

"And?"

"And they got him in the crotch."

Clark grimaced in sympathy. "Man, those accountants play hardball. No pun intended."

That got a snort of laughter from me. "Yeah, and now we owe them a pizza-and-beer Friday lunch."

"But you won."

"We cheated," I said, poking him in the chest. "You're not an official team member."

"Playing by the rules isn't one of my strengths."

No kidding.

"China," a voice interrupted, and I looked around to see Yari helping Cindy hobble from the shack. "We're calling it a day. You in for dinner?"

That's me. China Mackenzie followed by a last name fifteen letters long and mangled by all who tried to pronounce it. So everyone knew me as just China Mack, or simplified even further, China.

"Sorry. I have plans tonight."

Yari and Cindy both stared.

"What?"

"But we *always* go to Cracker Barrel after," Cindy said.

She was right. My small squad of fellow gamers and bad paintballers always stopped by the local Cracker Barrel for dinner after paintball. Not only did they serve pancakes for dinner, but they didn't bat an eye at our paint-splattered camo gear. But I'd promised Bonnie that I would be her guinea pig tonight for a new dish she was trying. Never ceasing in her attempts to graduate from culinary school, she was determined to master the technique of something called *sous vide*.

My friends knew how set in my ways I was, so my deviation from a tradition that wouldn't make a "normal" person bat an eye had them looking at me as though I'd just announced plans to give up my IT consultant career in favor of yodeling for a living.

I shrugged. "Trying to, you know, be more flexible."

"More?" Yari said. "I've never known you to be flexible at *all*."

"Hey," I protested, "you're one to talk." Yari's consternation at unannounced visitors was legendary. You had to make an appointment to stop by his apartment. Literally.

That shut them up and they all muttered their goodbyes, grumbling as they left about how they shouldn't have done this in the spring with the pollen count so high. After a few moments, Clark and I were alone.

"You didn't have to do that, you know," I said, turning to him. "We would've made it out."

He raised a dark eyebrow. "Yeah, but not without being covered in paint and bruises."

His dry assessment made me grimace, though he wasn't wrong. But I was distracted when he pushed his fingers through his hair. His very black, very soft hair that fell over his forehead just so. Eyes the color of the Blue Screen of Death studied me beneath winged eyebrows that arched just enough to make you wonder if his Supermanesque looks were at odds with a wicked streak.

In short, he was gorgeous and someone I—a five-foot-two, average girl who wore glasses and whose greatest hairstyling achievement was a ponytail—would never have dared to speak to just six months ago. But things change. Clark had gone from enemy, to employee, to friend, to . . . something else. I wasn't sure what to name that *something else*, though I'd broken up with Jackson Cooper—my erstwhile fiancé—to see if Clark and I could be that *something else* that would turn into *something more*.

But making the decision and then having the courage to act on it were two entirely different things. Guilt ate at me from breaking up with Jackson. It paralyzed me in my relationship with Clark, whose penetrating gaze saw too much, and I glanced away.

"I should say thank you," I said, trying to cover up the sudden awkwardness I felt. "It's the socially accepted protocol."

"Well, we must always do what's socially acceptable, mustn't we." His voice had an edge to it that I didn't understand, but when I looked back at him, he was gathering my gear. "Let's get out of here," he said. "Before the accountants recover."

Having a man to carry my stuff was still relatively new to me. I'd been mostly friendless and absolutely boyfriendless before Jackson and Clark had come along. Speeding through high school and graduating college, then MIT for grad school by the time you were nineteen, had a negative effect on developing social skills. While other people my age had been shopping for prom dresses, I'd been building my own computer.

I led the way out of the place, stopping to discard my paint gun and splattered armor. I'd ridden here with Cindy, so I followed Clark to his car. He stowed my gear in the trunk while I climbed into the passenger seat.

I was a car aficionado—something I'd picked up in an effort to have a subject in common with my older brothers, Bill and Oslo—so I could appreciate a nice set of wheels. Clark's didn't disappoint. A fully loaded Porsche Cayenne in steel gray, which suited him. Sleek, fast, and decadent. And yes, I was still talking about the car and not Clark. I think. Maybe.

"So you're at Bonnie's tonight?" he asked, distracting me from my mental comparison, which had morphed into "riding" euphemisms.

I adjusted my ponytail, a nervous tic I couldn't break. "Yeah," I answered absently, mentally switching gears to what cut of meat Bonnie would be massacring tonight. "Though I'll probably need to grab a Big Mac afterward."

Clark chuckled, a low, throaty sound that made butterflies swirl in my stomach. Reaching over, he slotted his fingers through mine.

His palm was rough and his fingers were calloused. I had the wayward fantasy of what those hands would feel like touching me . . .

"China."

"Yeah, what?" I asked, startled from my fantasy.

"I said your name twice," Clark said, shooting me a glance. "Where were you?"

My cheeks flooded with heat and I hurriedly looked away. "Just thinking about work."

"Damn. I was hoping you were thinking about sex."

My gaze shot back to him, and I nervously pushed my glasses up my nose. If I was bad at social skills, I was downright miserable at witty repartee, so a comeback was beyond me, not to mention any kind of sexual innuendo. Though judging by the glint in Clark's eyes, he wasn't expecting me to *say* something so much as *do* something.

The problem was, we hadn't *had* sex yet.

I mean, yes, we'd kissed and cuddled on the couch, and I'd been all hot and bothered, but something was holding me back. I just didn't know what it was. So I'd kept Clark at arm's length the past few weeks, at least, physically. We'd gone on dates and I'd made him watch the entire first season of *Star Trek: The Original Series*, which honestly hadn't done me any favors. The women's dresses were so skimpy and short on that show that he'd teased me mercilessly until I'd put on my Uhura dress to model for him.

As if sensing my discomfort, Clark's wicked grin faded. "What's going on, China?"

I pretended to misunderstand. "About what?"

"Every time I try to get close to you, you push me away."

I looked out the windshield so I didn't have to meet the accusation in his eyes.

"Why?" he asked. "I thought you decided to give us a shot."

"I am," I protested. "We've been spending a lot of time together."

"That's not what I mean and you know it." There was a bitterness in his voice that made me swallow hard.

The sun came out from behind the clouds, and I winced at the sudden glare. Clark let go of my hand and slid on his sunglasses. He didn't take my hand again.

We didn't speak for the rest of the ride home, which was incredibly uncomfortable, and that's coming from someone for whom a lack of conversation was usually a relief.

Clark grabbed my stuff from the trunk and walked me to my door. I unlocked it and stood hesitantly in the doorway.

"Do you want to come in?" I asked. "I don't have to be at Bonnie's for another hour."

"Are you going to talk to me?"

I blinked. "I'm talking to you right now."

He snatched his sunglasses off, and the look on his face instinctively made me take a step back.

Clark could turn on the nice-guy, take-me-home-to-meet-your-mama persona in a blink, but it was just that—a persona. In reality, the life he'd led had carved him into steel and stone, clothed in cynicism and suspicion. Those with any sense took one look at him and quickly looked away, unnerved by the innate menace that oozed from his pores. He was dangerous and he didn't bother hiding it.

Like now.

"Stop deliberately misunderstanding," he snapped. "You've put us on hold and refuse to tell me why." He paused, and when he spoke again, his voice was softer. "I took a chance on you. I haven't tried to have an actual relationship in years. You're keeping me at arm's length with no explanation."

"I-I don't know what to tell you," I stammered.

He slid his sunglasses back on. "If you figure it out, call me."

Before I could think of anything else to say, he was gone.

Bonnie's dinner was as bad as I thought it'd be, not that it mattered. I wasn't particularly hungry anyway. Which was a good thing, considering that her dream to become a chef was about as likely as her discovering dark matter. Grams would've followed that up with a *Bless her heart*. But I still showed up weekly, like clockwork, to try out her latest experiments.

"All right, what's wrong?" she finally asked. I'd been half listening to her rattle on about her latest troubles in her pastry class and how she'd repeatedly asked for additional assistance because the teacher was "smokin' hot."

"What do you mean?"

She rested her chin in her hand and her elbow on the table. "You've hardly spoken since you got here, and the only thing you've eaten is the polenta."

"It was really good," I said. I always tried to compliment at least one of the dishes she served me.

"Whatever." She dismissed my comment with a wave of her hand. "You're having boyfriend trouble. I can tell." She narrowed her eyes. "Is Clark being an ass?"

Clark wasn't her favorite person, not least because his and my relationship had started out so rocky. Then again, pretending to be interested in me as a cover—Clark's intro into the Life of China—hadn't endeared him to me either. (At least, not for a while.) But she'd given him her reluctant blessing when I told her I'd broken off my engagement with Jackson because I thought I might be falling for Clark.

"No, no," I hurriedly replied. "He's been great. It's just . . . We had an argument today. He says I'm holding back from him."

She frowned. "Holding back how? Like feelings and stuff? He knows you're not someone who can just spill her guts."

"No, I mean maybe that's part of it. But sex, too." I was embarrassed to be talking about sex with Bonnie, but who else was I going to talk to about it? Grams? She'd probably give me advice and tips and step-by-step how-tos, which would lead to mental images I'd never be able to unsee.

Bonnie leaned closer across the table, her eyes like saucers. "Oh my God, is he bad in bed?"

I rolled my eyes. "You have seen him, right?"

She shrugged. "It happens. All looks and no game."

"Well, I wouldn't know. Yet."

Bonnie's mouth gaped. "You mean you haven't slept together?"

I shook my head.

"Why not?" she asked.

Examining my feelings wasn't my strong suit, but I tried to put into words what went through my head when Clark began kissing me. "I think it's guilt," I said. "I still feel so much guilt for hurting Jackson. And with Clark, it almost feels like I'm cheating, because all I can think about is how I was selfish and hurt an amazing guy who loves me. What if I made the wrong decision? What if Clark and I don't work out, and I end up regretting breaking up with Jackson? Once we sleep together, there's really no going back."

With that last sentence, I felt relieved. Yes, that was what was at the heart of it all. Uncertainty. The looming possibility of regret. It was keeping me frozen in place.

Bonnie mulled this over for a minute, taking another sip of her wine and refilling both our glasses.

"I get it," she said at last. "Impulsive isn't your thing. You're always sure of outcomes when you make choices. But love isn't a sure thing. And you're never going to know if you don't try."

"But what if I'm wrong?" I couldn't get past that *what-if*.

"You can't go into a relationship with one eye on what you're going to do if it doesn't work out," she said. "You have to be all-in. And if it doesn't work out . . . Yeah, it totally sucks. But there's always a chance that it *will* work out."

It was common sense, but hearing words of wisdom and feeling it inside were two different things.

"And as for Jackson," she continued, "you have to trust in love at some point. Say you go all-in with Clark and it's great for six months, then it blows up in your face. You don't know what Jackson will be feeling, or what you'll be feeling. Relationships aren't black-and-white. If you and Jackson are meant to be, then it'll happen."

Trusting in ephemeral things like *fate* and *love* was as unthinkable to me as wearing my summer Endor *Star Wars* pajamas in the dead of winter.

"I mean, after what Clark did, I think he really cares about you, China."

What she was talking about was when he demanded that medics take blood from him to put in me as they were taking us both to the hospital via medevac helicopters. Injured himself, he couldn't really afford to lose the blood either, but since I was much smaller and had lost more, the medics had made a decision. Helped along quite a bit by Clark's threats of bodily harm to them if they didn't do as he said. This, I'd been told afterward by one of them as he'd come to check my status.

Of course, we'd both nearly died that night at the hands of his brother, once thought dead, but who'd been released from captivity by the Libyan regime. Tortured for years, he'd lost his grip on reality and had been consumed with the desire for revenge. Unluckily for me, one of those torture methods he'd learned had been nicking the carotid and letting someone almost bleed to death. You could do that to someone again and again, never quite letting them die each time.

Once had been enough for me. And Jackson had ended up saving both Clark and me that horrible night. I'd repaid him by breaking his heart.

Guilt clawed at me again. "Jackson's never going to forgive me," I said glumly.

"Do you need him to?"

I shrugged. "Selfishly, I'd feel better. But I know it's not going to happen."

"How about if you *forgive yourself*," she said, reaching across the table and taking my hand in a strong grip. "You did what you needed to do. Sometimes people get hurt. It doesn't mean the time you had together wasn't worth the pain in the end."

I raised an eyebrow. "Now you sound like that Garth Brooks song."

"I *love* that song!" Bonnie started singing as she rose and picked up our plates.

She was off-key and definitely tone-deaf, but it still made me smile.

I was still smiling when I drove back home, even humming the tune as I unlocked my door. Bonnie was right and she gave good advice. I was thinking too hard about all this, and maybe—just maybe—being too hard on myself.

It was dark inside and I felt a pang at the emptiness. Mia, my niece, still lived with me, but she was gone for the next two weeks on vacation with a friend who'd invited her to her family's beach house in Florida. School had gotten out early this year due to a lack of snow days to make up, and she'd left two days ago. I already missed her cheerful presence, even if she did have a propensity for not putting the dishes in the dishwasher correctly.

The glow of my fish tank beckoned, and I wandered over. The Doctor—by now his eleventh incarnation—swam lazily in the blue depths. I'd gotten him because supposedly it was relaxing to watch fish swim. In reality, it was just more stressful because invariably I forgot to feed him or I overfed him, resulting in too many floating goldfish I'd had to dispose of. The thought of what I'd do—or forget to do—if I had an actual kid made me shudder.

The hair suddenly prickled on the back of my neck, and I froze. It felt as though I wasn't the only person in the room. As if I was being watched.

I broke out in a cold sweat, remembering all too well when Clark's brother had ambushed me and my dad in the dead of night. Dad had lost his life protecting me, a scene that still played out in my nightmares.

A lamp flipped on, and I screamed, nearly jumping out of my skin as I spun around. My terror morphed into shock, then anger.

Kade Dennon was sitting in an armchair, one ankle resting on the opposite knee, and he looked utterly at ease, despite my scream.

"Do you always have to make an entrance?" I snapped, my pulse still racing. My knees were about to buckle, so I made it to the couch before collapsing. "You scared me to death."

"A hyperbole? Coming from Ms. Literal?"

I shot him a look. "An often-used hyperbole to express extreme terror. What do you want?" Because no way was he here just to say hello.

Kade Dennon was some kind of special assistant/BFF to President Blane Kirk. He'd taken over Vigilance—the government's very own supersecret spy software that tracked users online and in meatspace—after the assassination attempt on Kirk, and we'd struck up a tenuous working relationship. Whereas you knew instinctively that Clark could and probably had killed people, with Kade, you knew he had and didn't lose any sleep over it. Their looks were remarkably similar, though Kade was a good decade or so older than Clark.

Now he had the gall to look hurt. "Can't I just be checking up on you? My favorite five-foot hacker?"

"I'm five two." Even my driver's license said so.

A ghost of a smile. "Of course you are."

"I'm fine. Just peachy. So you can go now. Lock the door on your way out." Though obviously locks weren't a deterrent to unwanted government visitors.

His slight smile faded. "I'm here with information."

Kade's "information" had never done anything but put me in mortal danger, so it was with a heavy sense of trepidation that I asked, "What kind of information?"

"It's about Mark Danvers. Daddy Dearest."

The name was the equivalent of a stun gun. I felt like I had been suddenly submerged in subzero water. Everything inside me seized up—muscles, lungs, brain.

"My dad is dead," I said in a voice I barely recognized as my own. "He was shot to death in his own home."

"Yeah, I'm no psychiatrist, but you might want to see someone about that." Kade's feet dropped to the floor, and he leaned forward, bracing his elbows on his knees. "Whatever you want to call him— sperm donor, whatever."

"Why should I care?"

"Wanted to give you the heads-up," he said. Leaning back casually in the chair, he shrugged. "We think he's back in the country. Given his reputation and skills, you should keep an eye out."

"An eye out for what?" I asked.

Kade looked at me. "This guy has been around a long time in a profession with a life expectancy a decade less than most third-world countries. Ever wonder how he managed that?"

I shrugged. "Not really."

"The guy is a shadow. You won't see him when he's coming, and you won't have any warning. He's got the instincts and training of a professional killer. And he's extremely good at staying alive."

I frowned. "Why are you telling me this? Do you know something I don't?"

"That list is long," he quipped, "but in this instance, I know something very important that you don't."

I waited, barely breathing.

"Such as . . . Mark Danvers is the man who murdered your mother."

Kade had explained what he knew—that Danvers and my mom hadn't been in touch after they'd met in China. That he had no knowledge that she'd gotten pregnant with me. And although my mom had worked as a sleeper agent for the CIA for years, for some unknown reason, the agency had decided to terminate her a few years later.

"Why would they do that?" I asked. "The CIA isn't some third-world mafia you can't ever leave. She was a sleeper agent."

"I don't know," Kade replied. "What I do know is they instructed Danvers to do the job, and he reported it as complete after the car accident."

The car accident that hadn't been a car accident.

Now I stared up at the ceiling of my bedroom, blankets tucked up precisely just so under my arms. I'd managed to choke down my two Fig Newtons before bed tonight, even though I didn't really want them. Routine was comforting. Usually. Not tonight though.

Unable to sleep, I dug in my bedside drawer for the letter Grams had given to me. A letter my mom had written just before she died.

My dearest China,

I know this must come as a shock to you, after all this time. The first thing I want you to know is that your dad—the man you know as your father and who raised you—is a good, good man. He loved me far more than I deserved. I was lucky indeed to have met him, and I didn't regret a day we spent together, or the two wonderful boys we had.

I didn't—until I met Mark.

He was everything I'd ever dreamed of. Dashing and charming. Exciting and dangerous. We instantly made a connection. The job we were doing was dangerous, which probably contributed to the intensity of our feelings. It was then that I regretted choosing security over a dream.

You were the product of our love, Mark's and mine. I would have done almost anything to be with him—anything except leave your brothers without a mother, and break your dad's heart.

I told no one but Grams what had happened, though of course your dad figured things out. He was never a stupid man. He should have divorced me, but God love his soul, he loved me too much. I wish I could have loved him as much as he loved me.

I think that there may be people who would like to use you for their own ends, my dear. Mark had many enemies within the CIA and other agencies. I've been worried, lately, that I may have been discovered here, in the backwoods country of Nebraska. Which is why I'm writing you this letter. Just in case I'm not around to tell you all of this. I hope I am, but the future is never guaranteed. I hope I've hidden you and your true parentage well enough.

Please take care, dear China, and know that while your biology may have been a falsehood, the love of those closest to you has always been true.

All my love,

Mom

My mother had been murdered. It hadn't been my fault she'd died in that car wreck.

The idea was difficult to wrap my head around. I'd harbored guilt for being the only survivor that night all my life. My mother had been everything good in my world. And in a horrifying instant, my life had changed forever.

And to think the man she'd been so madly in love with—my biological father—had killed her . . . it was too much to process.

Love. Bonnie said I should trust in love. My mother had loved Mark, and he'd betrayed her. I'd loved her more than anything, and she'd died. Jackson said he loved me, but he couldn't forgive me for ending us, which I thought was something you did when you loved someone.

Love opened you up to being hurt. It was akin to not only someone pointing a loaded gun at you, but handing it to them, too. You just had no idea how long you'd have until they pulled the trigger.

Clark and I had something, there was no denying that. I liked him and cared about him. But there was a thick wall between us that had *Jackson* written all over it.

I glanced at my phone for the fiftieth time in the past thirty minutes. I hadn't heard from Clark all evening. He usually texted to at least say good night, no matter where he was, and he'd been in a few different time zones the past several weeks. But tonight . . . nothing.

It made me ache inside. The wall said *Jackson*, but the hurt inside my chest was all Clark.

I'd been told I was more like a guy than a girl, which sounded rather insulting, but was more a reflection on how I could turn off one side of my brain and completely focus on work. An ability I put to use the next morning. Although Sunday was technically laundry and admin day, I spent a few hours working on a consulting gig I had writing a mobile app. Maybe it was because that meant I didn't have to think about anything other than the code on the screen.

The growling in my stomach come late afternoon made me realize I'd forgotten to eat lunch. A glance in the fridge showed only a box of leftover Thai, various condiments, Red Bull, and ingredients for Mia's salads that were slowly decomposing.

My one indulgence to "spontaneity" was going through the drive-through of Freddy's, a fast-food burger joint that had the best french fries on the planet. Thinking of it gave me a pang, as Jackson had loved Freddy's, too. Then I had an idea.

Freddy's wasn't just up the block, and by the time I went through the drive-through, put everything inside a cooler (I hated when my car wafted with the odor of grease), then drove to Jackson's neighborhood, twilight was nearing.

I still had the key code to open the imposing gates to Jackson's upscale neighborhood. Well, *upscale* was putting it lightly when faced with multimillion-dollar estates with things like personal tennis courts, heated pools, and guesthouses.

As I drove the winding road that meandered through the neighborhood, I started to rethink this oh-so-great idea. Was I just going to show up at Jackson's house, after not seeing or speaking to him for more than two months, with a bag of Freddy's and pretend we were buddies?

I approached Jackson's driveway . . . then kept going. I'd loop around the neighborhood one more time and rethink this plan.

That looping "one more time" became six more times, then seven, as I agonized over what to do. By the time I'd decided to just forget it—because by now I was sure the food was cold, despite being in a cooler—I was on loop ten. I was just passing Jackson's house for the last time when someone stepped into the street in front of my car.

I slammed on my brakes, my wheels screeching to a stop a mere foot from him. Headlights cut through the gathering shadows to the figure standing in front of me.

Jackson.

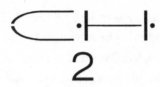

2

Time stood still for a moment, which was silly. Time can't stop. But my breathing did, before my lungs reminded me that they required oxygen.

Jackson walked toward my side of the car and bent down to the open window.

"You going to drive around the neighborhood all night? My security men tend to frown on that. They like to throw around words like *stalker* and *restraining order* when a woman drives by my house a dozen times in a row."

I found my tongue, which could still form words, I was glad to know. "It was ten. Not twelve."

He shrugged. "My mistake." A pause. "Did you want to come in?"

Seeing his face brought back a lot of bittersweet memories. A breeze drifted through the open window, carrying the scent of his cologne, which sent a sharp stab of something close to regret through me.

"If you want me to," I said.

He studied me for a moment, as though considering, then gave a brisk nod. "Come in."

Walking into Jackson's house was both familiar and strange. As always, he was dressed for business casual in slacks and a dark polo shirt, even though it was the weekend. His hair was brown with burnished-gold highlights, and it had been cut differently. It suited him, making his jaw seem more angular and setting off his eyes. He'd always dismissed his eye color as "just brown," but there were too many gold flecks in them to be merely "brown."

He took the cooler I was toting. "What's this?" he asked.

"I was hungry and thought you might be, too," I said, watching as he bent to open it. The familiar smell of grease and salt hit me.

"Freddy's," he said, his lips curving in a small smile, which quickly faded. He stood. "Sorry. I've already eaten."

"Oh. Yeah, right. I mean, of course you have." I pushed my glasses up my nose and shifted my weight from one sneakered foot to the other.

"Did you want to talk? Or did you just come by to say hi?"

Did I? At the moment, the coolness in his gaze and voice was making me regret this stupid idea to come here.

"I had a visitor last night," I said, not even realizing before I started that I was going to tell him. "Kade Dennon. He had information about my"—The words *my father* stuck in my throat—"Danvers."

Jackson frowned. "He'd better not be sending you on another mission. Danvers is dangerous."

A rhetorical statement. Danvers was dangerous and Jackson should know. Danvers had been the one who'd literally held a gun to Jackson's head six years ago, on an operation that had deliberately sacrificed US soldiers as decoys.

"No, not a mission. He wanted to tell me that Danvers . . . killed my mom." Saying the words aloud broke something inside me, and my vision blurred.

Jackson wrapped his arms around me, enveloping me in his embrace. Any further words were impossible. My throat was too full for any speech, and tears wet my cheeks and Jackson's shirt.

He led me farther into the house until we'd reached his study. We sat on a leather sofa I'd never particularly liked because if I scooted so my back was resting against the cushions, my feet couldn't touch the ground. It made me feel like a toddler, but I didn't protest.

"What happened?"

I related the conversation between Kade and me between sniffles. Jackson handed me a box of tissues, and I noisily blew my nose. My glasses had dried wet spots on them now, so I scrubbed them with my T-shirt while I talked.

"And he didn't say why he was telling you this?" Jackson asked.

I shook my head.

"I don't like it."

"I'd rather know the truth," I said. "If he really did kill my mom . . ." The thought trailed away, but a whisper inside my head that was rooted in anger wanted vengeance.

Jackson glanced off into space for a moment. He was frowning, but what he said next was unexpected. "So why are you here, China?" His gaze swung back to mine. The softness that had been there earlier was gone. He wore what I called his "game face," a blank expression designed to give nothing away.

"I-I guess I just wanted to . . . talk to you. See you." I shrugged and pushed my glasses up my nose. "You're my friend."

"You can't have it both ways," he said stiffly. "You can't break off our engagement, then go back to the Friend Zone. It doesn't work like that."

"I have no idea how it works," I said helplessly. "I missed you."

A shadow of pain crossed his face and was gone. The guilt that had been a ball of lead inside my stomach expanded. This had been a bad idea.

"I didn't mean t-to do something wrong," I stammered, trying to explain. "I don't have many friends, and you're important to me." My throat threatened to close up, but I kept going. "I don't know what to do so that I don't lose you completely."

Jackson abruptly stood, leaving me feeling even more like a kid playing a grown-up's game on the too-big couch. He paced, shoving a hand through his hair.

"I don't know if I'm capable of giving you what you want," he said at last. "I can't do this halfway bullshit. Pretending I don't love you so that I can watch you with Clark and still be your friend? I can't do that. I shouldn't *have* to do that." His voice was full of frustration and bitterness. He stopped pacing and faced me. "I think you should go."

Tears of heartbreak spilled onto my cheeks as I struggled from the depths of the couch.

"I'm s-s-sorry," I managed to stammer out, then hurried for the front door, hoping I could make it to my car before I broke down completely. Jackson didn't try to stop me.

Sheets of rain greeted me when I tore open the front door. Of course, because fate loved me like that. I ran outside into the storm. Sobs were stuck in my chest, and I wanted to escape with what little dignity I had left.

The sobs refused to be held back as I ran, blurring my vision. The rain pelted me, soaking through my clothes in an instant. I barely spared a thought for my leather seats as I yanked open my car door and got behind the wheel. I didn't start the car. I just sat there in the driver's seat of my badass muscle car and bawled like a baby.

I didn't know what to do. Jackson and I had been through so much together. I thought if I gave him space, I'd eventually earn his forgiveness. Obviously, I'd been wrong.

I'd underestimated how much it would hurt.

The only way I could have Jackson in my life was to get back together with him, and I couldn't do that. Though being rejected by him and denied even a platonic relationship felt like being ripped from the inside out. It was selfish of me, I supposed.

But I had made this choice, and I had to live with the consequences. I had to shut it down, close it off. That was the only way I could deal with it. By *not* dealing with it.

I drove home in a daze, on autopilot. How had I gone from two awesome men wanting me, to neither of them now speaking to me? I'd bungled everything and I had no idea how to fix it.

My grandma called on Sunday while I was putting away my laundry. Mia had rearranged my closet a few months ago by color instead of fandom, and I decided tonight would be a good time to fix it.

I toggled my Bluetooth headset. "Hi, Grams."

"China Girl!" she exclaimed. "You aren't gonna believe what happened to me the other day."

My Grams lived in the most eccentric retirement community I'd ever heard of down in Florida. They had an underground poker ring that had been repeatedly broken up by the cops. They had Viagra Wednesdays, which had led to the untimely—and embarrassingly compromising— death of one of Grams's "gentlemen callers," as she liked to put it. That had led to her earning a reputation of being so good in bed that you took your life in your hands. Most would view that as a deterrent, but Grams had them lining out the door. And just a couple of months ago, she'd turned down a marriage proposal.

"I dunno," I said. "I don't know if there's anything you can come up with anymore that'll shock me." I moved three of my *Supernatural* fandom shirts to the right, and six *Doctor Who* T-shirts to the left.

"I was on the television!"

That gave me pause. "It didn't involve the police or a judge, did it?" I wouldn't be a bit surprised.

"Of course not, though I wouldn't mind being on that Judge Judy's show. I like her. She and I could be bosom friends. But I'd have to sue somebody, and I've yet to run across someone I'd need to sue."

"Give it time, Grams."

"There was a *tornado*, honey. I was out driving and I saw it, so I just did what those men on the television do, and followed it."

My jaw gaped. "You *followed* it?" I screeched. "Are you crazy?"

"Ow, honey, stop yelling in my ear. And no, I'm not crazy. I'd never seen a tornado before, and there it was, ripping up a field. It got a couple houses, too, but luckily no one was hurt. But the news crew came, and I got to be on TV! Isn't that exciting?"

"No! No, it's not. Promise me you'll never do that again." Only my Grams would turn into a septuagenarian storm chaser.

She grumbled, but then promised. "Now what about you?" she asked. "What are you up to tonight?"

"I'm rearranging my closet." *Sherlock* fandom shirts went before *Supernatural,* and *X-Files* were all the way at the end of the rack.

Silence. I moved a few more shirts.

"Oh no. What's happened?"

"Why do you think something happened?"

"I know you, and when you're upset, you go on one of your . . . obsessive arranging sprees."

"That's not true," I protested. Then I thought about it. I'd rearranged her refrigerator when Jackson had gotten arrested, throwing away everything past its expiration date. I'd ordered all the spices in my kitchen cabinet by cuisine of origin when they'd canceled *Firefly*. And after watching *Iron Man 3*, I'd gone through the laborious process of relabeling all my Tupperware containers with my label maker to indicate allowed substances. "Okay, so maybe it is true."

"So what happened? You and Clark have a fight?"

Grams had supported my decision to break off the engagement with Jackson. She'd said if I was having doubts, then it was best to take a step back rather than do something I'd regret.

"Yeah, kind of."

"About what?"

"Jackson. I feel like I can't move on when I've hurt him so badly. Then I thought I'd go by and try to see him, just be normal friends, and he practically kicked me out."

"Well, honey, you did break off the engagement." Her gentle reminder just made me feel worse.

"How do I get over the guilt? I don't want to feel this way anymore."

"That just takes time. People hurt each other. It's the nature of life. You could just as easily have been the one hurt instead of him."

"I *am* hurting. I still want to keep our friendship."

She sighed. "That may not be possible. You'll just have to accept it and move on."

Accept it. Just like I'd had to accept the loss of my mom. The gaping hole she'd left had never been filled until Jackson came along. I'd let him into that space, and now he was gone.

We talked a bit more after that, but it was mostly her keeping the conversation going. I was too lost in my thoughts. Finally, we said goodbye. It occurred to me to tell her about what Dennon had said Danvers had done, but it was her daughter we were talking about. She'd buried and mourned her years ago. I didn't want to bring up such a painful topic. I was having a hard enough time dealing with it.

I spent the rest of the evening trying not to think as I finished my closet. Too much had happened too quickly. Six months ago, my life was scheduled and ordered and predictable. I had pizza every Monday night and never missed my Sunday pedicures. Jackson had been my boss, then my boyfriend. Now he was no longer there, but Clark didn't fit so easily into the hole left in my life, and I wasn't sure I wanted him to. It would be too painful when the hole became vacant again.

Jackson and I were similar creatures. Being together was easy. Clark was harder. He hadn't been bullied growing up because he was smarter than all the other kids. He could carry on a normal conversation without having to resort to default weather talk. He knew when someone was being sarcastic, or was angry, or sad. He didn't need someone to decipher normal human interactions.

Clark was a friend who cared about me as much as I did about him. He had a job that was dangerous and didn't lend itself to settling down. What he wanted from me was to be more than friends, but less than the whole love, marriage, baby carriage thing. There was a phrase for that. I'd heard Mia use it before.

Friends with Benefits.

Yes, that's what it was. I was relieved to have remembered the term. That sounded like just the thing for Clark and me. No long-term commitment or talk of love. Just enjoying each other's company. And no-expectations-that-I-couldn't-meet sex. I wouldn't hurt him the way I had Jackson so long as we both knew up front what the expectations were, or lack thereof. No guilt. No fear of failing. I knew Clark wanted to have sex with me. He'd made that perfectly clear. And now that I'd sorted through what I was able and wanted to give, I was ready, too.

I glanced at my cell. Still nothing from him. I guess he had said for me to call him, right?

Taking a deep breath, I dialed and waited. When he answered, I blurted out the first thing on my mind.

"Can you come over?"

I was out of breath, waiting by the door. As soon as we'd hung up, I sprang into action. Running upstairs to Mia's bedroom, I tore through her closet for something sexier than the current faded blue jeans and my *GOT GOT?* T-shirt. She'd wanted to wear an outfit I'd vetoed last week . . . white jeans and . . . there it was.

Shedding my clothes, including my Victoria's Secret blush-pink demi bra, I pulled on her jeans and the black shirt. Though it wasn't much of a shirt. It was a halter that tied around my neck and around my waist, leaving my back bare. Its neckline plunged nearly to my waist. Yanking out my ponytail, I ran a brush through my hair. Mia said I had great hair. Dark-chestnut, it was thick and wavy, and I had so much of it that I usually just wore a ponytail.

"If you wear a ponytail with that outfit, I'll never do smoky eyes on you again!" I could almost hear Mia berating me inside my head.

There was nothing I could do about the glasses, and I was hopeless with makeup. I'd add heels, but chances were likely I'd topple over in them, and wouldn't that just spoil the mood?

I had a couple of candles I'd bought for emergencies—you never knew when the power might go out—so I lit them and dimmed the lights. Out of breath, I glanced around my duplex. It was tidy. It was always tidy. The candles looked nice. What was I missing . . . ? Music. Of course. Seduction included candles, wine, and music. There was wine in the fridge, so just one last box to check.

"Alexa," I said, activating my Amazon device, "play seductive music."

The strains of "Let's Get It On" by Marvin Gaye filled the room. Oh, geez. A little too obvious.

"Alexa. Play romantic music."

Céline Dion, "My Heart Will Go On." The Titanic? Death and disaster? Um, no.

"Alexa. Play music for sexual relations."

"Push it. Push it good. P-push it real good!"

Gah! From bad to worse.

There was a knock at the door.

"Alexa. Stop music." Better silence than her playlist. I was so going to deduct a star from my review.

I took a deep breath. I was nervous. My bare toes clutched at the carpet, then I made myself calmly walk to the door. I pushed my fingers through my hair, fluffing it one last time, then opened the door.

I had to catch my breath. Clark did that to me, and tonight was no exception.

Wearing jeans that clung to his molded thighs and a black T-shirt stretched to cover his wide shoulders, he looked like every woman's fantasy of a bad boy, complete with a motorcycle parked in my driveway.

And he was looking at me as though he wanted to rip my clothes off and devour me . . . in the best possible way. A shiver went through me.

"Come in." I stepped back. His blue-eyed gaze remained fastened to mine as he moved forward, pausing for just a moment when our bodies were closest, then past me into the room. I got a good whiff of him—a trace of spicy cologne and the scent of his skin that was pure Clark.

Oh boy.

"Um, I have wine," I said, nervously pushing my hands into the back pockets of my jeans.

Clark's gaze dropped to my chest. "Nice top."

I glanced down. My position was thrusting my breasts forward, my nipples poking at the fabric. Instinctively, I wanted to shift and hunch my shoulders, but considering Clark's gaze had grown even more intense, I quelled the impulse.

He wanted me. He *really* wanted me. That was how a man looked at a woman when all he had was sex on the brain. I didn't feel awkward and geeky anymore. I felt like one of those models who could strut down a runway clad only in lingerie and know she was sexy. *I*, China Mack, was sexy. The look in Clark's eyes told me so.

The slow burn in the pit of my belly was like drinking a shot of whiskey, melting away the nerves and turning my jitters into anticipation.

I smiled and walked into the kitchen, brushing my fingers against his arm as I passed by him. He followed and watched as I got two wineglasses and the bottle of wine from the fridge. It was already uncorked, so I poured and handed a glass to him.

"Cheers," I said, clinking my glass against his. We both took a drink. The cold liquid slid across my tongue, and I saw Clark watching my throat move as I swallowed.

Turning, he set his glass on the counter and approached me. Silently, he took the glass from my hand and set it aside, too.

"What are—"

My words were cut off as he kissed me.

This wasn't one of those start-slow-and-build-up kind of kisses. His hands were buried in my hair as he held my head, his mouth searing mine. His tongue was hot and urgent, sliding against mine. My back was against the wall, and my arms were around his neck, holding on for the ride.

Clark's hands slid down to my butt, then the backs of my thighs. He lifted me up and my legs wrapped around his waist, all while he was still kissing me. He pressed me against the wall, and I felt the hard length of him even through two layers of denim.

Hooboy.

All thoughts fled against the onslaught of his passion, and I was swept away. His hand slid inside my neckline to cup my breast, and I moaned into his mouth. His hips ground against mine, and suddenly I wanted our clothes gone.

As if he'd read my mind, my feet were back on the floor, and he was pulling my top up over my head. I managed to get his shirt off before he attacked my jeans and shoved them down my hips. I kicked them aside as he lifted me in his arms again. This time, the jeans covering his erection provided a pleasant friction against my panties.

I pressed my breasts to his chest, kissing his neck and jaw. The slight stubble rasped against my skin. I found the pulse under his jaw and sucked lightly. Each step he took rubbed his cock between my legs, an unbearably pleasurable frustration.

He deposited me on the couch.

"Why not upstairs?" I asked as he unbuckled his jeans.

"Can't make it that far."

When he pushed his jeans down over his hips and his cock sprang free, I fervently agreed. He wasn't wearing anything under his jeans, which gave me pause for a moment as I pondered the hygienic implications of that, but then he was on his knees and tugging my panties down my legs, so I decided I'd discuss it with him later.

He pushed my thighs apart and looked at me, and I don't mean my eyes. He stared until I began wondering if something was wrong. Last time I'd checked, all had been A-Okay Down There.

"You're so beautiful," he murmured.

Having Clark utter such a compliment about the most private part of my body was one of the most amazing things that had ever happened to me. Genitalia was, by and large, not always particularly attractive. A man's penis could look rather comical if you thought about it too hard, especially when it wasn't erect. And women . . . Well, I'd never given that part of my body much thought as to how it stacked up to other women.

But Clark was staring as if he were Moses and I was the Promised Land, though a Bible reference seemed a bit blasphemous, given the current situation.

My fingers lifted his chin so his eyes met mine. "Thank you," I said with a small smile. "So are you."

He turned, brushing my fingers with a kiss, then lowered his head and pushed me back against the couch.

His tongue touched gently at first, just a swipe against me. It still took my breath away. His tongue probed deeper into my folds, and my eyes slammed shut. So hot and soft . . . oh dear Lord . . .

I'd already been half-primed, and it didn't take long before I was moaning and teetering on the edge, but he pulled back, teasing me. I made a sound of protest and opened my eyes.

The heat in his gaze as he watched my face could've melted a slab of ice. I couldn't look away, watching as he lowered his head again.

This time he slid a finger inside, gently pumping as he licked my swollen clit. The dual sensations were overwhelming, the sight of his dark head between my thighs so erotic, I wanted to brand the image into my mind.

Clark was making noises, moaning as he licked and sucked me. His finger moved faster and I felt my orgasm build. My eyes slid closed and my breath caught. I exploded in a wave of pleasure, cresting, and wrenching a cry from my throat.

I was too sensitive and tried to squirm away. But Clark's hands held my hips in position. His tongue gentled, but was unrelenting, coaxing my body for more.

"I can't," I breathed, gasping for air. Stars were still exploding in my vision.

"Shh," he murmured against me. "Yes, you can."

His gentle stroke turned firmer, and faster. Then he put his lips around the bit of flesh and sucked.

I screamed as another wave of pleasure ripped through me, more intense than before. My nails dug into his shoulders as my body shook under the onslaught of ecstasy. I'd never in my life had such an intense orgasm, and belatedly, I felt a wet spot on the couch.

Clark sat back on his haunches, a smug look of satisfaction on his face.

"Oh my God, did I do that?" I asked, completely embarrassed. I'd never made a wet spot before. Usually, the guy did that.

"Yep," Clark said with a shit-eating grin. "I hit the jackpot."

I had no idea what he was talking about, but he didn't look grossed out and was still sporting a raging hard-on, so I decided I'd Google it later. And dry-clean the couch cushion.

He rose and scooped me up again, this time like a damsel in distress. He headed for the stairs.

"I thought you couldn't make it that far?" I asked.

"I couldn't. Had to taste you. But now I want a bed. Rug burn sucks."

We reached my bedroom and he flipped on the light. He tossed me onto the bed crosswise. I was about to turn around the right way when he grasped my knees and spread them apart. He knelt on the bed between my legs. Reaching between us, he guided himself into me.

I didn't know why, but that was always one part of lovemaking that I especially enjoyed. Maybe it was the visual act of being taken by your man, the feeling of possession. It probably hearkened back to caveman days, but I liked it. A lot.

We both groaned as he slid inside me, stretching and filling me.

"Damn," he groaned, his eyes squeezing shut. "You are so wet and tight."

Both good things, according to *Cosmo*.

He kissed me, and I could taste myself on his tongue. Wrapping an arm around my waist, he pumped his hips, sliding out and back inside me. It felt exquisite. And I couldn't stop kissing him. The feel of our bodies, naked and joined, felt so . . . *right*.

Breaking off the kiss, he turned us so he was on his back, his legs stretched out and me crouched on my knees above him.

"Fuck me, China."

The words sent a thrill through me, and he didn't have to tell me twice. I braced my hands on his chest, letting my legs do the work as I rose and fell on him. It was my turn to watch him, and he was beautiful. His forehead was slightly damp with sweat, his eyes the deepest blue I'd ever seen. And he was looking at me as if the sun, moon, and stars were in my face.

I was so sensitive, it was a sweet ache. I went slow, savoring the feel of him and memorizing the moment. He reached up, stilling me, and slid his hands into my hair, pulling my face down to his.

The kiss was sweet and deep, a lover's kiss in the most intimate way, his body deep inside mine.

He turned me onto my back and lifted my legs to rest my ankles on his shoulders. He pushed inside me, slowly, going so deep that it made me gasp. There was a twinge of pain, and I winced.

"I'll take it slow," he said, his voice a rasp of sound.

We gazed at each other, him pressing my legs closer to my chest as he withdrew and pushed inside again. It was incredibly erotic and sexy, him looking at me as he took me. And a huge turn-on. Soon, it didn't hurt anymore, and he sped up, his eyes sliding shut.

"You feel so fucking good, baby. So good."

Abruptly, he switched positions again, putting my legs down so they could wrap around his hips. He moved fast, fucking me hard, and I knew why the missionary position was a standby favorite. I felt another orgasm building. Then he stopped.

I brushed his hair back from his face and kissed him, my breasts crushed against his chest. He surrounded me and filled me. I was his.

He broke the kiss off and moved fast and hard inside me. He was breathing hard, his back slick with sweat, and I felt the pulse of my orgasm. Clark paused, buried deep within me, as I cried out. Tears leaked from the corners of my eyes at the pure, sweet bliss.

When the waves had subsided, he moved again, clutching me to him. I could hear the sound of our bodies coming together, then he gasped, holding his breath, thrust into me once, twice more. His body shook with the force of his orgasm, his deep cry echoing in my ear.

He collapsed on top of me, sliding slightly to the right so he wouldn't crush me. Sweat mingled on our skin. My heart was racing and I still felt aftershocks clutching at his cock inside me. I held him close, and both his arms were wrapped around me.

He kissed me and I ran my fingers through his hair. Lifting his head slightly, he looked at me. His eyes were the softest I'd ever seen them, devoid of the usual cynical distance he kept as a shield between him and everyone else. His lips were red and slightly swollen, curving into a hint of a smile. He brushed my hair back from my face and lightly pressed his lips to mine, lingering for a moment.

He flopped onto his back, hauling me with him against his side with one arm and tucking pillows under his head with the other. I rested my head on his shoulder. His eyes were closed and his fingers trailed a slow pattern down and up my back.

"Passing out already?" I teased.

"Just enjoying the afterglow, baby." His lips shifted in a smile, and his eyes cracked open to look at me. "Because that was amazing. You are absolutely amazing."

My cheeks heated with pleasure, and I smiled back. "You weren't so bad yourself."

We lay there in bed for several peaceful minutes. I listened to his heartbeat, felt the rise and fall of his chest.

"You have a really slow pulse," I commented after a while. It couldn't be more than forty-four beats per minute or so.

"I know. Any slower and I'd be dead."

His quip made me laugh. "I, for one, can attest that you are very much alive."

"I run a lot," he said. "Keeps the heart in shape. You should exercise, too. Sitting in front of a computer all day isn't good for you."

"I exercise my mind," I retorted.

"Your mind is an organ, not a muscle."

"It still needs to be worked. Studies have shown that playing brain-training games keeps neural connections in the brain strong, potentially helping to prevent cognitive diseases like dementia and Alzheimer's." I shuddered. Those diseases were my worst nightmares.

Clark was quiet, then said, "My mom died of Alzheimer's."

I twisted a little so I could see his face. He was staring off into the distance. Clark had never talked about his family with me. I hadn't even known he'd had a brother until a few weeks ago.

"About ten years ago," he said. "The disease . . . It's awful. It's one thing to know what it is and what it does, but something else entirely to see it happen to someone you love."

The pain in his voice made my chest hurt. I wrapped my arm tighter across his chest and listened.

"I think the worst times were when she'd have these flashes of knowing what was happening to her. Those were terrible. Losing your mind bit by bit is tolerable so long as you don't know it."

"I'm so sorry," I said. "I can't imagine."

"She was a good mom," he continued. His fingers still mindlessly traced the skin of my back. "My dad died of a heart attack when I was little. She raised us on her own, worked two jobs. We joined the military to pay for school. I was just glad she passed before that last mission."

He meant the one where his brother had died, except he hadn't really died, but had been captured.

"Of course, by then, she didn't remember she even had sons. I was just the 'sweet boy' who'd come see her and bring her favorite dough-nut. We'd sit outside by the lake. It was a good facility. The best money could buy."

Something clicked inside my head. "Is that why you did contract work?" I asked, putting the pieces together. "Because of the money?" Killing people for a living—government sanctioned or not—paid very well.

Clark looked down at me. "You should see some of those places. Disgusting and horrifying don't begin to cover it. The smell, the people who work there . . . Unless you have money, they don't give a shit. I put her in a place I could afford at first. Then one day I came by—"

His voice broke and he stopped. His throat moved as he swal-lowed, then he continued. "She was sitting in her own filth. No one had checked on her for hours. I knew then I had to do something. No way was I going to let my mother be treated like that." His voice vibrated with anger. "Even at the expensive place I put her, I still had to bribe people to take special care of her. But at least I had the money to do it."

"At a personal cost," I said softly.

He shrugged. "It was worth it."

"So why didn't you stop after her death?"

He looked at me again, the despair in his eyes physically painful to see.

"Because I was good at it. And most of the time, I was one of the good guys. I could do the things no one ever wants to admit we do. So I stayed. I went freelance after that last mission, but I dealt more in information then." His chest rose and fell on a long sigh.

We were quiet then as I processed what he'd just said. Clark had been through so much loss, and painful losses at that. He'd lost his brother in more ways than one, and his betrayal had to have cut deep. And his mother . . . I couldn't imagine my mom not knowing who I was and how painful that would be.

"I've never told anyone about her," he said after a while.

I rolled over so I was lying on his stomach, chest to chest, and looked in his eyes.

"Thank you for telling me." I pressed my lips to his breastbone for a long moment. I could feel the thump of his heartbeat echoing mine. Or perhaps it was the other way around. I rested my head on his chest with a sigh.

His fingers tangled in my hair, gently pulling through the long strands. It was soothing. An intimate gesture between lovers. I closed my eyes and breathed in the scent of him. Of us. For the moment, I was at peace.

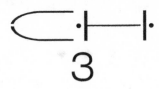

3

I woke up to a bounce on the bed and drops of water hitting my face and arms.

My eyes flew open.

Clark was on all fours, caging me. He was naked and smelled like soap. He shook his wet hair again, and droplets flew. His grin was a sight to behold, which was saying something, considering a naked Clark was pretty darn breathtaking. But his smile was open and made his eyes crinkle at the corners, the dimple on his cheek out in full force.

"Wake up, sleepyhead," he said.

I glanced at the clock and groaned. "It's barely five in the morning." And still dark outside. *Ugh.* "Please tell me you're not one of those annoyingly cheerful people in the morning."

"I am when I've had amazing sex with an incredible, gorgeous, clever, funny woman who is still naked." He pressed a quick kiss to my lips.

"Who is she? I'll kill her."

He laughed at my joke. Not something I was able to pull off on a regular basis.

"I have just enough time to take her to bed again before I have to go."

The words *I have to go* ricocheted inside my head, but then he was kissing me in earnest and placing my hand around his already rock-hard cock, so I thought I'd come back to the subject of where he was going afterward.

◆ ◆ ◆

That old wives' tale of men being especially sexually . . . enthusiastic . . . in the mornings was another adage that proved true. I was pleasantly sore and worn out when Clark was through with me.

But the sheets were dirty, and I needed a shower, and Clark was getting dressed. I sat up in bed, pulling the sheets up underneath my arms and reaching for my glasses on the bedside table.

"Where are you going?" I watched him pull on his boots and tie them.

"I have a client I'm meeting this morning. A new client."

"What kind of work are you doing for him?"

He finished putting on his shoes and turned to me, pulling me onto his lap, sheet and all.

"Don't worry. It's not dangerous."

"Your idea of dangerous and mine aren't the same thing," I grumbled.

His lips touched my forehead. "It's sweet of you to worry, babe, but I'll be fine. I'll be in touch later today."

After he left, I fell into my usual routine, adding washing and changing the sheets to my list. It was early, but no sense in not getting a jump on the day. And I had a satisfied smile on my face. This Friends with Benefits thing with Clark was what I needed, as were the multiple orgasms.

I was sitting at my desk, deep inside coding an online portal for a health clinic, when the doorbell rang. Rubbing my eyes under my glasses, I headed for the door. No one was there, but UPS had left a package for me.

Cool! It was probably the latest batch of T-shirts I'd ordered from RedBubble.com. Not that I needed any more. It was a guilty pleasure. When I wanted to procrastinate, I popped open a browser window and shopped for the latest T-shirts.

But it wasn't T-shirts. It was a box. A wooden box, about the size of a shoe box, with intricate carvings on the outside. It was unique and looked old, like an antique. A letter was in the package as well, and I opened it.

China,

We were going through the house, clearing out some things, and found this. Neither of us could open it, but we thought you might be able to.

Hope you're doing well.

—Bill

My brothers had decided to rent out the house once my dad died, but there was forty years of accumulated stuff that needed to be gone through first.

I sat down on the sofa with the box, resting it on my knees. It was heavy, but the wood was smooth. Tiny, nearly invisible cracks showed in different areas, and I realized with a thrill that this was a Chinese puzzle box.

I loved puzzles. The more complicated, the better, and this one looked to be a doozy. I grabbed a can of Red Bull from the fridge and went to work.

The boxes were made of tightly connected moving parts. The trick to opening them was to move the parts just the right amount and in the right sequence. Sometimes you'd move a piece only a fraction, then come back to it later and slide it the rest of the way.

It took me almost an hour, but I finally got the box open. A sequence of fourteen specific moves had opened the outer box, revealing another box. That one required twenty-one moves before opening.

I was almost afraid to look at the contents. This box had to have belonged to my mom. She'd been the one to put puzzles together with me. Dad had hated puzzles because he'd said they were boring.

Taking a deep breath, I peered inside, half expecting that it might be empty. But it wasn't. At the center of the box lay a single MiniDV cassette tape and a thin notebook about the size of my hand.

My hands shook as I took them out. There was a label on the tape with the word *China* written by hand. By my mom's hand. I could tell by the writing. I flipped through the notebook. Page after page was filled with her writing. It appeared at first glance to be a personal journal.

My mind was spinning in circles. A videotape and journal, from my mom, hidden inside a Chinese puzzle box. Had she intended to give it to me at some point, but hadn't had the chance? It was obvious she'd only meant it for me. No one else in our family could've opened the box.

I had to play it. But I needed a mini-camcorder. I'd had one, a few years ago, but wasn't sure where I'd put it. I scrambled upstairs and dug through my office closet. I had a place where I kept outdated tech equipment . . . and there it was. Bottom of the pile, covered in dust. I grabbed the cables that went with it and hurried back downstairs.

My heart was pounding and it wasn't just because I'd run. My fingers trembled as I struggled to hook up the cable to my television. I told myself if I'd stop hurrying, it would go faster, but I couldn't make myself slow down.

Finally, I had everything connected and turned on and was ready to press "Play."

The television screen flickered to life. I saw the inside of the barn at home, the scene warbling as the camera was placed and steadied. Late-afternoon sunlight filtered through the windows. Then my mom walked into the frame.

My breath came out in a rush. I'd been holding it.

She was prettier than I remembered, and smaller. When I was little, she'd seemed larger than life. Looking at her now, I could see where I'd inherited my small stature. She sat on a stool that had been dragged into the frame. Wearing jeans and a white blouse with her hair loose and long, she looked younger than her thirty-nine years.

Once she'd situated herself on the stool, she looked at the camera and smiled.

I paused it, staring at the screen. My knees shook and I sat heavily on the couch. I pressed "Play" again.

"Hi, sweetheart," my mom said. "I know that it's you watching. Only you could've opened that darn box. It took me a while, but I doubt you needed much time." She smiled again.

"Now you're probably wondering, why this video? I wanted to tell you something—tell *someone* the secret—in case I'm . . . not around anymore."

I winced, an ache blooming inside my chest.

"You may or may not remember me working at a little company called Fortress Securities, depending on how old you are when you get this. I worked there for a while, an undercover assignment."

I remembered. Mom had been away for six months. It had been right before her death. She'd only been back for a couple of months when the accident had happened. The farm had had a particularly bad crop season, and we'd needed the money. So Mom had gotten a job that paid really well, only it had been out east somewhere. I couldn't remember where.

"The CIA thought that a Chinese national—Liang Chen—was a spy. He was a programmer at the company. I was sent to get close to him and find out his mission.

"That was about six months ago, before the new year, and everyone was consumed with fears about the Millennium Bug. Y2K. The New York Stock Exchange had bid out the project to update their UNIX systems. Fortress got the bid two years ago. They'd been working on the software for almost a year by the time I got there and befriended Chen.

"It was only after the software had been delivered that I'd gained his trust enough for him to tell me what he'd done." Her voice was deadly serious. "Chen had been directed to write in a back door to the software. A back door that could give someone control over the market. Circuit-breaker rules put in place after the crash of 1987 would prevent a crash like that from happening again. But with this backdoor code, someone can disable or even rewrite those rules.

"This knowledge is dangerous. I'm afraid Chen might've had an attack of guilt and confessed that he told me. He's been acting weird in our interactions lately. And if he *did* tell them, they'll be coming after me."

She stopped talking, staring off into space for a moment, her face thoughtful, then she looked back at the camera. "If this tape still exists and you're watching it, that means the worst has happened. That I was right and that they hunted me down." Her eyes filled with pain. "I have so much more I want to tell you, explain to you. I can't hardly bear the thought that I won't."

Her voice was choked and she had to stop. A tear splashed her cheek, and she quickly swiped it away and forced a smile.

"But maybe I'm wrong and just being paranoid. Omaha is a long way from New York. I've hidden you and me well. If the worst does happen and you get this video, I wanted you to know that my death wasn't an accident, which is probably how they'll make it appear." She paused to clear her throat.

"I'm also leaving my journal. The one in which I kept the memories Mark and I made together. I hope you'll read it and perhaps understand. I hope one day you'll find a love that burns as hot and intense as ours did." Her face had softened when she spoke of him.

"I hope you know I love you," she continued. "You're the very best part of my life, and I'm so proud of you. No matter what you choose to do with your life, I know you'll be brilliant at it. Take time to be happy. We only get one chance at this. Make sure you can live with the choices you make."

There was a voice off camera. I thought I recognized my dad, calling her. She heard it, too, because she glanced away for a moment.

"That's your dad. I have to go. I love you, China. Forever and always."

She kissed her fingers and blew the kiss. Then she waited. We used to do this together, whenever she left. I blew a kiss at the screen, tears streaming down my face, and watched her mime catching it. Then she walked toward the camera, and the video ended.

The screen went dark as the tape kept playing. I was in shock. Part of my mind clinically analyzed the signs. Clammy hands, rapid pulse, nausea churning in my stomach, my breathing too rapid and shallow. Seeing and hearing my mom move and speak had been traumatic enough. Processing what she'd said compounded that by a factor of a thousand.

How could this be? It didn't make sense. Danvers was the one who'd murdered my mom, not some hit man hired by the Chinese. Kade had seemed very sure about it, and surely he'd know, given his position in the government stratosphere. Could Danvers have been a double agent? It seemed unlikely. Which meant perhaps he *hadn't* killed my mom.

With hands that shook slightly, I opened the journal and began reading.

A foolish idea, the diary began, *putting my thoughts on paper. Rule #1 of spy craft: write nothing down. But what's happened to me . . . I feel as though I must write it. Must keep record of the magic that's touched my life. Perhaps I feel that if I don't, it won't be real. It'll fade away as the memories grow dim with time. And I can't bear the thought of that.*

I remember the night I met him. We were in Hong Kong. I was waiting in a bar to meet my contact. I wore a blue cocktail dress. I was drinking tonic water with lime. A man stepped up next to me and I glanced over . . . and lost my breath.

He was . . . perfection. At least, my kind of perfection. Square jaw, deep-set blue eyes, strong brow. His smile was warm while also being slightly self-mocking. He embodied cocky confidence with an edge of abashment—a high school heart-throb quarterback who accepts his own popularity, though he doesn't quite understand it. He was also my contact.

I was filled with a sense of anticipation and inevitability. I no more had the power to turn away from what sparked between us than I could have forced the moon from the sky. I never wanted to be unfaithful. And after Mark, I never would be again. He was my savior and my doom.

I closed the journal, too overwhelmed to read more, and sat on the couch for a long time, thinking. I rewound the tape and watched it again. Then again, memorizing everything she said. I was still there when there was a knock on my door. Moving on autopilot, I got up to answer it.

Jackson.

As if I hadn't been through enough today.

I had buried my heartbreak somewhere deep inside, and patched it over with Clark. I could look at Jackson now without feeling the guilt and sense of loss. I couldn't handle the kind of rejection he'd dealt me last night, not again. Apathy was my armor.

"Why are you here?" I asked, echoing his question last night.

"I came . . . to apologize." He let out a long breath. "I wasn't prepared to see you last night, and I'm afraid I didn't react very well. I was hoping we could talk."

I thought about it for a long moment. Letting him in wouldn't be just literal, but figurative as well. He'd shut me out of his life, and I'd spent last night coping with how much that had hurt. I didn't know if I could handle another painful conversation. But shutting the door in his face wouldn't be very helpful to either of us.

Wordlessly, I stepped back and held open the door. He brushed past me and I closed the door behind us.

He stood awkwardly in the middle of the room. I saw his glance land on the dismembered puzzle box and study it, then he turned toward me.

"Last night, you made a gesture of friendship," he said. "And I threw it back in your face. I regret that. I hope you can forgive me. I was . . . hurting. And perhaps I wanted to hurt you back." His gaze drifted away, as though he couldn't quite look at me while he said that. "It's small of me, I'll admit. And petty."

"It's okay," I said hastily. "I get it." And I certainly didn't want to rehash anything from last night. Burying it seemed a much better—and easier—thing to do. He didn't need to know how much he'd devastated me. I nodded at the couch. "Want to sit down?"

He sat on one end of the couch, and I took the other. "Do you want something to drink?" Social protocol rules kicking in.

He shook his head. "No. Thanks." He studied me. "You look great," he said. "I forgot to mention that last night."

"So do you." Jackson always looked great. He hadn't been voted one of the World's Most Eligible Billionaires—twice—for nothing.

"I do want to be friends," he said. "I miss you, too. Being apart has been . . . difficult."

The guilt clawed to get out of its cage inside my gut.

"But I realize now," he continued, "I moved too fast. We're at different points in our lives, and I didn't take your feelings under consideration enough. I pushed you too hard."

I didn't know what to say. It was the first time he'd admitted that anything about our breaking up was his fault and not mine or Clark's.

"Someone like you, especially," he said. "I was thoughtless and selfish."

I missed the last part because I was focusing on the first part. "What do you mean, someone like me?"

He gave me an odd look. "You know. Because of . . . how you are."

My breath caught at the stab of pain his words caused. I'd always thought that Jackson was the one person who didn't see me as "odd." That he understood what impact my intellect had on my day-to-day understanding of life and people.

I cleared my throat against the sudden lump in it. "I didn't realize you'd categorized me."

"China, that's not what I meant—"

"But it's what you *said*."

"I'm sorry." His voice was soft and he reached out and covered my hand with his. "It wasn't meant to be derogatory in any way. You are who you are, and I didn't mean for it to sound as though you're less than anything but amazing. Truly."

I studied his eyes, trying to gauge his sincerity. Reading people was something I always struggled with, which was why I relied on the words they said. It meant that I sometimes didn't get nuance or body language, and that I tended to take things more literally than intended. Words were important.

"Okay," I said at last.

He smiled a little and squeezed my hand before letting go.

"Was that all?" I asked, quelling the impulse to tighten my ponytail.

"Not entirely, no." He shifted, turning to more fully face me. "I thought we should talk about Clark and moving forward."

My eyes widened. "That would probably be very uncomfortable."

He shrugged. "Nevertheless."

"What about Clark did you want to discuss?" And I really hoped he didn't ask if we'd slept together, because I was a shitty liar.

"I think it's a good thing that you're choosing to explore a relationship with Clark."

I stared. "That's . . . not what I thought you were going to say." I couldn't possibly imagine that he was serious. Unless he was "over" me, as the saying went. But that seemed improbable, given how he'd acted last night. "Why exactly do you think it's a good thing?"

"Because you have nothing to compare us to. You said yourself that ours was your first real relationship. That I was your first love. I think once you have some time, you'll realize that what we have is special and rare."

"So . . . you're just going to wait around for me?" His gaze was steady and I could find nothing in his expression to cue that he was joking.

"You're worth waiting for."

My breath caught. It seemed impossible. Not only had he forgiven me for the choice I'd made, he still cared enough to hope we'd get back together. I didn't know if I should hug him or cry. My feelings were in a muddle. I was grateful and relieved, but I was afraid, too.

"Jackson," I said carefully, "I can't promise you anything. I don't want you waiting for something that may never happen. I can't do that to you. I can't hurt you again."

"It isn't up to you. This is on me. It's my choice. I don't want to pressure you, but I don't want to disappear from your life. You wanted to be friends. That's what I'm offering. If at some point you want to talk about us, I'm all ears."

Maybe it wasn't what I'd pictured, but he was saying we could be friends. That I could still talk to him and see him. I realized I was too weak and too selfish to say no.

"Okay. I'd like that, too."

His smile was satisfied and familiar. It was the one I saw when he closed a business deal. "Good," he said. "Now, do you want to talk about your mom? You were pretty upset about it."

Funny he should ask. "Actually, there's more." I explained about the puzzle box, then showed him the tape. I didn't mention the journal. It felt too much like betraying my mom's trust. I kept my composure this time, though I didn't watch. I watched Jackson instead. He focused on my mom, his brow furrowing. His eyes widened slightly when she talked about the back door. Leaning forward, he rested his elbows on his knees, his hands loosely clasped.

It felt good to have him here. I'd missed his familiar presence. I wasn't sure how to process everything he'd said, but I'd think about that later.

"What do you think?" I asked once the tape stopped playing.

Jackson let out a deep breath as he turned to me. "I think that is a massive bombshell your mother just dropped on you."

"Do you think it's possible? What she said was done by Chen?"

I'd thought through how it could've been done and come up with a couple of different coding scenarios, but wanted to see if he'd think of something that I hadn't.

"I'm sure it could've been done," he replied. "The question is, does the back door still exist?"

I could tell the idea intrigued him, as it had me. "If the CIA knew about it, I can't imagine they wouldn't have fixed it by now."

"Or maybe they can't. They would've had to go public with the news. The fact that a foreign agency was able to compromise the New York Stock Exchange would've done as much damage to the market as crashing it."

He was right. "So it could still be there."

"We should certainly find out."

"We?"

He gave me an odd look. "You don't want my help?"

"No. I mean, yes, I do. I'm just surprised that you'd want to."

His lips twisted. "Friends help each other, right?"

I didn't answer. The question was rhetorical.

"Thank you," I said. "Yes, I think it's something we should find out. I want to know what really happened to my mom, the reason she died. And who actually killed her."

Jackson got to his feet. "I'll start researching what happened to that company and its employees."

"Thank you." I followed him to the door just as it swung open.

Clark walked in, saw Jackson, and stopped in his tracks.

"Clark, good to see you," Jackson said, and he actually sounded as if he meant it. He closed the distance between them and held out his hand.

"What the hell are you doing here?" Clark didn't shake his hand, and he didn't sound glad to see him, though I would have known that purely by his choice of words instead of the growl in which he'd said them.

Jackson's arm lowered to his side. "Stopped by to see China, of course."

"Maybe she doesn't want to see you." Clark stepped closer to Jackson, invading the socially acceptable eighteen inches of his personal space. "I know *I* don't."

"It's not up to you." I half expected Jackson to respond in kind to the venom in Clark's voice, but he remained placidly calm and matter-of-fact.

"Clark," I intervened, "it's okay. We've worked things out."

Clark's attention turned to me, and he raised one eyebrow. "What have you worked out, exactly?"

He wasn't growling anymore, thank goodness, but the ice in his voice wasn't much better. I pushed my glasses up my nose as I stammered out an answer. "Well, um, you know, that we can be friends. Jackson and me," I corrected, in case he thought I meant us.

"Friends," Clark echoed flatly.

"That's right," Jackson said. "China and I are going to be friends. Isn't that great? I miss her and, well," he shrugged, "she misses me. You don't *mind*, do you? After all, I only want what's best for her. Which is what *you* want, too, right?"

I had a hard time reconciling his words with the way he said them, as if he was issuing some sort of medieval throwing-down-the-gauntlet challenge, covered in sticky sugar. They were still too close to each other.

Clark's lips slid into a smile that wasn't at all friendly. "Well played, Coop."

Jackson's shrug was modest. "This isn't my first rodeo." His voice lowered. "You'll fuck it up eventually, and I don't mind waiting."

I winced and braced myself for a physical reprisal from Clark, but he held himself in check.

"You seem awfully sure," he sneered.

"I know your type. You like the pursuit and the victory. Sticking around isn't in your playbook, not a man like you."

"You know nothing about what kind of man I am." Clark's eyes glittered with malice. "But right now, I'm the kind who's going to kick your ass if you don't get out."

There was that threat of violence I'd been expecting. The silence so thick and heavy, I could hardly breathe.

Jackson glanced at me, the hard lines of his face softening. "I'll speak to you soon," he said.

"Um, yeah, okay." I watched him leave, swallowing hard before switching my gaze to Clark. He wasn't watching the door. He was watching me.

"What's going on, China?"

"Nothing," I said. "We had an argument the other night when I went by—"

"You went to his house?"

Oops. Guess I hadn't mentioned that, and judging by Clark's tone, that was a Bad Thing. "I just wanted to say hello, talk to him." I shrugged. "I missed him. I told him I wanted to be friends. He said he couldn't. I left. Tonight, he said he's changed his mind, that we *can* be friends." I left out the part about him wanting to wait around to see if I changed *my* mind. He'd already given Clark that message himself.

"That's what you want." His voice didn't go up at the end, though I answered it as if it was a question.

"Yeah, I think so. He and I have a lot in common. I don't have a lot of close friends, and I hate to lose the few I have."

"You heard him, he's still in love with you and thinks all he has to do to win you back is wait us out."

"I told him I couldn't promise that I'd want to get back together. He seemed okay with that."

Clark's eyes widened slightly and his whole body went still. I had the distinct feeling I'd said something wrong, but I didn't understand what. I wasn't responsible for Jackson's actions.

"Are you fucking kidding me right now?" Clark asked.

I was at a loss and threw up my hands in exasperation. "What? What did I say? I don't understand why you're upset."

"You're already planning on what you're going to do when this ends between us," he retorted.

I still couldn't see where I'd gone wrong. "What am I supposed to do? I'm sorry if it seems callous. I didn't intend to hurt your feelings." I just wanted to end this conversation. Too much had happened today that still had me reeling. An argument with Clark was the last thing I wanted to deal with.

"You didn't hurt my fucking feelings, China!" His yell made me jump. He lowered his voice. "I'm . . . upset . . . because you've already doomed our relationship to failure. You assume it's not going to work out."

I was confused. "And you don't think that?"

His expression was stark. "I think I may be falling in love with you."

I felt as though he'd tossed one of those flashbangs. A loud and bright stun grenade, designed to disorient, impair vision and hearing—it all described my current state.

I stood in silence, staring at Clark, my jaw agape.

"Say something," he coaxed.

I shook my head. Slowly at first, then with more vehemence. "No. No. I don't want to hear this."

"You don't want to hear how I feel?"

"You and I are friends. Close friends. I care about you. We have fun together. And last night we saw that we're obviously very compatible in bed. Love isn't part of that."

"You're not making sense," he said. "I can fuck you but I can't love you?"

I flinched, though his crassness just ignited my already fraying temper. "Yes," I snapped. "That's exactly right. Jackson wanted all that from me. Love, marriage, kids, the works. Well, if there's one thing I know, it's that loving someone only gets you pain and betrayal."

50

"That's not true—"

"Yes, it is!" Now I was yelling, but I couldn't seem to stop. "My mother was *everything* to me. And she *died*. All my life, I thought it was my fault. Do you know what that's like to live with? Now I find out that the man *she* loved, my sperm donor, betrayed and killed her! Can you imagine how she must have felt if she knew at the end that he was the one?" The thought had been hiding in the back of my head all day, too painful to give voice to.

I stopped to take a breath, seething with anger not wholly directed at Clark. He said nothing, just watched me, his expression unreadable.

"So no, don't tell me you love me. I don't want to feel obligated to love you back, just so I can go through the pain of loss and betrayal. It's not worth it."

I stalked past him, snatching up my keys from the table. The walls were closing in on me.

"Where are you going?" he asked to my back.

"Out. I'll understand if you're not here when I get back." I slammed the door shut behind me and burned rubber out of the driveway.

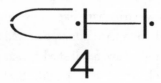

4

I didn't think, I just drove. Now that I'd given a vent for my anger, it boiled out of me. Not so much at Clark, though he'd triggered it, but at Danvers.

How could he have done that? What kind of monster would kill the woman he loved? Had he said anything to her first? I didn't want to think I shared DNA with someone who could do that. But Kade had been so sure and had access to information and files that I didn't. He had no reason to lie to me.

I struggled to remember that night. It was something I'd tried to forget. I'd been at a weekend camp at the University of Nebraska Omaha. A class of incoming freshmen computer-science majors, and me, the eight-year-old freak. The weather had been bad that day, with snow and ice on top of the five inches already on the ground.

Mom had driven the pickup truck, a more-than-a-decade-old Ford with a rusting frame and peeling paint. The heater worked, mostly, though the defrost could barely keep up. I'd been apprehensive, watching Mom clutch the wheel in a white-knuckled grip as she leaned forward in her seat to try to see out the windshield better.

I tried to remember the sequence of events, but it escaped me. All that came back to me was the aftermath of waking up in the hospital. The accident itself was buried in my memories. Psychologically, no doubt I'd been overwhelmed with the horror and tragedy of Mom dying, so I'd blocked it.

I'd always been glad of that, but now I wished I could remember. How had he done it? How had Danvers made it look like an accident? And how had I escaped? It probably would've been easier to kill me, too. He hadn't known I was his kid. I couldn't imagine that his scruples, if he had any, would've prevented the murder of a child. After all, he'd murdered his lover.

Why? The Why was killing me. Had it been as Mom had feared? That the Chinese had sent someone to kill her, and it hadn't been Danvers at all? Or had the CIA double-crossed her and decided she needed to be eliminated, then sent Danvers to do the dirty work? That's what Kade had said happened. I had no reason to doubt his version of events, other than an emotional need for my mom not to have been betrayed by the man she loved.

My anger gradually faded as my tires ate up the asphalt. I felt better behind the wheel of my Mustang. It knew me and I knew it. Behind the wheel, everyone was the same, for better or worse. It didn't matter how smart you were or how well you could grasp the concept of sarcasm.

I didn't want to go home yet. I regretted losing my temper with Clark. I didn't usually get angry, not like that, much less yell at someone. I was embarrassed, and I didn't want to face an empty home if he'd decided not to stay. I'd practically told him to leave. Considering it looked as though we wanted different things in our relationship, it wouldn't surprise me if he'd decided to cut his losses now.

That was one thing too much to handle today: losing Clark.

I found myself pulling up to Retread, my favorite nostalgia store. The familiar, comforting scent of musty books and decades-old trinkets, vinyl records, and assorted detritus reached me as I walked inside, and I took a deep breath.

At the sound of the bell clanking against the door, Buddy—the store's owner—popped his head up from behind the counter. He looked confused when he saw me, his brow furrowing. Pushing his glasses up his nose, he glanced at his Apple Watch.

"It's a Monday," he said by way of greeting.

"Hello to you, too." I smiled a real smile. Buddy wanted nothing from me. Expected nothing. He just knew I had a penchant for buying used Harlequins to send to Grams, and a freakish knowledge of Chia Pets.

"You're never here on a Monday night," he persisted. "Only Saturdays. You okay?"

No, but I was getting there. "Grams said she's out of books," I lied. "Thought I'd come see if you had any new stock."

He was still looking at me as if I had two heads and one eye, but shook himself out of it. "Um, yeah, sure. There's a couple of boxes in aisle five that are new."

Aisle five was a joking euphemism we'd come up with for the maze of pathways and clutter that eventually led to the farthest corner of the store. Shelves stacked nearly to the ceiling barely let much light into the tiny alcove. Two boxes, overflowing with paperbacks, sat stacked on top of each other.

I sank down to the floor, sitting cross-legged. I'd get my jeans dirty, but I didn't care. I started digging through the boxes, sorting them into genre. Western romances, contemporary romances, those with a mystery, Regency, and the Highlander ones. I saved the last stack for myself. I had a thing for a man in a kilt. One of them caught my eye. *The Outlaw Highlander*. I settled back against the wall and started reading.

The thing I loved about reading these books was that I could get lost in them the same way I could get lost in coding. Everything else disappeared for a while, including my life. It was relaxing and gave my brain a break. The novels weren't high literature. They were just meant to entertain, provide a break from reality, and then deliver the happily ever after that life seldom did.

I was deep into chapter ten when someone sat down next to me. I jumped, startled.

"Any sex yet?" Clark asked, nodding at the book I held.

Unexpected relief flooded me at the sight of him. Then I smelled the delicious scent of baked tomato-and-cheese and saw he had a pizza box next to him. My stomach growled loud enough to be heard two "aisles" away. I hadn't eaten since breakfast.

"No intercourse yet, but plenty of second base," I replied. "How'd you find me?" I eyed the pizza.

"Well, I waited for a while, then Reggie came by with your usual order, even though you hadn't called it in." A dark eyebrow lifted. "I think he was worried about you."

Reggie had been my pizza-delivery guy now for almost five years. Same order. Same time. Every Monday night.

"So anyway," he continued, "I figured you'd end up somewhere comfortable, somewhere that you knew. Thought I'd try here."

"Why?"

His brow furrowed. "I just told you why. It's familiar to you."

"No, I mean why come looking for me? We argued. I yelled at you. We disagreed."

He shrugged. "So? Couples fight. We had a fight. I got over it."

There was something else he wasn't saying. I could tell. "That's not all," I said, watching him carefully. "What else? Did something happen?"

He reached for the pizza and opened the box. Handing me a slice dripping with cheese, he said, "I watched the tape."

Ah.

I bit into the slice and chewed. Clark started on his own slice. It was quiet while we devoured the food. Buddy poked his head around the corner.

"I smell pizza," he said.

"Have some," I offered. There were two slices left so I gave him the box.

"Thirsty?" he asked. "I have beer."

"Sure."

He disappeared with the box, and when he came back, he handed a cold bottle of beer to each of us. "Store's closing in fifteen minutes," he said.

"Got it."

He went away again, leaving Clark and me alone. We sipped our beers. I wasn't a huge fan, but there was something about pizza and beer together that was a perfect pairing. The same with hot dogs and beer.

"You want to talk about it?" Clark asked. I knew he meant my mom.

"Not at the moment." I finally felt back under control. I didn't want to rock my emotional boat right now.

He nodded and took another sip of his beer. Staring straight ahead at nothing in particular, his long legs stretched out in front of him, ankles crossed, Clark seemed relaxed. And exuded sex appeal.

I observed him covertly as I drank. His hair, inky black and soft, thick enough to run my fingers through. The bone structure of his face was beautiful. High cheekbones, a strong jaw, narrow nose, and full lips. A shadow darkened his cheek and jaw—stubble that didn't succeed in marring his perfection.

Broad shoulders stretched the cotton of his T-shirt. His chest was deep. From the side, he was as thick as two of me, all of it hard muscle. His skin was soft, his arm lightly dusted with dark hair. As he took another drink, my gaze caught on his hand.

Thick fingers, rough but not calloused, lightly gripped the bottle. I knew what those hands could do. I'd seen him kill, but I'd also seen him be exquisitely gentle touching me.

Images from last night flashed through my mind. It had been amazing sex. I didn't know if this was usual, or if I'd just been incredibly lucky in my choices of Jackson and Clark for lovers. By all rights, I didn't have the kind of physical appeal that should've been enough to attract either of them. Science had shown that people tended to date and marry a partner with roughly the same attractiveness level. I was a few levels below both of them.

I certainly wasn't going to look a gift horse in the mouth. And speaking of mouth . . .

I set aside my beer and took off my glasses. Getting on my knees, I turned and straddled Clark's thighs, resting my palms against his chest.

His lips quirked as I took the beer from him. "Want something?"

"Uh-huh." I figured he could stop me at any time. He hadn't left, so the parameters I'd set on our relationship must be acceptable to him. I reached for the hem of his shirt and slid my hands underneath the cotton.

I sighed at the feel of his skin, tracing the hard line of muscles in his chest and abdomen. It was a sigh that was part awe and part longing. He was the kind of man women saw and instinctively knew they'd never be able to have. Yet here he was, letting me stroke his flawless body.

"Just so we're straight," he said, drawing my gaze to his eyes. "You're just using me for sex, right?"

I leaned back a little and cocked my head to one side. "That's a rather callous way of putting it, but perhaps technically true."

"It won't work, you know."

Judging from the hard length of him I could feel pressing against me, "it" was working just fine. I glanced down to check.

"Not that," he said, rolling his eyes. "This whole Friends with Benefits thing you want."

"Why won't it work? It's an extremely logical solution."

He leaned forward, his hand sliding underneath my hair to curve around the back of my neck. I was suddenly aware of how small and fragile my neck was. His blue-eyed gaze was penetrating, and I could feel the rise and fall of his chest under my fingers.

"Because it never does. Trust me."

He said it with such absolute certainty, it sent a chill through me. "Does that mean you're turning me down?" It had to be. "But then . . . why did you come here?"

"I came here because I was worried about you. You've had some big shocks. I wanted to make sure you were okay and didn't do something stupid."

The words stung, though they shouldn't have. "My IQ is far above mental incapacity. I don't need a caretaker. I'm fine." It felt weird touching him now, and I yanked my hands out from under his shirt and tried to climb off him.

His hands gripped my hips and yanked me back onto his lap. "I'm not saying you're mentally incapable. I'm saying I was worried. And no, I'm not turning you down. I just don't think things are going to go according to your plan."

Footsteps behind us and I glanced over my shoulder. Buddy took one look at me straddling Clark, turned beet red, and scurried away.

"I'm closing now, China," he called out. "Leave through the back door when you're . . . um . . . done."

We heard the front door close and the clank of the dead bolt being thrown.

"Does that mean I can ravish you?" I asked.

His lips twitched. "I'd love for you to ravish me."

Permission requested and granted. I grinned and leaned forward, my eyes slipping closed as I slid my hands around his neck. When our lips were an inch apart, he suddenly stopped me, pressing a finger against my mouth. My eyes popped open.

"Except, no kissing."

I stared, his finger still pressed against my lips, a question in my eyes.

"Kissing is personal. Intimate. Loving," he said, caressing my lips with a featherlight touch. "And it's unnecessary for sex. Pleasurable, yes, but unnecessary. After all, we're just scratching a biological itch, right? With the most convenient partner. So no kissing."

Logically, he was right, but . . . I didn't like the idea of not kissing Clark. I didn't see a way I could argue with him though. Slowly, I nodded.

His smile was thin. "Good. So we understand one another. You may proceed with promised ravishing."

I smiled back, but with considerably less enthusiasm. How strange that we were going to have sex, but I felt as though I'd just been rejected. Emotions were so unpredictable and volatile. I hated dealing with them, so I didn't.

I shoved the emotions to the back burner. The reality was, I had a good man—though he might debate the adjective—here with a drop-dead-gorgeous face and a body that could hold his own with Thor. I'd be a fool not to take advantage. Not to mention, his cock seemed locked and loaded. I wasn't one to let a good erection go to waste.

Grasping the hem of my shirt, I tugged it off and over my head, letting it fall from my fingers. My breath caught at the way Clark was looking at me. Smoldering looks were something only in Harlequins, but here was one in real life, and it was directed at me.

I stripped off his shirt next and took a moment to admire the view, lightly caressing the bulge of his biceps. Veins stood out slightly from his skin, and I traced them up his arms to his shoulders, grazing his collarbones, then down to brush his chest and nipples. A shiver went through him and his hips jerked up as he pulled me down.

His cock ground against me and a surge of heat flooded my center. He was still gazing into my eyes, looking as though he was barely holding himself back from ripping off my clothes. Reaching behind my back, I unsnapped my bra, letting the straps slip down my arms. I brushed it aside.

Clark's gaze tore from mine, dropping to my breasts. The Adam's apple in his throat bobbed as he swallowed. I slid my hands up to cup his neck and pulled his head toward my breasts. Eagerly, he lapped at my left nipple. I watched. His eyes were shut and his hands gripped my hips, tugging me closer toward him. His tongue flicked my nipple and I gasped. His eyes slid open, his gaze burning into mine.

I couldn't look away. Watching him was incredibly erotic. He flicked his tongue again and an answering thrill went from my nipple to my clit. I moaned, then gasped again as his eyes slid shut and his mouth closed over me, gently sucking.

My fingers dug into his shoulders, and distantly I thought he should be glad I didn't have long nails. He released my breast, now wet and heavy with arousal, and turned his attention to the other, repeating the same delicious torment. I ground against his cock, my clit aching for relief.

Reaching between us, I groped for his belt. He leaned back and watched me undo the belt, then I went to work on his jeans. He helped, pushing them down and off his legs, taking his shoes and socks with them. Now he was fully naked and sitting on the floor, but he didn't seem to mind.

I jumped up and got rid of my jeans, panties, and shoes, my eyes glued to his cock. It stood, proudly erect, jutting from his body. He was thick. And long enough to make a difference. Like the rest of him, his penis was a masculine work of art.

I knelt between his legs and placed my hands on his thighs, lightly covered with soft fur. Clark didn't manscape, but he was well groomed. My hair was in a ponytail, which meant I could use both hands.

Bending over, I gave a light lick to the tip, gratified when he hissed a breath through his teeth. Starting at the base, I ran my tongue slowly up along his shaft, tracing the tip. I cupped his balls, gently squeezing, as I laved the head of his cock with my tongue.

He groaned and I took him in my mouth, my lips covering my teeth, my tongue stroking the sensitive underside of the head. I wrapped a hand on the now-wet shaft, sliding down as I took him deeper.

There was extensive literature on how to perform fellatio correctly, and I'd done my fair share of studying the technique. Clark must've approved of my skill because he was gasping out curses.

"Holy shit," I heard him say, and I smiled around his cock. I sped up, then paused to take him all in. His hips lifted and I relaxed my throat.

"Fuck," he ground out. He was breathing hard and I glanced up just long enough to see him watching me, his hands in fists at his side. His eyes were dark, the pupils dilated, and he was focused on me with an intensity bordering on ferocity.

I was already aroused—I liked doing this, giving him pleasure—and the sight of what I was doing to him made my clit even more swollen. I moaned around his cock, my eyes slipping closed as I moved faster, pumping him with my hand and my mouth.

Suddenly, he pulled me up and off him. Grabbing my waist, he lifted me. I was aching for him and eagerly straddled his thighs. I watched him guide himself into me, and we both groaned.

"Fuck, you are so wet," he hissed, his brow creased almost as if he were in pain.

I was beyond words, my entire attention focused on where our bodies connected. I rose and fell, riding him. Sweat broke out on my forehead. I hovered on the edge, moving faster. Clark's hands gripped my hips, taking over as I tired.

My arm was wrapped around his neck, the other hand gripping his shoulder, when I unthinkingly leaned forward to kiss him. At the slight brush of my lips against his, Clark's eyes shot open. Threading his fingers through the ends of my ponytail, he pulled. I let out a startled cry at the twinge of pain, my head tilted back and exposing my neck to him.

My heart was racing as he kissed my neck, nipping at the skin underneath my jaw. The fur on his chest was rubbing against my sensitive nipples with every movement up and down his shaft. I was so close, it was nearly unbearable.

Taking over, he lifted me and brought me down as he thrust up. It was hard and deep and felt so good. I squeezed my eyes shut as he did it again and again. On the third time, my world exploded and I cried out, clutching at him as I came apart. He groaned in my ear, his hips jerking as he emptied himself into me.

I was gasping for air, my heart thudding in my ears. I collapsed against him, my head resting on his shoulder, nestled against his neck. We were both sweating, my breasts mashed against his chest as he regained his breath, too.

That warm feeling of contented bliss was abruptly shattered when Clark unceremoniously moved me off him and got to his feet.

"Cuddling isn't part of the deal," he said, extending a hand to me and helping me up. "I'll get dressed if you want to use the restroom." He was already reaching for his jeans.

I felt as though a bucket of cold water had been dumped over my head. Clark wasn't even looking at me, just zipping up his jeans. My nakedness was suddenly mortifying, and I spun on my heel, grabbed up my clothes, and hurried to the bathroom.

It was a single toilet room and I locked myself in. Numbly, I cleaned up the remnants of sex staining my thighs. Clark hadn't been kidding. If Friends with Benefits was all I wanted, then that's all I'd get. The sex had been good—really good—but I was shut out from where Clark had let me in last night.

He'd said he was falling for me. Perhaps his distance was a form of self-preservation. Or maybe he had been exaggerating when he'd said that. A man like Clark falling for a girl like me?

I looked in the mirror and all I saw was the same China. Hair in a ponytail, no makeup, my nose slightly marked by the indentation of wearing my glasses all the time. I had beautiful lingerie, but I was no Victoria's Secret Angel.

I was thin and short, the only features to my credit on the Beauty Scale were my blue eyes and my hair. I wasn't toned with firm abs and an ass you could bounce a quarter off. My breasts were a C cup, but Victoria was being generous. My nails were bitten, unmanicured, and it had been weeks since my last pedicure.

Suddenly, I wished I could be . . . more. More of what deserved to stand next to Clark. I'd never gotten my self-esteem from my looks, which was a good thing. It had always come from my brain. But now, when I *wanted* to make myself look as good as possible . . . I had no idea how.

I twisted away from the mirror and began dressing. It didn't matter. I didn't know why I cared. I'd told Clark I didn't want some kind of ephemeral happily ever after with him, so I shouldn't feel inferior. He obviously didn't mind having sex with me, so I had to be attractive enough to elicit a sexual response. Or maybe he just had a really strong sex drive, and a stiff wind would do the trick, too.

The postcoital bliss was a distant memory by now, and I shelved my disappointment and . . . whatever else I was feeling that made me want to go back and bury myself in those Harlequins. Last night I'd felt fulfilled and important after sex. Tonight I felt like . . . a thing. Not valued or special, just someone who could be easily replaced.

This must've been what Clark meant when he said it never works.

Well, he was wrong. I needed to adjust, that was all. My expectations needed to change. Unmet expectations were the death of every relationship.

I took a deep breath before exiting the bathroom, determined to cope and deal like a grown woman should. Sex without strings. Lots of people did it. The television said so. I could do that. I'd been given many challenges in my life, and I'd passed them all. This one would be no different.

Clark was waiting, scrolling through his phone. He glanced up at the sound of my footsteps.

"Ready to go?" he asked, handing me my glasses. I nodded.

I followed him out the back, turning off the lights and making sure the door locked behind us. I didn't take the Harlequins because I hadn't paid for them. But I knew Buddy. He wouldn't sell them out from under me.

Clark had parked about half a block away from me. As we passed my car, he paused.

"I took the tape," he said. "I want to get it analyzed. Make sure it's the real deal. Is that good with you?"

I couldn't find a reason to disagree, though a part of me stung at the thought of being out of possession of the one thing remaining of my mom.

"It's fine," I said, my voice like cardboard. The pep talk in the bathroom hadn't really done much for me.

Clark frowned, squinting at me. "You okay?"

"I'm fine. Just tired." A standard excuse everyone universally accepted, no matter how illogical. The truth was, the vast majority of people didn't care and didn't want to get involved in your shit. Social protocols demanded they inquire when it was obvious something was off, but secretly, they were relieved when they could push it aside and label it as Nothing to Worry About.

"Okay. Catch you later."

His parting words were given over his shoulder as he headed toward his car, and I had to press my lips together against the gasp of pain they elicited. *Catch you later.* It was something you said to a casual acquaintance you played softball with twice a summer, not what you said to a woman you'd just had sex with on the floor of a retail store.

I stumbled to my car door, tripping over some irregularity in the concrete that I couldn't see. My eyes were blurry, but it was just because of the streetlight. Not because I was on the verge of crying. That would be ridiculous and juvenile. And that would make it two days in a row.

My keys felt clumsy in my hands, and it took forever to find the right button to unlock the door. Finally, I slid behind the wheel and slammed the door, taking a moment to breathe in my safe space.

There was a game I remembered playing, somewhere, when I was a kid. It was a board game, of a sort, for a single player. Shoot the Moon was its name. Two chrome rails stood parallel to one another. The controls moved them either farther apart, or closer together. A metal ball was balanced on the rails, and you had to try to keep it on the rails as long as you could, scoring points depending on where it dropped.

I felt like that game. Barely staying on the rails of my life, wondering when the ground was going to fall from under me, moving faster and faster toward a destination I didn't know anymore.

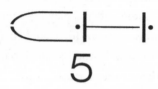

5

I was able to get away to meet Mark three months later. We met up in London. I'd never felt such anticipation, or the thrill that came when I laid eyes on him again. We rented a cottage in a tiny village and hid away from the world for five blissful days.

We made love. Not sex, no. Love. He was my perfect match. He knew what I wanted before I did. He was strong yet gentle, overwhelming in his passion for me. I couldn't stop touching him, stroking his skin, his jaw, the slope of his shoulders. He had the most expressive eyes, and I could see everything he felt in them. The storm of passion, the placid calm of contentment. The deep pain of parting.

For five days, we ate, drank, made love, and talked. We teased and laughed, and he held me when I cried. Neither of us wanted to go. Parting *was torture. We swore to each other that we'd meet again. We had to. I couldn't bear the thought of this being goodbye.*

◆ ◆ ◆

The next morning, I decided I needed a plan. Something concrete. A checklist to follow to find out what really happened to Mom. And the first step was to learn the details about the accident that night.

The police station in Nebraska was a Google search away and had a website. Unfortunately, they didn't have an online request form—they were a small precinct and apparently not that high tech. I had to look up the phone number and speak to an actual person. *Ugh.*

"Now when was this?" the officer asked for the third time. He sounded older than dirt, and I had to talk really loudly because he was hard of hearing.

"January 12, 2000," I repeated. Leaning over, I lightly banged my forehead on my desk. "A car accident with a fatality."

"And how do you spell your last name again?"

Okay, I couldn't blame him for that one. I slowly repeated each letter, all fifteen of them.

"And you say you were involved in the accident?"

I banged my head again. Harder. "Yes."

"Okay, miss." He didn't try to pronounce my last name. "You'll need to provide proof of identity. You can mail or fax us a copy of a government-issued photo ID . . ."

I had an app for that and was faxing a copy of my driver's license as he continued.

". . . and then we'll get back to you within three to five days."

"I just faxed my ID," I said. "Why will it take so long?"

"Sweetheart"—he sighed, sounding tired—"we got boxes stacked in the basement that go back fifty years. It'll take me some time to dig through them."

I heaved a mental sigh. "Okay. Thanks."

We hung up and I made a carefully precise check mark on my list, then added another item at the bottom. *Receive Police Report.* The items were now out of chronological order, and I almost rewrote the list when there was a knock at my door. It was Jackson.

"So I found more info on that company," he said. I stepped aside to let him in. He carried a manila folder and handed it to me as he passed by. Flipping it open, I began reading as he continued to speak. "They've been in business for twenty-five years. They started small, with no more than a handful of employees. The job they did for Y2K compliance is what put them on the map."

I followed him to the couch and sat down. "It's strange that such a small company would get that high profile a job."

"Agreed. My guess is that someone who knew this company would be an easy place to put Chen must've helped. Someone on the inside, maybe."

I glanced up at him from the file. "If we can find that person, they might know how to access the back door," I mused. "Or even tell us if it still exists."

"I suggest we go to New York and meet with the current owner," Jackson said. "He might know more of the history of the company. There wasn't much in the public records until they went public back in 2005."

"We?"

"I have a plane," he said. "Plus, without my name, you won't get in the door. But he'll meet with me."

He was right. Jackson's presence would make it much easier. I was glad to not go alone, but being with Jackson in such close proximity made me leery. I didn't want to lead him on or hurt him any more than I already had.

But he was the one who suggested it. "Are you sure? You don't mind?"

"Absolutely. Go pack. I'll call my pilot."

Okay, then.

I packed on autopilot, mindlessly grabbing clothes and checking items off my *Things to Pack for an Overnight Trip* list. I wondered what would have happened if Jackson hadn't been willing to help me. The thought of being around him for a couple of days was appealing, and at the last minute, I tossed in the little makeup bag Mia had made me buy and stock with bottles and tubes and brushes. I added Mom's journal, too. It hurt to read it, but she'd written it and deserved to have it read.

When I came back down to the living room, Jackson was just hanging up his phone. "Ready?" he asked.

"Just a minute." I tossed a few fish flakes in for the Doctor. He was swimming around pretty steadily. He seemed healthy enough, but that was always the case before turning belly-up. "Okay. Ready."

Lance, Jackson's butler/chef/driver/whatever-else-he-needed, met Jackson at the airport with an overnight bag for him. He smiled when he saw me, and I smiled back.

"Miss China," he said, "it's so good to see you again. We've missed your warm presence in the house."

I caught the *we* and opened my mouth to ask if he was using the royal "we" when I realized he must have meant Jackson. A subtle message? I was amazed that I'd caught it.

"I've missed being there," I replied.

Jackson rested his hand on the small of my back and guided me up the stairs. The touch surprised me, but I didn't mind. It was comforting to know he could still touch me in a casual way.

We were settled in our seats and in the air before I gasped, remembering.

"What?" Jackson asked. "Are you okay?"

I hesitated. "It's just . . . I forgot to tell Clark I was leaving town." I thought for a second, frowning. "Though I guess, technically, I don't have to."

Jackson's face had gone carefully blank. "Why is that?"

"Because we're just . . . friends," I said. "I mean, it's not as though I need to ask permission." Then why did I feel a nagging sense of having done something wrong?

"You're just friends." A statement. Not a question. And his tone had been one of disbelief.

"Yeah. I mean we're *good* friends . . ." I really didn't want to discuss the Benefits part of Clark's and my relationship. "But it's not like I'm going to marry him. I don't want that." And even I could sense we'd gone into This Is Awkward territory.

"Marriage is a big deal," he agreed.

I felt so awkward. "I mean, yeah." I babbled on. "And over half of marriages end in divorce, which is awful. Then there are the ones who *should* get divorced, but don't. I mean, look at my parents. My mom met someone else she fell head over heels for, but stayed with my dad out of *obligation*." The word tasted sour. "And the man she loved so much, betrayed and killed her. Marriage is a farce."

Turning, I looked out the window, staring unseeing at the clouds. Jackson was facing me, seated in the chair on the other side of the table, and I could feel his gaze on me.

"Would you like something to drink?"

The soft sound of the flight attendant's voice made me turn. "Um, sure. Do you have Red Bull?" I doubted it, but it was worth a shot.

She smiled. "Of course. Mr. Cooper has been stocking it since your first flight with us."

Oh. Well, that was thoughtful.

Jackson asked for coffee with cream, and the attendant headed to the galley to get our drinks.

"You stocked Red Bull for me?" I asked.

"Well, I certainly don't drink it," Jackson said. "Tastes like deer piss."

I burst into laughter at the look on his face. "That would mean you've actually caught a deer and tasted its urine," I teased. "Otherwise, how could you possibly compare the two?"

"You're underestimating the capability of the human imagination," he replied, resting his ankle on the opposite knee. "And they do sell deer urine. I could taste it, if I was so inclined. I'm not, but I could."

"What's the weirdest thing you ever ate?" I asked, suddenly struck by curiosity.

"Hmm, let me think." He squinted a little in concentration. "I think it would have to be octopus. Not because it's odd or weird to have eaten it, but because the tentacles were still moving."

I stared at him, jaw agape. "You're kidding me. That's so wrong." I shuddered just thinking about it. "If I ever visited the Far East, I'd starve. I don't do weird food."

"They have McDonald's there."

"Yes, but I know it's not proper McDonald's. American McDonald's. They've made it all weird." I made a face and Jackson chuckled. I shrugged. "I have the palate of a twelve-year-old, what can I say?"

For a moment, we both were smiling, and the weight I'd carried around inside my gut since I broke off our engagement lifted.

"I've really missed you," I said. "I don't know if you want to hear that or not—"

"Of course I do," he interrupted. "Selfishly, I'm glad you've missed me. It gives me hope."

I shook my head. "Don't. Don't say that. I can't be responsible for your happiness. I will fail you."

"I don't believe that."

"People are inherently selfish. They hurt those they care about. Even when they don't want to. It's inevitable."

"Pain in life is inevitable," he said. "I agree with that. It's naive and foolish to think you'll go through life unscathed. But neither can you fear the hurt so much that you wall yourself off from people and close relationships. I think the vast majority of people would say that they'd still choose the same path, even if it ended badly."

The attendant brought us back our drinks, and I thought about it. I wondered what my mom would've said to that. If she'd have still chosen to fall in love with Danvers, knowing her life would end at his hands. I couldn't imagine that she would.

"I doubt my mother would agree with you," I said.

"Oh, I think she would."

My gaze turned skeptical. "Why on earth would you think that? She *died* because of misplaced love and trust."

"But she had you. I don't think even knowing how it turned out would've made her regret the path that brought you about."

Tears stung my eyes and I hurriedly looked out the window, gulping down my Red Bull to conceal my emotion. To his credit, Jackson said nothing more. He rose and retrieved his laptop, moving to another table so he could work, and leaving me to my thoughts.

Jackson changed into a suit before we landed, making me glance down at my own attire. Jeans and my *S.P.E.W.* T-shirt.

"I don't think I'm dressed appropriately," I said. Programmer Business Casual was fine for work, but not for meeting with the CEO of a company who managed assets worth more than $150 billion.

"It's New York," Jackson said, straightening his tie. "We'll stop somewhere."

Clothes shopping. One of my least favorite activities. The only thing I enjoyed shopping for was lingerie. The perfect bra still eluded me despite drawers full of them in my bedroom.

We landed in New York to beautiful weather. The sun was shining in a cloudless, brilliant blue sky. The temperature was a crisp sixty-eight, making it deliciously warm in the sun. I lingered on the tarmac for a moment, breathing it in. Closing my eyes, I took a moment to feel the sun on my face. Vitamin D was good for the body. Sunshine was good for the soul. The majority of light on my skin was from the glow of a computer monitor.

A black sedan was waiting for us, and Jackson held the door open for me to get in while the driver stowed our luggage in the trunk. I realized, somewhat ruefully, that I was pretty darn spoiled by Jackson's lifestyle. They said money couldn't buy happiness, but it sure made life easier and more pleasant.

I looked out the window as we drove into the city. I'd never been to New York before. The number of taxis in the streets was incredible. It seemed as though every other car was a taxi. Traffic was heavy and we moved at a snail's pace.

"Charlie, let's make a stop at Bergdorf Goodman," Jackson said.

"Yes, sir."

"That sounds expensive," I said.

"It's New York. Everything is expensive."

It wasn't as though I was destitute. I made good money and had a healthy savings account, but it seemed frivolous to spend a lot of money on one outfit. I saw a Forever 21 up ahead. "What about there?"

"You want to go into a meeting wearing a twenty-dollar dress and ask the CEO to believe you know what you're talking about and aren't just some weird tinfoil-hat conspiracy theorist?"

I pushed my glasses up my nose. "Well, that's one way of looking at it."

"Clothes are your first impression," he said. "They make a statement. You want it to be the right one."

The driver pulled up outside a beautiful building on the corner of Fifth Avenue. I craned my neck to see, then nearly fell out of the car when the driver opened the door. He caught my arm and stopped my tumble.

"Thanks." I recovered as gracefully as I could.

"I'll call when we're ready," Jackson said, rounding the car to where I stood on the sidewalk. "I'd guess a couple of hours or so."

"Yes, sir."

"A couple of hours?" I protested as Charlie drove off. "To buy an outfit?"

"Have you ever been to New York before?" he asked.

"No."

"Then we should stay a day or two. Go to the theater. Sightsee. You could use a few days off."

His phone rang before I could reply, and he glanced at the screen. "Go on inside," he said. "Personal shoppers are on the fourth floor. I'll be up in a minute."

The doors were intimidating in and of themselves, but the inside made my jaw drop. Champagne-colored carpet, chandeliers, and people dressed in clothes nicer than anything I owned. And that was just the employees.

To say I didn't fit in would be an understatement. A woman passed me with a diamond on her finger the size of a marble, expensive perfume wafting in her wake. I felt like I was the round peg, and this square hole was really uncomfortable.

I took a deep breath. I was a grown woman. I had four degrees and a six-figure job. This would be simple. A shopper would make it even easier, and quicker. So . . . fourth floor it was.

Making my way through the store to the elevators, I rode it to the fourth floor. An opulent lobby greeted me, clothes tastefully displayed—not on racks, but one complete outfit at a time.

I wandered forward, drawn to an elaborate evening gown in rose silk. The neckline plunged, as did the back, soft lace in the V inserts that would be see-through when worn. The skirt flowed to the floor, a slit concealed up one side. It looked exquisite, like something a princess would wear.

"May I help you?"

I jumped, startled, and whirled around to see that a woman had approached me. She had an I'm-paid-to-be-friendly smile and was dressed simply in a black just-below-the-knee skirt and white blouse. Her black heels were sensible but classic.

"Um, yeah." I pushed my glasses up my nose. "I need to buy a business outfit. Can you help me?"

She glanced at my ponytail, her gaze drifting down my T-shirt to my jeans and worn tennis shoes. "The clothes we have here are very . . . exclusive. There is an excellent Lord & Taylor down the street. Or perhaps Macy's might be a better choice for you."

A flush of embarrassment crept up my neck, but anger burned as well. I narrowed my eyes.

"Are you implying that I'm not good enough to wear these clothes?"

Her lips thinned. "No," she said, her voice curt. "I'm implying that you can't afford them. And I don't have time to waste on a tourist wanting to try on designer clothes as a lark, no doubt posting photos to Instagram and Twitter and sucking up my entire afternoon with your nonsense." She paused to take a breath and continued more calmly. "So please show yourself out."

I was pissed now. "Excuse me," I said to her retreating back, my voice like ice. "I am a customer and you are paid to help me. Or shall I tell your manager that you've not only insulted a client but refused to sell me merchandise? Your position here might be in jeopardy if I were to do that.

"Not to mention that it's grossly out of date and out of touch to assume I can't afford the clothes here just by looking at me," I continued. "I realize you may have to deal with tourists, but you shouldn't assume." I took a breath. "Now. I need a business outfit. Will you help me or not?" Though at this point, I should probably have just asked for a different salesperson. But for some reason, she'd pushed my buttons.

Her eyes were wide and she took a moment, then smiled thinly. "Of course. You are correct. My apologies, Miss . . . ?"

"China," I said. "You can call me China."

It was at this moment that the elevator doors opened, and Jackson stepped out. He spotted me and walked over to stand behind me. He glanced at the saleslady and our standoff, a question in his eyes.

The lady's mouth gaped. Obviously, she'd recognized him. Her face paled.

"I-I'm so sorry . . . China," she stammered, dragging her gaze from Jackson to me. "It was a long weekend and I shouldn't have taken that out on you. Please accept my most sincere apology."

I wanted to roll my eyes but refrained. Of course it would take a man showing up for her to take me seriously.

"What's going on here?" Jackson asked.

"She thought I should leave because I obviously can't afford any of their clothes," I replied.

Jackson's gaze turned cold. "Maybe we should go elsewhere."

"No, no, that's not necessary," the lady hastily interjected. "We have many things that would complement China's beautiful coloring and figure."

I took pity on her. She probably *did* have to deal with annoying tourists, and, considering my attire, I shouldn't blame her for assuming. Though she *had* been rude about it.

"It's fine," I said to Jackson. "I'm sure . . ." I waited, looking at the lady.

"Brenda," she said.

"I'm sure Brenda will be able to help me," I finished.

Her relief was evident in her smile. "Absolutely. Follow me, please."

Brenda showed Jackson to a seating area and took me into a private room before scurrying off to find clothes. I was surprised that she didn't even ask my size, but when she returned and I began trying on clothes, I could tell she hadn't needed to ask. She had me pegged perfectly.

Usually, business trousers were too long on me, but the petite in the ones Brenda brought fit perfectly. Black with a thin pinstripe, they hugged my hips and tapered to hug my ankles. The blouse was thin, crimson silk with a scoop neck and short sleeves. Brenda slipped on a jacket that matched the pants. A jacket would also be too long, but this one hit right at my hips. Buttoning the single button at my navel pulled the fabric in to accentuate my waist.

Brenda brought a pair of shoes the exact same shade as my blouse. They were closed toe with an open insole and a tiny strap that buckled around my ankle. The heel was only a couple inches high, but it was skinny. I wasn't positive I wouldn't break an ankle, but I decided to try anyway.

When she stepped back and I saw myself in the mirror, I was stunned. Surely the woman staring back was a different China. Yes, I looked young, but my ponytail and glasses fit the outfit. *Business Chic* is what Mia would've said. Feminine without being provocative. In short, I loved it.

"I'll take it," I said. "Do you have more stuff like this?"

Brenda smiled, a real one this time. "Absolutely."

As she headed out of the dressing area, Jackson walked in. "Give us a second," he said to her. She nodded and disappeared.

"What do you think?" I asked, doing a slow 360.

He looked me over from head to toe, and smiled. "Perfect."

I could've sworn his gaze lingered on my ass.

I shrugged off the jacket, carefully replacing it on the hanger. "She went to get me a few more things. Another outfit or two wouldn't hurt."

The blouse was sleeveless and had a single keyhole button behind my neck. I struggled with it for a minute before Jackson stepped forward.

"Here, let me."

I bent my head and waited. The soft brush of his fingers against my skin gave me goose bumps. He was close enough for me to smell his cologne and feel the heat of his body. It took him longer than it should've to undo the button. When he did, I lifted my head and caught our reflection in the full-length mirror.

Jackson was looking down at me, his hands settling on my shoulders before drifting down my arms in a light caress. The expression on his face was pained.

Settling on my waist, he tugged at the fabric, untucking it from my pants. He lifted and I obediently raised my arms so he could take off the blouse. It floated to the floor. Bending, he pressed his lips to my bare shoulder.

I shuddered, my eyes slipping closed. His lips moved closer to my neck, and I tilted my head to the side. I heard him breathe in deeply, as though reacquainting himself with my scent. The thought brought tears to my eyes.

He touched me and kissed my skin with such tenderness, it was nearly reverent. Grasping his hands in mine, I crossed my arms over my chest, enclosing myself in his embrace.

My skin was pale against the black of his suit, my bra a matching black lace. Even with the red heels, he still stood head and shoulders above me. His head was bowed and his eyes were closed, his lips an inch from my ear. I could feel the warmth of his breath and the beat of his heart.

Jackson slid his hands from mine and stepped back. His eyes met mine in the mirror. His expression was blank now, the pain from before gone.

"I'll send Brenda in," he said, and left the room.

The rest of the session was a blur, my mind preoccupied with Jackson. I took what Brenda suggested for another two sets of business attire, then decided to leave, wearing the first outfit.

When I finally emerged, Jackson was waiting in the padded chair, one ankle resting on the opposite knee while he thumbed through his phone.

Brenda hovered nearby and glanced uncertainly between Jackson and me. Ah yes. The bill.

"Allow me," Jackson said, reaching for his wallet.

My pride reared its head. "No." That came out more sharply than I'd intended. They both looked at me. "I can pay for my own clothes, Jackson, but thank you for the offer." There. A socially acceptable thanks-but-no-thanks.

Jackson's lips twitched slightly, and he lifted his arms in a gesture of surrender. "As you wish."

I reached for my backpack. Brenda visibly winced at my *Buffy* wallet but took my credit card readily enough. The total was enough to make me think the fabric here was spun from fairy dust and angel wings. I could've bought another Iron Man. Or two.

"Hungry?" Jackson asked once I'd signed the receipt. "I set up the meeting for four this afternoon."

It was almost one and I hadn't eaten all day. "Yeah, that sounds good."

"There's a place on the seventh floor here that's good. And has a great view of Central Park."

The host recognized Jackson with a smile and nod, leading us to a table for two. The chairs reminded me more of thrones, plush and with backs that curved up and over my head. Way over my head. I was just glad my feet didn't dangle. Once we were seated, our faces were half-hidden from any casual observers.

The table was right next to a window with a smack-dab center view of Central Park. It was a gorgeous view, with spring flowers blooming and foliage gradually filling out the trees.

The menu was full of things that I wouldn't eat, including lobster mac and cheese. Why would they ruin a perfectly good bowl of mac and cheese by putting the rubbery innards of an exoskeleton in it? I'd always wondered how hungry the first person had been who'd looked at a lobster or crab and said, *Hey, I wonder if I could eat that?*

I went with a plain roasted chicken breast. "Can they leave off the asparagus sauce?" That didn't sound like something I'd like.

"Of course," the waiter said. "And for you, sir?"

"I'll have the filet. Medium rare."

"Very good, sir."

The waiter left us and I sipped the white wine Jackson had ordered. I felt decadent, wearing designer duds, eating a gourmet lunch in New York, overlooking Central Park, and drinking before five. Lifestyles of the rich and famous.

My cell buzzed and I glanced at the screen. Clark.

"I should take this," I said to Jackson.

He nodded and rose. "I'll give you privacy."

"Hi," I answered as he walked away from the table and went to take a seat at the bar.

"The video is authentic," Clark said.

"I figured as much. I put a request in today for the official police report of the accident. I don't really remember what happened."

"You don't think it was an accident anymore, obviously."

"I think her death was too coincidental, given what she said on the tape."

"I've got a buddy at the CIA. We do favors for each other, usually under the radar. I'm going to have him look up your mom's case file. If she was an agent, she must've had a handler. Maybe they're still around."

"Thanks. That's a good idea."

There was a pause. "Where are you?"

I pretended ignorance. "What do you mean?"

"I mean, I went by your place and you're not there. So where are you?"

Time to bite the bullet. I grimaced. *Ugh.* Bad choice of idiom. "I'm in New York."

"New York? Why?"

"I want to meet with the man who runs Fortress Securities. I'm hoping he knows more information about the company's history back then, or anything about malicious code in the Exchange that might've been found between then and now." I conveniently left out any mention of Jackson.

"I see." His voice was ice. "And I'm betting you didn't fly commercial."

I didn't say anything.

"Why didn't you call me?" he asked. "I would've gone with you."

"It's not that I wouldn't have wanted you to, but Jackson has the clout to get a meeting with this guy," I said. "He offered to help." I glanced toward Jackson, who was half-turned toward me, his elbow resting on the bar.

"I bet he did."

Irritation bit at me. "What does it matter?" I snapped. "You aren't my boyfriend or my boss. I don't need your permission."

Silence met that and I immediately regretted my words. It wasn't that they weren't true, but I'd said that in a way Mia would've described as bitchy.

"That didn't come out right," I hastily added. "I meant—"

"I know what you meant." He cut me off, his tone suddenly as casual as if we were discussing the weather. "You're right. We're just fuck buddies. Have a good time in the Big Apple." He ended the call.

I had the feeling that hadn't had gone very well, despite his change in tone. His use of the term *fuck buddies* was needlessly vulgar and made me flinch.

"Everything okay?" Jackson asked, taking his seat.

I nodded and forced a fake smile. "Yep. Everything's fine."

He looked like he was going to ask another question, but our food arrived. I concentrated on not getting anything on my clothes, and Jackson didn't pursue my phone conversation. I knew he had to have guessed it was Clark, but I certainly didn't want to talk about it. But it had sucked the joy I'd been feeling right out of me.

We finished lunch and Jackson accepted the check the waiter handed him.

"We can go dutch," I offered.

Jackson shot me a look and slid his credit card into the black leather folder. I put my *Buffy* wallet back in my backpack.

The drive to the Fortress offices took forty minutes. It passed mostly in silence. I people-watched, which in New York I realized could be an Olympic sport. I craned my neck to see around Time's Square, my eyes wide at the huge glowing billboards and masses of tourists.

"Oh my God! Did you see that?"

I spun toward Jackson's window as we drove by. He looked out. "What?"

"There's a man wearing nothing but a cowboy hat, underwear, and a guitar!"

"Oh. Yeah, that's the Naked Cowboy. Makes his money off taking pictures with tourists."

"Does he do that year-round?" It couldn't be a healthy profession in winter.

Jackson chuckled. "I doubt it."

I saw others dressed as Spiderman and even a Wonder Woman. "Aren't they worried they'll be sued for copyright infringement?"

"They're probably more worried about paying their rent than being sued."

That was probably true. Maslow's hierarchy of needs would deem a roof over one's head more important than the threat of litigation.

Fortress Securities was housed in a skyscraper on Wall Street. We got out of the car and had to go through security—showing our IDs and walking through metal detectors—before being allowed to approach the elevator bank.

My ears popped as we zoomed to the thirty-fifth floor. I followed Jackson off the elevator into the reception area of Fortress. Glass and metal and modern decor greeted us, meant to impress without being ostentatious. My stomach tightened in knots, and I was suddenly very glad Jackson was with me.

Jackson gave his name to the receptionist, who looked like a slightly older version of Mia. Her eyes widened and she smiled so brightly at him, I was surprised not to see our reflection in her pearly whites.

"Right this way, Mr. Cooper."

She led the way to a corner office buried deep in the building, her hips sashaying in a skirt two inches shorter than mine on legs five inches longer. Knocking on a door, she opened it to reveal an outer office that housed a secretary sitting at her desk, and couches and chairs.

"Please have a seat. Joan will take care of you. And my name is Tess, if you need anything, Mr. Cooper." Another smile for him as she ignored me. If I wasn't so used to it, I'd be offended.

We sat as Tess whispered something to Joan, then left, closing the door quietly behind her. Joan murmured something into the headset she wore. Five minutes later, she walked us into the inner office.

The view made me catch my breath. Sunlight glittered off the sky-scrapers of Lower Manhattan, the streets and noise far below. Between the buildings, I could see the Freedom Tower, stretching toward the sky.

"Jackson, how good to finally meet you."

A man rose from behind a spare glass-and-metal desk, rounding it to come shake Jackson's hand. He was older than Jackson, perhaps late forties, and his smile showed perfectly even, white teeth. His suit screamed dollar signs, and he wore it as someone used to nice things. His eyes were shrewd and gleamed with intelligence and vitality. This was a man at the top of his career and in the prime of his life.

"Bruce, it's good to meet you, too," Jackson replied. "This is China Mack, a colleague of mine."

I put on my Polite Smile and shook his hand. His grip was warm and firm.

"Pleasure to meet you," he said. "Please, come, sit down. Tell me what I can do for you." We followed him to a seating area, and each of us took a separate armchair. "I was certainly surprised to hear from you. We don't exactly operate in the same marketplace."

"We have some information you might be interested in," Jackson said. "And were hoping you'd be able to answer some questions for us."

"Of course."

Jackson looked at me. "It has to do with something that happened before you took over as CEO," I began. "Information has come to light about the work Fortress did back in 1999 for the New York Stock Exchange, specifically, the Y2K compliance-software update."

Bruce stiffened ever so slightly. "What about it?"

"We have credible intel that the software was compromised," I said. "That there was a back door installed by an employee of Fortress at the behest of a foreign power."

Tension gripped Bruce and his eyes narrowed. "How the hell did you find out?"

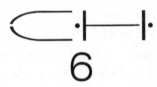

6

"So it's true," I said, ignoring his question. "How long did it take to find it?"

Bruce's lips pursed. "I'm not saying anything else without counsel present. You can show yourselves out." He stood.

"Wait," Jackson said, rising, too. "We're not here to blackmail you or the company. We're not talking about going public. This is personal."

"What are you talking about?" Bruce asked.

"Just hear me out," I said. "Please."

He hesitated, then sat down again. Jackson did the same.

"My mother knew about the back door because the man who did it told her. It's possible she was killed for knowing that information. I'm trying to find out if she was, and if so, who was responsible for her death. Any information you have on the company or software could help me."

"And why should I help you?" Bruce asked. "If I validate your information, you could use it against me. If it went public that Fortress had at one time knowingly compromised the New York Stock Exchange, it would destroy our company as well as have ramifications for every trade we made during that time when the software was installed."

"Are you sure you were able to really remove the software?" I asked. "And reverse anything it might have done? It had to have taken you time to replace it, and during that time, it would have continued to run the Exchange. You didn't go public then for the same reasons. The Exchange would've had to shut down for who knows how long. It would've destroyed the economy."

Bruce's face was like granite.

"We could help you," I offered. "Jackson and I can look at the software you replaced, find out exactly what it did and what the back door was intended for. We can report to you quickly and quietly, and if there's anything you need to retrace and correct, you won't have to tell a soul."

"I know Jackson could do something like that, but you're barely older than my daughter. Why should I believe you?"

"China's skills are exceptional," Jackson said before I could reply. "She's worked for me, and I can vouch for her abilities. She can do what she's promising."

Bruce was thinking about it. I could tell.

"You want to make sure all the cobwebs are clean, don't you?" I prompted.

"All right," he relented. "I'll give you access to the old software, but it has to stay on property. You cannot make a copy, and you will use our equipment on a separate network to examine it."

"Agreed."

"It was in place for nine months before they realized something was wrong," he said with a sigh, leaning back in his chair. "This was before I was CEO, so I'm relying on secondhand sources. I wasn't directly involved.

"The matter was fully disclosed to me when I was offered the position," he continued. "To my knowledge, the back door was in place but was never accessed. It was found via a code review post-Y2K. Everyone kept it quiet, and it was fixed with a software patch thirteen months postdeployment."

"That's a long time to have a back door available to the New York Stock Exchange," Jackson said.

"We monitored the vulnerability closely, and to our knowledge, no one accessed it."

"But you aren't one hundred percent sure," Jackson said.

"This was over fifteen years ago," Bruce said. "If someone had accessed it, we'd know by now."

"Let's take a look at that software," I said, "as well as a database of transactions for those thirteen months."

"That'll take some time to pull together," he warned.

"We've got time."

Bruce set us up in a conference room where he had three IT people produce four computers with three monitors each and establish a network between them. Someone else brought in a portable hard drive.

"Here's the software as it was delivered in 1999," he said. "Both the uncompiled and compiled files. I'll have someone bring you the database when it's ready."

It took a few minutes to copy the software, and I shed my jacket while I waited. Jackson did the same and also loosened his tie.

"How do you want to do this?" he asked.

"We'll start at the top and work our way down," I said. "It would go faster if we took separate modules, but I don't want to miss anything. Two sets of eyes are better than one."

A ding from the computer said the file copy had finished. We each took a seat and went to work.

Reviewing someone else's code is like reading their handwriting. One person's capital *S* may look different from someone else's, but it's still an *S*. Coders had their own ways of doing things, and in most cases, there were about a dozen ways to skin the same cat—an idiom

I'd learned but thought was truly barbaric. If you looked carefully, you could identify how many developers were involved in the same project. By the time three hours had passed, Jackson and I had identified five main styles, which we creatively referred to as Coders A, B, C, D, and E.

"We need to take a break," Jackson said, rubbing his eyes. "How many lines have you done?"

I glanced at my screen and did the math. "Three thousand or so. You?"

"About the same."

Technically, reviewing more than five hundred lines of code an hour wasn't advisable, but Jackson and I also weren't your average programmers. But he was right. We needed a break.

"A Red Bull sounds good," I said.

Just then, Bruce popped his head in. "I'm heading to dinner," he said. "Care to join me?"

Jackson and I glanced at each other, and by silent mutual agreement, he said, "Sure."

A limousine took the three of us to a steakhouse, and I felt like a dwarf walking between them, as both Bruce and Jackson had several inches on me. The maître d' took one look at his auspicious guests (not me—them) and had to conceal his elation. I assumed patronage by famous, rich people helped any restaurant's standing, though this establishment seemed to hardly need it. The tables were full and the bar held a crowd of people, yet we were led toward the back of the restaurant. It was quieter there, and we were seated at a circle corner booth by the window.

I hesitated about how we were going to sit, but it seemed both men were averse to sitting side by side in a booth, so the dubious honor of being the middle of the sandwich went to me. At least it was big enough so we could spread out. The table was set with a white linen tablecloth and napkins, and silverware so polished, it shone.

Bruce ordered a bottle of wine for the table as I looked over the menu, which was basically meat, meat, and more meat. And potatoes about five different ways.

I chose an entrée at random and ordered. The men ordered as well, and the waiter went away.

"How is it going?" Bruce asked.

"There's a lot of code to go through," Jackson said, "but we're making headway. So far, nothing out of the ordinary."

"Something's been bothering me," I said. Bruce turned toward me. "I was wondering how Fortress—a relatively small and unknown firm—got such a high-profile project. I know it was before your time, but still, maybe you know how that happened?"

Bruce grinned. "Actually, I do. It's called nepotism, and it's because my grandfather had a seat on the Exchange. If Fortress could land that account, the future of the company was secure."

I frowned. "But you didn't work for Fortress at that time."

"No, but I was eyeing it to buy. The company was ridiculously undervalued. The deal ensured its future, and I bought it."

Wait a minute, that didn't fit with what we'd guessed. If Bruce's grandfather was the one who'd pushed the deal through just so Bruce could buy the company, then he couldn't have known about the spy. Except . . .

"How did you first hear about Fortress?" I asked.

"Oh, I don't know." He sighed, then he frowned, thinking. "You know, now that I think about it, Grandfather may have been the one to mention it. But that was months before this project was bid out, much less awarded."

"Are you and your grandfather close?"

He nodded. "I'm the only son of an only son, and my dad died when I was young. He's been like a second father to me."

A grandfather devoted to his grandson, who just happens to point out what a great investment Fortress Securities would be only months before helping them land a lucrative and game-changing contract. A contract that would result in someone being able to secretly install a back door into the New York Stock Exchange.

It all sounded too coincidental not to mean anything, and when I glanced at Jackson, he looked like he was tracking the path the same way I had.

"Is there any way we could meet with your grandfather?" Jackson asked.

"Sure," Bruce replied. "He's out of town today but will be back tomorrow. I can set something up. But I can tell you, he won't know anything about this back door. He's over eighty years old. Technology to him is a pen that takes weeks to run out of ink." He smiled at his own joke, and I reflexively did the same.

The food came then, and conversation between Jackson and Bruce turned toward business and tech. I half listened as I ate, concentrating on what I'd seen of the code so far and the most likely way to insert a back door.

"Wait a second," I burst out, belatedly realizing I'd just interrupted their conversation.

"What is it?" Jackson asked.

"Of course, I should've thought of it before."

"What?"

"The back door. We're assuming he could've installed it at any point during development. But actually, there would have been a very small window of time to do it without anyone else on the team knowing. He had to have done it at the last minute. All we have to do is find the previous version in backups and run it against the final version. That'll at least narrow it down to showing us what was added last."

Jackson turned to Bruce. "Do you have backups for the previous versions, too?"

Bruce nodded. "We should. We keep our project backups in case it's necessary to roll back at some point. And like most developers, we hate deleting files."

I was ready to go right then, but the men looked at me askance when I said we should just leave. Jackson still had half a steak to eat, and Bruce had about the same. I sighed. Of course. Don't come between a man and his steak.

"The backups are in storage anyway," Bruce said, looking at his phone. "I'll send IT a message to retrieve them. It'll take a bit. But the good news is that the database is ready."

I cooled my heels and tried not to fidget. I watched Jackson cut a bite, put it in his mouth, chew, and swallow. It was like he was eating slowly on purpose. Another cut. Another bite. Another swallow. My gaze followed the meat from his plate, to his fork, to his mouth, then back down to his plate.

Bruce excused himself from the table for a moment, but then I returned to watching Jackson eat. Finally, he put his utensils down, sighed, and swung his gaze to mine.

"I feel like I'm being watched by a rather persistent—and hungry—Yorkipoo."

I frowned. "Why a Yorkipoo?"

"Because they're cute, small, very smart, and they don't shed."

Huh. Well, I'd been called worse. The important thing was, "Are you done?"

"Yes, China." He sighed, gave one last longing look at the remnants of steak on his plate, and signaled the waiter for the check.

We'd paid by the time Bruce returned, and he politely thanked Jackson. I'd caught a glimpse of the bill, which had been close to $700. The bottle of wine had been old and French, and the steaks, Wagyu. To billionaires, thousand-dollar dinners weren't a big deal, but I made a mental note to make sure Bruce took us out again and didn't conveniently disappear to the bathroom when it was time to pay the tab.

The limousine wasn't waiting outside, but a town car was instead. I got in first, then the men. Bruce sat on the seat facing backward. We headed back to the office.

Even at this hour, traffic was horrendous. I was checking my phone while Jackson and Bruce chitchatted. A sharp turn made me look up from the screen. We were driving down a tight alley.

"What's this?" I asked.

Bruce glanced out the window. "Probably a shortcut to avoid traffic."

The buildings on either side were dark and rundown. We passed a dumpster overflowing with garbage, and I caught a figure huddled on the ground next to it. A homeless person. Seeing one always sent a pang of sympathy through me.

The car slowed to a crawl, then stopped, the engine idling.

"Why are we stopping?" I asked, my senses crawling.

"I don't know."

Bruce twisted around in his seat to speak to the driver just as my window began to roll down. Automatically, I glanced up to the open window. My breath froze in my chest.

The "homeless" man stood outside my door, an automatic pistol pointing directly at me.

Several things happened very fast. I heard Jackson shout, "Get down!" Before I could obey, he shoved me none too gently to the floor. The boom of gunshots thundered in my ears, as well as the sound of shattered glass. Bruce yelled, diving for the opposite side of the car. Jackson was a sitting duck, his body covering mine.

Reaching up, I yanked the door handle and shoved as hard as I could. There was a solid thump of the door colliding with a body, and the bullets stopped. In a flash, Jackson was out of the car, nearly stepping on my head in the process. He flew at the attacker, who'd stumbled back. The guy raised his gun just as Jackson hit him, and I screamed.

They wrestled, Jackson's hand locked around the man's wrist, the gun between them. Jackson slammed his forehead into the guy's nose, and he grunted in pain as blood spurted.

The driver. He had to be in on it, I just realized.

I scrambled up from the floor. Bruce had jumped out the other side of the car, but I couldn't see where he'd gone.

I caught the driver's gaze in the rearview mirror. He looked surprised to see me alive. Asshole.

Thrusting my arms over the seat back, I locked one around his neck in a choke hold. He was a big guy with a bald head and thick neck. I grabbed onto my forearm, grunting with the effort of squeezing.

He clawed at my arm, and I thought I was going to be able to hold him, but he reached up and grabbed my head. I tried to pull my head back, but he latched onto my ponytail and yanked so hard, tears came to my eyes. My grip on his neck loosened, and suddenly I was flying over the top of the seat, my back slamming into the console.

I cried out in pain and heard another gunshot outside the car. I couldn't see Jackson or the attacker, but they were the least of my current worries.

The driver slammed his elbow down into my breast. Excruciating pain shot through me, so bad that I couldn't catch my breath even to scream.

"Fucking bitch," the driver snarled, smashing his fist into my cheek. Pain exploded in my head. I heard the flick of a switchblade, looking up just in time to see the blade glittering above me.

Adrenaline poured through my veins in a cold rush. My head was under the steering wheel, which gave me a perfect view of his Man Spread. I slammed my fist into his crotch as hard as I could.

He howled, his eyes closing, and I grabbed his arm holding the knife, pulled myself up, and sank my teeth into his skin. He grunted and tried to shove me away as blood touched my tongue. I wanted to vomit—human blood contained so many pathogens—but if I let go, he'd kill me.

He seized my ponytail again, yanking. Somehow, I twisted around, my jaw still locking on his hand. I used his body as a human jungle gym, kneeing him in the stomach and stepping on his injured crotch.

My head was numb, but he yanked anyway, and I couldn't stop him from pulling my head back until I had to let go with my teeth.

Blood dripped from his hand, and his eyes were livid with rage and pain. I was wedged between him and the steering wheel, straddling him—a grotesque perversion of an intimate position. My throat was bare and too vulnerable. My eyes were glued to the knife. I had both hands locked around his arm, straining to hold the blade back, but it was coming inexorably closer. I wasn't going to be able to stop him.

The door flew open and Jackson was there, gun in hand.

"Let her go." The muzzle was level with the driver's head. The knife stopped coming.

I gasped with relief as the driver let go of my hair, the pressure on my scalp easing, though it still burned like fire.

Reaching up, I pried the knife from his bloody hand. Jackson helped me out of the car. I stumbled, my body still in pain. As I looked up at Jackson, he caught his breath when he saw my face. I could feel blood dripping down my cheek, and I couldn't straighten all the way—the aches in my breast and back were still too much. I clutched an arm across my chest, cradling the injured party.

The look in Jackson's eye was pure, murderous rage.

"Get out of the car." Barely leashed violence threaded his voice.

The guy eased out, his hands raised. Jackson motioned him to stand with his back to the wall.

"Who hired you?"

The guy said nothing, a look of contempt on his face.

Jackson's hand flashed out, slamming the butt of the weapon against the side of his head. The sharp crack made me flinch.

"I'll ask again," Jackson said. "Who hired you?"

Blood dripped from the man's head, his lips curled in a snarl.

The gunshot made me jump as the man howled with pain and collapsed to the ground. Jackson had shot a bullet into his knee.

"That leg will never work right again," Jackson said, pointing the gun at his other knee. "Want to be a lifelong cripple?"

His voice was so cold, it sent a shudder through me. I'd never seen him this way before. Calculatingly hurting someone with such precision. It scared me.

"All right! All right!" The man's face was shockingly pale and twisted with pain. "Don't shoot."

"Then talk."

The man's gaze moved, looking between us. A sixth sense struck, raising the hairs on the back of my neck. I spun around just in time to see Bruce, pointing yet another gun at us.

I shoved Jackson to the side, tripping and falling with him to the ground just as a shot rang out. I rolled over, seeing the driver dead on the ground, a bullet through the center of his chest.

"You killed him," I blurted, looking up at Bruce. "You almost shot Jackson."

"I'll fix that now," Bruce said, still pointing the gun at us. "Drop the weapon, Jackson."

"What the hell are you doing?" Jackson asked. "You're going to kill us? Why?"

"You think I'm just supposed to trust you that this news won't get out? That Fortress installed a back door into the Exchange? My business will never recover. Now drop the weapon."

"I told you, we're not interested in ruining your business," Jackson bit out.

The muzzle of Bruce's gun swung my way. "Drop the gun or she goes first."

Jackson bit out a curse, sliding his gun across the concrete. Bruce bent and picked it up, his gaze remaining fixed on us.

"A mugging gone wrong," he said with a shrug. "It's New York. Those things happen."

I still had the knife, but I wasn't close enough for it to do any good, no matter my mad skills in throwing them. The idiom *Never bring a knife to a gunfight* ran through my head. I hadn't thought I'd ever actually experience that particular one.

We just needed a distraction. Anything that would make him glance away.

"You don't want to do this," Jackson said, trying to reason with him. "We haven't done anything to you, and I've given my word that we won't. Killing us is trouble you don't need. You don't think with who I am that there won't be an extremely detailed investigation? And you don't know this, but she," he nodded at me, "has the president on speed dial."

Not at all accurate, but I didn't think now was an appropriate time to correct him.

"A simple mugging isn't going to cut it."

Bruce frowned, thinking. "You're right. Get up."

A reprieve, maybe? I hid the knife in my palm and pushed it up the sleeve of my jacket. Jackson stood first and helped me up. I winced as every muscle in my body informed me of its presence.

Bruce reached into the front seat of the car and hit a latch. The trunk popped open.

"Get in," he motioned.

Well, this was just getting better and better.

We were almost to the car when Jackson lunged at Bruce. The gun went off as he knocked it from Bruce's hand, then he swung his fist at Bruce's face. The crunch of bone on bone was loud. I scrambled for the gun, but they were struggling and it got kicked farther away.

The sounds of them smashing into each other and into the wall sent panic through me. I glanced over my shoulder and saw Bruce land a nasty uppercut on Jackson, spinning him into the brick wall. Jackson exploded back, smashing his fist into Bruce's kidney, then the other into his cheek. Bruce went down. Was it over?

I saw it the same time he did. The gun Jackson had tossed away. It was inches from his hand. Bruce grabbed it.

Jackson lunged.

Bruce aimed.

I threw my knife.

The knife hit true, right at the base of Bruce's skull, in the sweet spot between the spinal cord and brain stem. Death was instant. His body slumped over, the gun clattering to the ground.

My legs gave out and I crumpled.

Jackson was breathing hard, his face battered and bruised. His mouth was bleeding and his jacket was torn. Reaching down, he riffled through Bruce's pockets, pulling out his wallet and cell. Using Bruce's finger, he unlocked the phone, scrolled, then took a photo of something with his own phone before tossing it back down onto Bruce's body.

"C'mon," he said, hurrying to me and helping me up. "We need to get out of here."

Three dead bodies lay in the alley, and they'd almost been us.

I began shaking uncontrollably. I couldn't tear my eyes away from Bruce's body. We'd just had dinner with him. Had he known the whole time that he was going to try to have us killed?

"China." Jackson's voice was loud. His hand was under my chin, turning my gaze to him. "It's okay. You're okay. Stay with me." He had his phone in his hand and hit a button. It was picked up almost instantly. "I have a situation," he said. "Priority one, code red. Send medic, guards, cleanup, and law." He ended the call.

"The police?" I squeaked. "How are we ever going to explain this?"

"Of course, not the cops. My lawyers."

He wrapped me very carefully in his arms. I hurt, but not enough to step back. I felt cold all over and I couldn't take a deep breath. My glasses had fallen off somewhere inside the car, but I wasn't about to try to get them.

I'd killed someone. Yes, he'd been going to kill us, but still. My knife was the one sticking out of the back of his neck. And it wasn't as though he was a stranger, like the other two.

I closed my eyes. Jackson was lightly stroking my hair. I focused on breathing. The scent of his sweat was mixed with cologne, and it was familiar.

Jackson employed the best, and the best turned up six minutes later in a flood of cars and vans. I was taken to a special black van outfitted on the inside like an ambulance. I clutched at Jackson, terrified to be apart.

"No," I protested when they tried to lift me up inside. "Don't leave me. What if someone attacks you again? Or me? We're not safe." Every sense of safety had fled, despite the dead bodies, which I couldn't see now, as they were being covered up by thick tarps. I had fistfuls of Jackson's shirt in my grip. He'd shed his torn jacket, tossing it at one of the people cataloging the crime scene.

"You're safe now," he said. "Look there. You see those men."

I looked. At least half a dozen men, wearing full tactical gear and toting some serious-looking weapons, surrounded us and guarded the entrance to the alley.

"Nothing is going to get by them," he said. "I promise, they will protect us."

Slowly, I nodded.

"Now you need someone to look at your injuries," he said. "So be good and get in the van, okay? Maddy will take care of you." He indicated a woman with a stethoscope around her neck. She was older, maybe in her midfifties, and petite, but looked as though she could take on one of those guards, and it'd be a toss-up as to who'd come out on top.

Maddy smiled at me, her expression warm and open, inviting me to trust her. "It's okay, China. I'm here to help."

I looked up at Jackson, uncertain. His lips curved in a reassuring smile, and he pressed a kiss to my forehead. "I'll be back soon. I promise."

Maddy helped me get my jacket and blouse off, making sure that the door was shut so people couldn't see, and examined me. She cleaned the cut on my face and the blood from the driver. Butterfly bandages sufficed to hold the skin together.

"You have some nasty contusions on your back and ribs, but I don't think anything is broken," she said. "You're going to really hurt tomorrow."

I hurt already. I didn't want to think about tomorrow.

"Take a hot bath tonight, that'll help. And I'll give you some pain medication. It'll help you sleep."

After giving me a shot, she wrapped a blanket around me, and I realized I was shivering. My clothes were torn and bloodstained, though my pants had escaped unscathed. I'd have to get the blouse and jacket cleaned and repaired. They'd cost way too much to merely discard.

Maddy left me alone in the van, and I waited. Now that the adrenaline and shock had worn off, I was hard-pressed to keep my eyes open. They kept drifting shut. I never knew what was worse: when you were so tired but were too uncomfortable to sleep (like on a plane), or when you were desperately tired but couldn't allow yourself to sleep (like while driving). They were both pretty miserable to me.

I was about to give up and lie down on the stretcher when Jackson appeared. He held out his hand.

"Let's go."

He helped me down from the van and handed me my glasses. I slipped them on, then wished I hadn't. The alley and bodies were in crystal clarity now, as though I needed an HD image of the crime scene.

We got into the back seat of a sedan, this time with two of Jackson's armed guards in the front. Another sedan, also filled with gun-wielding men, followed behind.

I rested my head against the back of the seat and closed my eyes.

The next thing I knew, Jackson was gently shaking me.

"China. Time to wake up. You can sleep again soon. Let's just get to the room, okay?"

I was lying sideways in his lap, and I thought I'd drooled some. *Nice.*

I shifted and sat up, holding in a groan at the aches and pains that brought. Jackson stepped out to the curb, then extended his hand to me.

The hotel was luxurious and exquisite, chandeliers and marble floors, fresh flowers and antique furniture. I hardly noticed. Jackson must've had someone else check us in because he took me straight to the elevator. Our suite was near the top floor. I was so drowsy now from the pain medication, it was hard to put one foot in front of the other. I had just enough energy to kick off my shoes and peel my trousers from my legs before crawling underneath the sheets. I closed my eyes and said a prayer that I wouldn't dream tonight.

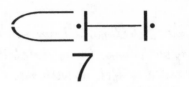

7

Six months later, Mark had an assignment in the most unlikely of places—Maui. I flew there and met him afterward. The honeymoon I'd always wanted but never had, with a man who was not my husband. A sad tale, but I wouldn't have traded that week for anything. My guilt wasn't enough to keep me from going to him.

To feel the intensity of joy after months apart . . . perhaps the only ones who would understand are military spouses. Mark's job was dangerous, and worry gnawed at me when we had to go days without communication. To be in his arms again was the sweetest pain.

Whenever we reconnect, our first time together is always a matter of ripping clothes off and coming together in a blinding need. I love that first time the most. To want and be wanted so intensely . . . it's like the most potent aphrodisiac, the most addictive drug.

Seven days in paradise with the love of my life. It was a place out of time. I'd never been happier, or more in love.

He asked me. Asked me to leave my husband and run away with him. I was elated that he asked, that he wanted a lifetime with me. I wanted that, too. More than anything.

But I couldn't. I had two young boys at home who needed their mother. If I turned my back on them, what did that make me? I'd end up resenting him for it, if I left my children. Our love would grow bitter and tainted. The very thing we had together would fall apart under the weight of regret.

Telling him no was the hardest thing I'd ever done. He begged me. Got down on his knees, took my hands in his, and kissed them. His eyes were filled with pain and desperation. I sobbed and he held me. That night he promised to never ask me again. It only made me cry harder.

◆ ◆ ◆

I woke from a (thankfully) dreamless sleep and made the mistake of stretching. My breath caught at the aches and stiffness in my muscles.

Glancing around, it took me a moment to remember the events of the previous night and where I was. A posh hotel room, though it was dim. The blackout curtains were drawn, so I had no idea what time it was. There was a clock, but without my glasses, I couldn't make out the glowing numbers.

Jackson was lying next to me on his back, sound asleep. A bruise darkened his jaw and I could see more on his ribs and abdomen. His hand lay on top of the sheets, his knuckles bruised and scraped.

It was a miracle we were still alive.

I edged as close to Jackson's side as I dared without waking him. He'd showered, because I could smell soap. It made me want to be clean, too, but I couldn't make myself move away from him.

The only reason he had been there last night was because of me. I'd nearly gotten him killed.

I settled my palm, ever so lightly, on his chest. I watched the rise and fall of his breathing and could feel the warm beat of his heart. It was so, so easy to take each day, each moment, for granted. That you'd have another day tomorrow, and more after that, to correct mistakes and fix things that hadn't gone the way you wanted them to.

But that was part of the problem, wasn't it. I didn't know which way I wanted my life to go, and I didn't have an unlimited time frame to decide. In fact, given the events of last night, I might have even less time than I'd imagined.

I fell back asleep to the sound of Jackson's steady breathing.

When I woke again, I was in the bed alone. Alarmed, I sat up and saw Jackson sitting at the desk with his laptop open in front of him. He glanced my way and I saw his gaze drop to my chest before lifting to my eyes. Oh yeah. I was only wearing my Victoria's Secret demi cup in black satin with the matching no-show panties. I tugged the sheet up.

"Good morning," he said. "I ordered some breakfast. It should be here soon."

"Thank you." The television was on, but muted. I read the closed-captioning. "I see they found Bruce."

"Yes. Since we were the last ones seen with him, the police want to talk to us. My lawyers are taking care of it."

"How?"

"They gave them a sworn statement from you and me about what happened last night, minus Bruce's collusion. Two men wanting to mug two billionaires? It's plausible."

I frowned in confusion. "Did I give a statement in my sleep?"

Jackson's smile was fleeting. "The lawyers took care of it. I hope you don't mind. That's what I pay them for. There's no need for us to speak directly to the police."

I was relieved, and grateful. Money was a more effective shield than bullets in some instances.

My body ached and I remembered the bath that Maddy had recommended. "Do you need the bathroom for a while?" I asked. "I'd like to take a bath."

"Be my guest."

I slowly climbed out of the bed, mindful of the aches and pains. Jackson was looking at me, his expression growing grim and forbidding as more of my battered body was revealed.

"Did the software all get uploaded?" I asked, partly to distract him.

"Yes. I've had a team of my people going through it back at Cysnet."

Although Bruce had told us we couldn't take the software off the premises, Jackson had ways around that. There were other methods of networking than Ethernet and Wi-Fi.

"Do you trust your people?"

"Each one was handpicked and hired by me," he said. "Yes, I trust them."

I nodded, then made my way slowly to the bathroom, feeling his gaze on my back the entire time.

The mirror wasn't kind.

I bruised easily, which didn't help, but even so, I looked like I'd been on the losing end of a serious can of whoop-ass.

My right eye was swollen and bloodshot, a dark bruise surrounding it. The cut on my cheek still had the butterfly bandages holding it closed, and a fragile scab had grown along the seam. My back and side were a mix of blue-and-purple bruises. Note to self: *Being thrown against the dash of a car left a hell of a mark.*

I started the bathwater as hot as I could stand, then slowly began stretching my muscles. By the time I'd brushed my teeth and climbed into the tub, I could at least move without every inch being fraught with pain.

Thirty minutes later, I was feeling mostly human. Freshly scrubbed and shaved (I couldn't stand not shaving), I wrapped myself in a voluminous white robe and grabbed a brush before leaving the bathroom.

Jackson was still at the desk, wearing a robe identical to mine. The suite was so big, there must have been another bathroom where he'd showered while I bathed. His hair was wet and his jaw was smooth.

"I have Bruce's grandfather's address and phone," Jackson said. "I think we should pay him a visit today."

"How did you get that?" It wasn't like you could just Google for that kind of personal info.

"It's what I took a photo of off Bruce's cell last night."

Ah yes. Now I remembered. I'd been in such a daze, I hadn't even though to ask what he'd been doing.

"That's kind of callous, isn't it?" I asked. "His grandson just died."

Jackson's eyebrows flew up. "Seriously? You're worried about his feelings and social niceties? His grandson tried to kill us."

I shrugged, muttering, "Just thought I'd mention it."

Jackson motioned to the closet. "I had your clothes brought over that you bought yesterday. And I sent the other outfit to be cleaned and mended."

"Thank you." It was nice to have someone else around, just to help. It grew tiresome, adulting. As simple a thing as taking care of my clothes for me was appreciated. It was one less thing I had to worry about, and I already had plenty to worry about.

Breakfast had come while I'd been in the bath, and the smell of bacon and eggs made my mouth water. I headed for the table room service had set and reached for the coffee urn.

"Want some?" I asked.

"Sure."

I poured two cups as Jackson closed his laptop and came to sit at the table with me. Dinner seemed forever ago, and I was surprised by how ravenous I was. I managed to polish off my entire plate of bacon, eggs, and hash browns, plus a pancake, an order of toast with jam, and two cups of coffee. I caught Jackson staring at me as I added some more syrup to the last two bites of pancake.

"What?" I asked, suddenly self-conscious. Had I dripped syrup on me? I glanced down, but the robe was still a pristine white.

He shook his head, grinning ruefully. "I don't know where you put it. How you can eat the way you do and still look the way you look."

I forked a bite of pancake. "I have good metabolism." And sometimes, when deep in coding, I forgot to eat. I didn't tell people that, though, not since I'd mentioned it to Bonnie, who'd given me a look and informed me that I had to be a "special kind of stupid" to forget to eat. "I plan my day around mealtimes," she'd said.

"Be glad you do," he said. "If I ate like you, I'd have to work out twice as much as I already do."

"I didn't realize you worked out to keep from gaining weight," I said.

"Why else would I do it?"

"I don't know. Some people like working out," I said, which was about as easy for me to fathom as the people who insisted that they enjoyed eating kale.

"Working out sucks. I do it because I used to be a tubby kid, and I don't want to go back to *being* that tubby kid."

"You were overweight as a child?" Okay, that threw my mental imagery of his past all out of whack.

"Yep. Super smart, glasses, poor, and chubby. A good day was when I got to keep my lunch money."

Bullies. I'd had my share of them, too. Children could be the most vicious creatures on the planet.

"But I showed them," Jackson said, his lips twisting into a thin smile. "The best revenge is success."

I couldn't disagree with that. Being one of the most sought-after and eligible billionaire bachelors in the world wasn't an accomplishment many could boast of.

"I bet the high school reunion was *awesome*," I said, my imagination conjuring up images of Jackson showing up via helicopter on the football field.

He grinned. "Better than I imagined."

In another forty-five minutes, we were ready to go. I wore a sleeveless sheath dress in block colors of navy blue, white, and beige. The hem came to an inch above my knee, and I had on the same pair of red heels as yesterday. My hair was in the usual thick ponytail, and Jackson had returned my glasses. At the moment though, I wore a huge, oversize pair of black sunglasses, which hid my bruised eye. The rest of my bruises were mostly decorating my torso.

Jackson's security people led us out the back of the hotel—two people in front and two behind—to a waiting black SUV. One of the guards got in the front with the driver, and two more climbed into the car with us. The remaining guard watched the street as we pulled away.

The trip to Grandpa's house took us about an hour, though it was only about thirty miles upstate from Manhattan. The homes grew to gargantuan proportions, and the lawns were expansive. It would have been a beautiful drive, if I'd focused on the scenery. But I was on my computer, looking through code. I trusted Jackson's people, but I wanted to look for myself, too.

"We're here," Jackson said, pulling me out of my concentration.

I glanced up and saw we'd stopped in front of a beautiful brick home, built in a Tudor style. Though most Tudor homes I'd seen were cozy cottages. This was a cozy cottage only if your other house was the Kennedy compound.

The guards escorted us to the door, then tactfully stood behind us. Jackson knocked and rang the bell. A woman wearing a half apron answered. She held a brown feather duster and was Latina. I guessed her age to be midfifties.

"May I help you?" she asked. She was frowning, and it had the look of what her perpetual resting face must be.

"We're here to see Harrison Cummings," Jackson said. "Is he available? Tell him Jackson Cooper would like to have a word."

"Please come in," she said. "I will go inform him."

We stood in the foyer and I gaped as I looked around. Jackson's mansion was professionally decorated, but it was in a modern, masculine fashion. This house was done in a high-end rustic style that probably cost a fortune to look authentic. Antique bronze fixtures with the Edison bulbs made to look old, and heavy furniture that appeared to have grown out of the hardwood floor, it fit so well. A beautiful baby grand piano stood in the corner of the massive great room, opposite a stone fireplace that stretched all the way to the top of the vaulted ceiling.

"Wow," I breathed. "This is my dream house."

"You like it?" Jackson asked.

I nodded vigorously. "It's beautiful. And look at the view." The wall at the back of the room was floor-to-ceiling windows, showing a vast expanse of green lawn and property, edged with thick woods for privacy. It was peaceful and rustic, but only thirty miles from the city.

The maid appeared again. "This way."

Jackson had the guards wait, and we followed her down a short hallway to a small library. Despite the season, a fire burned in the grate of the fireplace, and an old man sat in the armchair directly to the right. A blanket covered his lap, and as we drew closer, his face appeared haggard with grief and age.

"Mr. Cooper," he said, his voice called up from deep inside his chest to reverberate around the room. "This is indeed a surprise. Do have a seat."

Despite his age and apparent frailty, he had an air of authority that only came with experience and years spent having others jump to do his bidding. Jackson and I sat on the love seat opposite Harrison.

"I take it you have additional information regarding the—" He paused to clear his throat. "The death of my grandson."

"Yes, sir. I have. But it's going to be different from what the police told you."

Harrison frowned. "What do you mean? You weren't ambushed and mugged? You both have bruises on your faces, and I see your knuckles are scraped and bruised."

"Yes, we absolutely were ambushed," Jackson said. "We're very lucky to be alive. Unfortunately, what the police didn't tell you—because I didn't tell them—was that Bruce was the one who set up that ambush. The targets were me and my colleague."

Harrison's mouth was slightly agape as he absorbed this information, then he snapped it closed. "That's preposterous," he sputtered. "Accusing my grandson of accessory to murder is ridiculous. What possible proof do you have?"

"We're two witnesses," Jackson calmly replied. "And he had a strong motive."

"What motive?" Harrison clearly thought Jackson was lying, his tone scathing.

I answered that one. "He was afraid that we would divulge the fact that Fortress Securities installed a back door via the Y2K software upgrade eighteen years ago."

Silence. Harrison looked from me, to Jackson, then back to me. He let out a long, tired sigh.

"I knew one day it would get out," he said, passing a gnarled hand over his forehead. "It's not something you can keep a secret forever. Not something that big." He looked up. "And you were going to go public? Ruin Fortress?"

"No," Jackson said. "We're trying to find anyone who knew about the back door. We're here because Bruce said you were instrumental in making sure Fortress landed the project, even though it was a small company that never could've gotten it without help."

"Are you with the government?" he asked, his eyes narrowing in suspicion.

"Why would you think that?"

"Because I was warned not to tell anyone."

"The government warned you?" I asked.

"No. The Chinese."

I'd thought as much, but it was good to hear it confirmed.

"Tell us what happened."

Harrison gazed into the fire, seeming to collect his thoughts before he spoke. "It was 1998. The Y2K problem was just showing up on the public radar, though of course the tech world had known about it for a long time.

"I had a seat on the Exchange and had been tasked with heading a committee that would send out requests for proposals on upgrading the Exchange software. We were in the midst of reviewing those bids and proposals when I was . . . approached. He was a very successful Chinese national with an international firm having offices in a dozen countries. I never would have expected it of him."

"Did he offer you something? Threaten you?"

"It was the strangest thing, to be sitting across a linen-covered table, sipping a lunch martini, and have a man in a five-thousand-dollar suit tell you that if you didn't agree to put Fortress Securities ahead of the other bids, your grandson would suffer an unfortunate accident." He gazed into the fire again. "I was . . . stunned. These are the things of fantasy and movies. They didn't happen to regular people. I told him he was being ridiculous and that I was going to report his threat to the SEC."

"What happened?" I asked when he paused.

He turned toward me and the look in his eyes was one of resignation. "They engineered a close call. A taxi, out of control, missed running Bruce over by inches. He leaped out of the way, suffered a broken arm. They assured me that next time, there would be no escape. So I listened. And I did as they said. I didn't ask why they wanted Fortress. I just made it happen."

"Then what?" There had to be more. Bruce hadn't tried to kill us just because we might cause him some bad PR.

"I encouraged Bruce to buy Fortress. No sense letting an opportunity go to waste. He's done very well with the company."

"That's not the whole story," I persisted. "Bruce said they found the back door and fixed it thirteen months later. What happened in the meantime?"

"Nothing," he said. "Whatever was supposed to happen, didn't."

"You're lying," Jackson said flatly. "As of now, your grandson died a victim of a crime. We know the truth. Do you want his name dragged through the mud? Because I have no scruples about letting everyone know what really happened."

He was silent, but we didn't waver, waiting him out. Finally, he spoke, and his voice was quiet and tense.

"The back door, we thought it would be used to crash the market, which is what we watched for. But we were wrong. We found out later, by tearing apart the software, that it had a very different purpose."

I waited, barely noticing that my hands were in fists in my lap. This was it. This was what had killed my mom.

"The software added one one-hundredth of a cent to every tenth trade, sending it to over three dozen accounts, scattered around the world. By the time we'd crawled through all the trades affected, we realized over five billion dollars had been stolen."

The words reverberated inside my head. Five billion dollars. That had been the price of my mom's life. Money. Not some high ideal of country or patriotism—no matter how twisted. Just . . . money.

"Excuse me." My voice sounded foreign in my ears. "Where is your restroom?"

Harrison, looking bewildered, pointed. Calmly, I got up and walked through the door. I was watching myself as if from the outside.

My heels clacked on the wooden floor, slow at first, then faster, as though someone were chasing me. I kept going until I slammed my palm into a half-open door and saw a sink and toilet. I barely made it in time.

I emptied the contents of my stomach and more, until I was dry heaving. Finally, I flushed the toilet and sat back on the floor, exhausted. Someone handed me a damp washcloth. I glanced up to see that Jackson had followed me. I couldn't be bothered to be embarrassed.

Wiping my face, I scooted until my back was against the wall, leaning against it with a sigh. I felt wrung out, and it wasn't just from getting sick.

Jackson sat down next to me, handing me my glasses, which I'd tossed away. He had my shoes, too, which he carefully set side by side on the tile. He leaned against the wall as well.

We said nothing. Jackson wasn't an idiot. He knew why I was upset.

He reached down and grasped my hand in his, threading our fingers together so our palms touched.

"Money," I said at last. "Stupid, dirty, senseless money. Nothing more than that." The icy rage inside burned colder than my despair, chilling me to the bone.

"I know."

Jackson let me absorb and adjust to this information in silence, merely holding my hand. I concentrated on breathing in and out until I didn't have to consciously do it anymore.

"Now what?" I asked.

"We have the why. You know who did it. I guess the answer to that question is up to you."

"I'm taking someone's word for it that Mom was killed and that Danvers did it. I still want to see the police report. Clark was also checking into seeing if Mom's CIA handler was still alive. Maybe they'd know more."

"Then let's get out of here."

The trip back to the city was quiet. I didn't bother opening my laptop. Instead, I watched the scenery go by outside the window. Jackson spoke on his cell, directing the team to find the code, which should be easier now that we knew what it did. I tuned him out after a while.

We were in the middle of rush-hour traffic when my phone buzzed. A text from Clark.

I have information. I'm in NY. Meet me.

I texted back. Okay. Where? When?

Top of the Empire State Building. Of course. Sunset.

Well, that was very specific. And touristy. And *Sleepless in Seattle*. Yet, it fit. I smiled a tiny fraction. Leave it to Clark to lighten my mood.

I checked my weather app. Sunset was in roughly two hours. By the time we got back to the hotel and I made my way to the Empire State Building, it would take me about that long.

"I think I want to get out and walk," I said, picking up my backpack.

Jackson looked at me as if I'd said I'd just sprouted wings and wanted to test them out. "Why would you want to walk? We'll be there shortly."

I didn't want to mention Clark and have him get all weird on me, so I obfuscated. "I need some time alone. I'm just going to walk around for a bit. I want to clear my head."

He looked unconvinced, but nodded. "Okay, but you're taking Julio with you." He motioned to one of the guards.

"I don't need a babysitter," I protested. "Unlike you, no one knows who I am. I'll be fine. Just one of a few million other people walking the streets."

The car was stopped and the sidewalk was right outside my door. I popped it open and slid out.

"I'll meet you back at the hotel later," I said, shouldering my backpack. "Don't wait on dinner for me." I shut the door and melted into the stream of humanity flowing down the sidewalk.

The light turned green and the SUV sat there for a moment. I knew Jackson wanted to send someone with me, but I was being partially truthful. I wanted to be alone for a while. A car angrily honked and the SUV sped through the intersection.

I was by Central Park West, and as I glanced over, the grass and trees of the park looked peaceful and inviting. I headed that way. Joggers passed me as I walked. I wasn't in a hurry. I breathed in the warm spring air and felt the breeze stir my hair.

I wondered if my mom had visited Central Park when she'd lived in New York. She must've. Everyone did, right? You couldn't come to the Big Apple and not step into Central Park. Maybe she'd visited Strawberry Fields—which was where I was headed.

I'd gotten my Elvis love from my mom, but she'd appreciated the Beatles. Not as a fan, but as an influence in popular culture. Honestly, I just thought they'd become as popular as they had been because of the

British accents. There wasn't an American alive who didn't love a British accent, especially teenage girls.

The *Imagine* memorial was more crowded than I thought it would be, with about a dozen people meandering by and taking photographs. I gazed at the mosaic for a few minutes, then moved on, making my way south through the park.

I passed a line of food trucks, pausing next to one that served Belgian waffles. A plateful of carbs sounded like just the thing. I ordered one with Nutella and strawberries, then sat on a bench to eat it, watching people go by.

I deliberately thought of nothing. I slowly ate my waffle, the warm chocolate melting on my tongue. The sound of traffic going by, people walking and talking, and planes overhead filled my senses. I closed my eyes, drinking it in.

Yesterday, I'd nearly died. I could've easily missed this experience. How many more experiences would I miss because of fear or hesitation? Thinking that "one day" I'll do it? What if that mythical and ever-so-evasive One Day never came? And would I be alone?

I was sure my mom hadn't thought her life would end so soon. When she'd been my age, she'd probably thought she had decades ahead of her. Time to get married and have children, watch them grow up and have children of their own. Time to travel and see the world, or at least the places that didn't serve disgusting sea creatures as a staple.

The premonition of being at a crossroads—or a fork in the road—was even stronger now. One path was marked *Jackson*, the other, *Clark*. Perhaps it was narcissistic of me to think I had two men waiting on a way forward with me, but I wasn't in the habit of lying to myself to make life sweeter. Did it make me feel guilty? Absolutely. But I hadn't made them choose their paths.

In Clark, I could have a safe Friends with Benefits relationship that, while perhaps not as emotionally fulfilling as I'd hoped, would also safeguard me from heartache. We could work together and . . .

play . . . together, without either of us risking our hearts. He'd said he was falling in love with me, but I didn't trust that. Clark didn't strike me as the Falling in Love type.

Jackson was the polar opposite, wanting love and marriage and family. On one hand, it was incredibly tempting to create my own "tribe" that was just mine. People who would love me no matter what. Yet that held a truckload of risk, and I'd yet to meet anyone who hadn't been hurt by someone who supposedly loved them.

It was like going down the rabbit hole, and there was no answer. Not yet. Not until I knew what had happened to my mom. The truth would set you free? I guess I'd find out.

I took my time making my way to the Empire State Building, stopping along the way to buy flip-flops, and stuff my red heels in my backpack. Heels were great for sitting. Not so great for walking.

When I reached my destination, I craned my neck to look up. It was beautiful and the height made me dizzy. The wind was chilly now, the streets shadowed from the setting sun, and I wrapped my arms around myself.

I bought a ticket for the 102nd floor and waited for the elevator. The line wasn't terribly long, and my ears popped on the way up. My stomach was trembling, though I didn't know if it was from nerves or anticipation. Clark still set butterflies to flight inside me, no matter what.

The observation deck was deserted, and when I stepped out there, I realized why. The wind took my breath away and made my eyes sting behind my glasses. A shiver overtook me. It was too darn cold out here. Clark would just have to ditch the movie reference and find me inside the gift shop.

I spun around and ran right into a man. "I'm sor—" It took me a fraction of a second to go from surprise to shock to recognition.

Clark.

He picked me up in a bear hug and held me against him. I was surprised, given our last conversation, but instinctively wound my arms around his neck, tightening him to me. He was deliciously warm, bracing his back to the wind and sheltering me with his body. The wind whipped my hair, and I buried my face farther into his neck, inhaling the scent of leather and skin that was all Clark. He held me so tightly, almost as if he knew I'd nearly not seen the dawn today. I didn't know why he wasn't mad at me anymore, and I didn't care.

Finally, he let me slide down his body until my toes touched the ground. That's when he got a good look at my face.

"What. The. Fuck," he ground out.

"If we're going to argue, can we do it inside?" I asked with a sigh. My teeth started to chatter.

He swung open the door and we stepped inside. I breathed a sigh at the warmth. Clark grabbed my hand and tugged me toward the elevators, but I put on the brakes.

"I want to buy a souvenir," I explained. His eye roll was epic. I ignored him and browsed the merchandise. There was a really pretty snow globe with the Empire State Building that I picked up, as well as a book describing the construction of the building during the Great Depression. Clark plucked them from my arms.

"I got it," he said, heading for the register. Though the place was filled with tourists, people took one look at him and got out of his way. I winced, thinking of what the look on his face must be.

He was back quickly and we joined a group of people herded into an elevator. My ears popped again on the way down. Clark held tight to my hand the entire time, staring fixedly straight ahead.

I didn't protest when he led us out of the building and down the street. We crossed a block and went into a bar called the Liberty. It was full, but not crowded. He led me through the bar to a set of stairs going down. The lower level had fewer people, which was nice. I wasn't much of a crowd person.

There was a grouping of leather sofas, and one of them was empty. That's where we landed. A waitress approached almost immediately. She had a piercing in her lower lip that was the size of a dime, with one of those circles in it to keep it open. Those things fascinated me. In earlobes, okay, I could kind of understand. But how did she keep food or liquid from coming out of the hole? I could see her gums and teeth through it.

I opened my mouth to ask when Clark elbowed me sharply. "Don't do it," he muttered.

Grudgingly, I obeyed, sending him a dirty look and rubbing my sore ribs. He'd hit a bruise.

He ordered drinks for us, and the waitress left. She was a cute girl, though the piercing marred the prettiness of her face, in my opinion.

"You said you had information," I began, wanting to bypass the whole what-happened-to-you conversation. Alas, it was not to be.

"Nice try," Clark said. "Start at the beginning, and don't even tell me that Jackson was involved, or I may kill him."

I hesitated too long and he cursed, lengthy and with great feeling.

"It wasn't his fault," I said, and with a sigh, began the story. When I'd finished, Clark looked slightly less pissed off, which would usually be a good thing, but instead he just channeled it into a glint of steel in his eye that was dangerous.

"Bruce is dead already, so don't get any ideas. We lived to fight another day, plus we found out what the software back door did." I pressed my lips together. "My mother died because someone wanted money. That's it."

Clark frowned. "What did you think it would be? Some high ideal? People don't kill for that. They kill for personal gain or revenge."

The words hurt and I stared at him. Clark's eyes softened and he pulled me into his arms.

"I'm sorry. That was a shitty way of putting it."

"No, you're right. I was just hoping that she'd died for something worthwhile. When you lose someone you love, you want it to be for a good reason. That their death serves a higher purpose somehow, in the grand scheme of things. Because she's lost to me forever. I don't want her sacrifice—my sacrifice—to have been for nothing."

"I don't believe anyone's death is for nothing," he said. I twisted in his arms to look up at him. "Everyone has an impact on somebody—their life, and their death. No one comes into or leaves this world without making some kind of difference, for good or bad."

"That's surprisingly deep, coming from you."

One corner of his lips lifted in a smirk. "I have all kinds of depth under this sexy-stud exterior."

I laughed and spontaneously hugged him. I didn't think I'd be laughing anytime soon, but leave it to Clark to prove me wrong.

The waitress returned with our drinks, giving me a look of disdain for my unbridled display of affection. Apparently, that was Not Cool, in her view.

I took a sip of my drink—clear, but sweet and tart at the same time—and asked, "So what did you find out?"

"The good news is, your mom's handler is still alive." He handed me a slip of paper. "That's his name and address."

"Then what's the bad news?"

Clark's expression was grim. "The address is for a retirement home, where he suffers from Alzheimer's."

Ouch. That hit a nerve for Clark, I was sure. Plus, who knew if he'd remember the answers to the questions I wanted to ask?

"So if we find out who got the money," Clark mused, "then we find out who ordered your mom's murder. Since Chen was killed, we can't assume only the Chinese were involved. The problem is, there's no rhyme or reason as to why the CIA would want her dead, then do nothing about the back door. Letting all that money spill through their fingers was a risky move. Why did they do that? Were they hoping it would lead to something—or someone—bigger?"

"I don't know," I confessed. "I don't want to believe that Danvers killed her. It had to be the Chinese, or maybe a subversion in the CIA itself." Hope springs eternal.

"Any word on that police report?"

I shook my head. "I thought I'd call tomorrow and check on it."

A huge black guy came over to us, wearing jeans and a tight T-shirt. His expression was no-nonsense.

"Excuse me," he said, directing his words to me. "May I have a word?"

Clark glanced at me. "You know this guy?"

"No," I replied, confused. "I don't think so. Do I know you?"

"No, ma'am. This'll just take a minute."

"She's not going anywhere without me." Clark stood, going toe-to-toe with the guy, whose gaze narrowed. Clark was dangerous, but this guy looked like he ate nails for breakfast.

I jumped to my feet, laying a restraining hand on Clark's arm. "It's fine," I said. The last thing we needed was an incident. "I won't leave your sight."

That seemed to satisfy Clark, sort of, so I followed the man until we were out of earshot. Clark was watching me like a hawk.

"Who are you?" I asked. "What do you want?"

"My name is Travis," he said. "Bridget told me about you."

"Who's Bridget?"

"Your server. I work security here. Thought I'd come down and see if you could use some help. I can call the cops, or just detain him"—he nodded toward Clark—"for a while so you have time to make other arrangements."

I wasn't following. "Why would—Oh." The light bulb went on. "He didn't hit me," I said with a sigh. "I got mugged last night."

Travis frowned. "Are you sure? Because you don't have to lie. There are people who can help."

"I swear. He'd kill anyone who hurt me." Which was the absolute truth.

"Okay, well, take this. Just in case." He handed me a card.

"I do appreciate it, though," I said. "That was kind of Bridget to notice and get involved."

He nodded and moved on. I went back to Clark.

"What was that about?"

"Just trying to do a good deed and save a woman in an abusive relationship," I said.

"Did you tell him you and Coop already broke up?"

I gave him a look and decided to ignore his dig at Jackson. "So when do we go visit this handler? What's his name?"

"Jim Dayle. He's in a place over in Jersey. Visiting hours are tomorrow from ten until four."

"Okay, then. That's what we'll do."

I took another swig of my drink, thinking, when a woman plopped herself down opposite us.

"Hey, baby," she said to Clark. "Miss me?" She transferred her gaze from him to me, then back. "We're still married, you know. Don't tell me I caught you cheating on me."

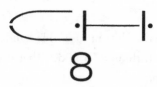

8

"Married?" I repeated, stunned. I turned to Clark. "Is she serious? You're *married?*"

The woman gave a tinkling laugh that grated on my nerves, right along with her thigh gap. She was lithe and tall, with thick, straight mahogany hair that fell past her shoulders. Her hair was shiny, her eyes were a chocolate brown with thick lashes, and with her sculpted cheekbones and full lips, she looked as if she could be Charlize Theron's brunette twin.

I clenched my jaw, waiting for Clark's answer. He rolled his eyes at me.

"Fuck, no," he said. "It's a fun little game she likes to play." His gaze narrowed as he turned back to the woman. "She thinks it's funny."

"It *is* funny," she said. "One of these days someone's going to slap you. That will be *hilarious.*"

"China, this is Gabby," Clark said. "Gabby, meet China."

"It's *Gabriella*," she corrected him, her gaze chilly.

"Whatever." He shrugged. "What the fuck do you want?"

"I have a job opportunity for you. What luck that you're in town."

"Do I want to know how you found me?" Clark asked.

She smiled, but it was thin-lipped and cold. "We have eyes everywhere. Or have you forgotten?"

Reaching out, she picked up his glass and took a sip of his drink. My eyes narrowed and I suddenly knew what the expression "the green-eyed monster" meant. I certainly felt as though I had a monster inside wanting to get out and begin plucking out the woman's perfectly arched eyebrows.

"I'm not taking jobs right now," he said, taking his drink from her. "Find someone else."

"But it's an old friend of yours," she wheedled, tracing the exposed skin of his neck and clavicle with one sharply manicured nail. "Remember Wirecutter?"

Clark stiffened ever so slightly. "What about him?"

I watched with satisfaction as he picked up her hand with two fingers—as though she were contagious—and removed it from his body.

"He's made an enemy. One who wants him dead." She shrugged one shoulder, as if speaking about another person's demise was akin to talking about the weather. "You were specifically requested."

"And he's here?"

She gave him a withering look. "I wouldn't be here, wasting my time, if he wasn't."

Clark glanced away and I could tell he was thinking. Gabriella reached into her designer handbag and produced a manila file folder. She handed it to him.

"Information is inside. It's likely to be out-of-date within twenty-four hours. Payment is five hundred thousand now, another five hundred once it's done. I'm assuming your account is still open?"

Clark's gaze swung back to her, and he gave a curt nod. She smiled. "Excellent."

She stood and blew Clark a kiss before heading for the stairs and exit. I turned to Clark.

"Please tell me you're not serious," I said. "You really just took a contract?"

His gripped my arm. "Will you keep your voice down?" he growled. "I'm not sure the bouncer heard you."

His sarcasm was hard to miss, but I lowered my voice. "Answer the question," I demanded. "Are you really going to kill this guy?"

"*This guy* deserves to die."

"Who are you to say that?" I was angry, not just at his attempt to justify murder, but that he'd think he was *qualified* to make that judgment on someone.

Clark loomed over me, his eyes a cold, blue fire. "I'm qualified to say that because I know what he's done." He stood, took some bills from his wallet, and tossed them on the table. Grabbing my hand and the folder, he pulled me along behind him up the stairs and outside.

I hurried to keep up with his long strides that were eating up the pavement. "Tell me, then," I said. "The least you could do is tell me what he's done."

"So you can judge for yourself?" he asked. "How about you just trust me?" He stopped and spun me around so my back was to the brick wall. His body pressed against mine, his hands locked around my wrists, holding me in place. "Or don't you think I'm capable of seeing the difference between right and wrong?"

His warm breath touched my cheek, and my heart skipped a beat. What had he said again? Oh yeah.

"Of course you know right from wrong," I said. "That's why I was shocked to see you accept the contract."

His eyes bore into mine and I saw nothing except him. The naked cowboy could've pranced right up and started singing "Rhinestone Cowboy," and I wouldn't have noticed. His hands clasped my arms in a firm hold that didn't hurt, but I knew I couldn't get away. His gaze dropped to my mouth, and I had the nearly irresistible urge to lick my lips. Scraps of memory, like photographs flipping through my mind's eye, hit me.

Clark with his head between my legs. His body on top of mine, moving inside me. My gasps and cries of pleasure. The sound of our bodies coming together, slowly at first, then faster and harder. How he looked at me when he was about to come.

Some of what I was thinking must've shown in my eyes, because Clark suddenly muttered a curse and abruptly let me go.

"Come on," he said. "My hotel's around the corner."

He wasn't kidding. The place was about a two-minute walk, a boutique hotel with a suit-clad doorman who smiled and held the door for us. The elevator was empty and waiting on the ground floor.

Room 407 was at the end of the hall, and Clark slid the key card into the slot. Inside, it was a gorgeous room, and I took a moment to appreciate it. The decor was deep purple along with white and silver. The king-size bed took up a whole corner close to the windows, which had a great view of the Empire State Building. It was dark outside and the building was lit up.

Clark sat down at the desk and began going through the folder. I sidled up next to him and peered over his shoulder.

There was a photograph of a man—large and roughened by life—unsmiling and with eyes devoid of humanity. Just looking at him sent a shiver through me. I looked down at the dossier Clark was reading.

"... *bodyguard ... Stasi officer ... Russian Mafia ... drug cartel ... human trafficking ... child pornography ...*"

His real name was Andrei Alexeev, and he'd gone from bad to worse, in careers where humanity and a conscience were a liability. Now he was an oligarch with thousands of henchmen at his fingertips and a global network of drugs and humans from which he soaked his billions.

Clark kept flipping pages. There were photographs. Lots of them. Victims, some so young that it was all I could do not to be ill. While there were pictures of him on an enormous yacht, surrounded by pencil-thin anorexic women with long legs and flowing locks of hair.

Photos of dead people followed. Clark paused at a photo of a man, flat gaze staring straight ahead, with a bullet hole between his eyes.

"Did you know him?" I asked.

Clark's fingers tightened on the photo. "Yeah." His voice was low and rough. "He was undercover CIA. You've heard of Aldrich Ames?"

I remembered. Yes, the CIA agent who'd spied for the USSR and Russia. I nodded.

"This man trained me. He was my mentor. Andrei had him tortured and killed when Ames leaked his identity. They dumped his body in the gutter and sent his teeth to the CIA for identification. The teeth had been extracted while he was still alive."

The look on Clark's face was like a punch to the gut.

"And you think your pain gives you the right to be his executioner?" I asked.

"I think someone has to be. And he's been gift wrapped for me and loaded with a pile of cash. Why wouldn't I?"

"Because it's wrong."

His lips twisted. "That's the difference between you and me. My morals are flexible. He needs to die."

"Someone else will just take his place," I argued. "Maybe someone worse."

"So I shouldn't take him out because evil exists and will always exist?" Clark snorted in disgust. "Take your altruism to the nearest prison. Let me know how that works out for you."

I'd never seen this side of Clark. Darkness, with eyes a bottomless pit of anger and hopelessness. He was the embodiment of the avenging, fallen angel, determined to atone for his sins by wiping out evil, no matter what it made him.

It made me unbearably sad.

"What do you need me to do?" I asked quietly.

There was a flash of relief in his eyes, and gratitude, then it was gone.

"I don't know yet. Maybe nothing."

"I'm not letting you do this alone," I said. "We're friends. Partners. Remember?"

A nearly imperceptible wince crossed his face, so quick I might have imagined it.

"You bet," he said flatly. "Have a seat and give me a minute."

I sank onto the edge of the bed and waited. My phone buzzed and I glanced at the screen. Jackson. I hesitated, then swiped and sent the autotext: Sorry, I can't talk right now. There. He knew I was alive, but didn't want to chat.

I waited—somewhat patiently—for Clark to finish reading. When he finally turned to me, I was more than ready to hear a plan. Anything to take my mind off my own issues.

"So he's staying at the Ritz," he said. "He's in town for only tonight, and he has a habit of ordering . . . entertainment . . . when he's in town."

"Entertainment?" I echoed. "Like pay-per-view?" Was there a fight this weekend?

"No, China," Clark said with exaggerated patience. "He orders a few high-class hookers."

"Oh. Well. That has to be way pricier than pay-per-view." I blinked twice and pushed my glasses up my nose.

Clark's lips twitched. "I'm sure. The thing is, if we can get with the hookers, then we'll get him when his security is the most lax and his guard is down. Men like him never expect a woman to be a threat."

"Good idea," I said, nodding. Then my brain caught up with The Plan. Wait a minute. "How are you planning to do that?" I had a really bad feeling about this.

"I'll be their handler," he said. "Get into the suite, take out some bodyguards, take him out."

O. M. G. "No," I said, instantly shaking my head. "You just showed me this guy's file. He's dangerous. If you get caught, he won't just kill you. He'll torture you." Bile rose in my throat at the thought of Clark's face in those pictures I'd seen.

"Then I won't get caught," he said, rolling his eyes. "Obviously."

His blatant disregard for his own safety made me angry. I also knew I wouldn't be able to stop him. He was already popping open a small laptop.

"Then I'm coming, too."

"Nope." He didn't even glance at me as he logged in to his computer.

"I can be a hooker. I've seen *Pretty Woman*."

His snort said it all.

"I know I'm not high-class hooker material. I'm not *low*-class hooker material. But I've cosplayed before. And you need backup."

"Your self-image is massively distorted," he said. "But regardless, you're not coming along." He reached for his cell and dialed.

"Who are you calling?"

"The only place in town who'll have what he wants—Hey, Simone," he said into the phone. "It's Clark . . . yeah, it's been a while. How's Clint doing? Still getting straight *As*? Awesome. Hey, I hear you have a special request for tonight at the Ritz . . ."

He kept talking, arranging to be the handler. I didn't know which was worse: that he knew a madam's number, or that they were on a first-name basis.

"You know my plans for him." He was still talking. "Somebody with a lot of cash contacted me." He paused, listening. "Arrange to have your guy ambushed. I'll fill in. Your hands are clean. Besides, no one's going to look too hard for revenge. They'll be too busy fighting to take his place."

A few more words and plans exchanged—time and place—and he hung up.

"Good to go," he said, glancing at his watch. "I'm meeting them in ninety minutes."

"Then I need to get ready." I headed for the closet, hoping he'd have what I needed.

Clark muttered a curse. "I said, you're not coming."

"You can't stop me," I tossed over my shoulder. I spied what I needed and pulled it off the hanger. A man's pristine white dress shirt. Perfect. I undid my thin red belt and set it aside.

"Your face is bruised," he argued. "No one's going to buy that you're a hooker."

"I had an unruly customer last night." I presented my back to him. "Unzip me, please."

I had to wait a moment, but he reached up to my zipper and slowly drew it down my back. A draft of air touched my waist, then the featherlight touch of his fingers in the small of my back. He drew a line down to the top edge of my panties and stopped.

"Looks like you had a helluva time last night." His voice was thick, and I remembered the bruises decorating my back and torso.

Well, that was enough to break the mood. Here I'd been getting hot and bothered, while he'd been visualizing how I'd acquired my battle scars.

Clearing my throat, I moved away, pretending nothing was amiss. "I'm fine," I said, stepping out of my dress. I was left in a matching set of bridal white-lace demi-push-up, teeny-tiny bikini underpants, and red heels.

"Damn, you look good," he said, his hands on my waist turning me to face him. I swallowed at the blue fire in his eyes. "Though I prefer your skin the way it usually looks, like the color of the clouds at sunrise. The palest shade of pink that's almost too perfect." His fingers grazed my abdomen down to my hip bone.

The desire in his eyes was impossible not to see. And I could feel heat burning in my belly. It would be so easy to take one step forward, straddle his lap, put my arms around his neck, and kiss him.

But kissing would open the door to love, and offering something I wasn't able to give. So I stepped back instead of forward.

I forced the fakest-sounding laugh ever as I turned toward the closet. "Wow, that's really . . . poetic. So much nicer-sounding than pale." I pulled on the dress shirt and began buttoning it. "Hope you don't mind if I borrow this? It's not really your style."

"You never know when you'll need to put on a suit." His reply was nonchalant, but something sad flickered in his eyes before it was gone.

I left the top button undone, then wrapped the belt around my waist. I folded back the sleeves several times until they were nearly to my elbows. I checked myself in the mirror. Not bad for an impromptu prostitute costume. I struck my best come-hither pose, which probably looked ridiculous, but one worked with what one had.

"How much would you pay?" I asked, only half teasing.

He was sprawled in the chair, his knees far apart, one elbow on the armrest. His body looked relaxed, but I could tell that every muscle was taut. I tried valiantly to keep my eyes from staring at the obvious bulge in his jeans.

Clark rose, taking his time about doing it, until all six feet, two inches of him stood a mere breath from me. I tipped my head back, watching his face as he concentrated on his shirt draped on my skin. He reached forward and I stopped breathing. He undid three more buttons on the shirt, excruciatingly slow, opening the V down to low between my cleavage. The soft brush of his fingers against my skin made goose bumps erupt on my arms, and my nipples puckered.

He slid the elastic band down my ponytail until it came off. My hair fell in a heavy mass. I watched his face as he worked his fingers into the strands, all the way to my scalp, gently drawing the strands to splay across my shoulders and back. His gaze seemed mesmerized by the thick, soft mass of my hair.

"There," he said quietly, seemingly oblivious to the sexual tension choking me.

The shirt came down to midthigh. The belt accentuated the narrowness of my waist while the low-cut neckline showcased my ample cleavage, courtesy of Victoria.

"One last thing," he said, reaching up and sliding my glasses off. Now I could only see him, nothing else. "Other than the shiner, you're perfect."

The air was thick in my lungs, making my chest heave in a way that drew his attention to my breasts, his gaze flicking downward. His hands settled on my shoulders, his thumb lightly stroking the exposed skin of my neck and clavicle.

I swallowed hard. "Are you sure that whole not-kissing thing is still in effect, right? Because it's not included in the Friends with Benefits package?" I asked, my voice breathless and probably not fooling anyone. I wanted to kiss him so badly, it was a physical ache.

"You're with him," Clark murmured, his fingers moving to caress my jaw while his gaze memorized my face. "And you should be. I was an idiot to think you could feel more for me. Look at what I've done, what I'm doing tonight. You should ditch me, baby. Go back to Coop, have a wedding that costs millions, and invite everyone who has ever been a shit to you."

I was barely breathing, but I didn't mind. I was painfully aware that I might not ever see Clark again. Funny how a brush with death makes you reevaluate your priorities.

I wish I knew what I wanted. Being with Jackson was comfortable and safe. Clark was right about that. We were perfect for each other, and the chemistry was fantastic.

But Clark . . . it felt as though I'd stuck my finger in an electrical socket and been shocked into life. It was addictive . . . and terrifying.

The Friend Zone was the only safe place I could put him, but it also killed me that that's where he thought he deserved to be.

His blue-eyed gaze penetrated mine, and I couldn't look away. There was more to Clark than what he let on, and I didn't want him to slide back into the dark shell he'd been in when I'd first met him.

"Please don't say that," I whispered. "You've saved my life. More than once. You're not evil, just . . . misguided on occasion." *Understatement, what?*

"You believe that because you *want* to, but that doesn't make it true."

"Let's not go tonight," I tried again. "Take me somewhere else instead. I've never been to New York before. Show me something I'll never forget."

His fingers traced the outline of my face from my temple to my jaw. "Aw, baby. I wish I could," he murmured.

"Please, Clark. I don't want anything to happen to you. Killing people isn't who you are."

His lips twisted. "You give me too much credit. You think it'll cause me even a twinge of conscience to put a bullet in this asshole's head?" He leaned even closer and enunciated each word. "I'd do it for free."

I watched him and he watched me.

"Still think I'm not evil?" he asked.

"Would you care if I didn't?" I replied.

A glint of appreciation shone in his eyes. His lips brushed my ear. "Anything," he whispered. "I'd pay any price you named."

My eyes drifted closed at the touch. I wanted him. Our chemistry when we were together was overwhelming. It clouded my thoughts and judgment. And it made me not care about losing either of those things.

He abruptly stepped away and I could breathe again, but the disappointment was acute. His words were still echoing inside my head.

"Here's the rules," he said. "Don't draw attention to yourself. Don't speak unless spoken to. You'll probably be shorter than the other girls, so use them as camouflage."

As he said all this, he was checking his handgun's magazine and slapping it back into place. It went in the back waist of his jeans, and he tugged his T-shirt down to cover it.

He crouched down and lifted one pant leg, sliding a lethal-looking knife into a holster and attaching it to his calf. "Do not try to get involved in what I'm doing, even if you're trying to help. You'll just get in the way." He tugged his pant leg down and lifted the other. A smaller pistol went into an ankle holster.

I'd never seen Clark get this armed before, and my face flushed when I realized it was . . . pretty darn hot. I had four degrees, a well-above-genius-level IQ, could pay my own bills and afford (mostly) anything I wanted to buy, within reason. Yet here I was, a throwback cliché, who thought a man—who already was hotter than sin—looked even more tempting when armed to the teeth. The phrase "panty-dropping" was a crude, though apt, way to describe how I felt watching him.

Clark stood, glanced at me, and froze. His eyes darkened. "If you don't stop looking at me like that, I'm going to take you to bed. Consequences be damned."

A shiver went through me at the way he growled those words, and I hastily looked away.

He held his leather jacket for me to put on, and I obediently slid my arms into the sleeves. It was wreathed in his scent, and I felt safer just wrapping it around me.

"Are you sure I can't wear my glasses?" I asked. "I'm no good after about four feet without them."

"We'll take them with us," he said, snagging them with his finger. He opened the jacket I was wearing, his eyes meeting mine, and slid them into the inside pocket. The back of his hand touched my breast, and I sucked in a breath.

"If you're insisting on doing this, you need to channel your inner *Pretty Woman*," he said. "You're not there to make friends, so no need to smile."

That was good, because my strained, polite smile wasn't believable under the best of circumstances. I doubted it would hold up to the I'm-really-a-hooker-I-promise scenario.

"Let's go." He took my hand and led me to the door.

A limousine was waiting for us downstairs, and when the driver opened the door, I was hit by a flood of female voices. I stopped in my tracks, anxiety hitting me hard. New people, and women at that. Women were usually colder to me than men, and I wasn't good at chattering small talk. I'd thought we'd meet them there or something, not that I'd have to share a ride with them.

Clark was talking to the driver, who rounded the car to get in the driver's seat. He looked at me standing immobile on the sidewalk.

"Wanna back out?" he asked.

Yes. "No."

"Then get in." He said it with the exasperation of a parent with a five-year-old wasting his precious time because I was too scared to go into the haunted house at the mall.

I took a breath and climbed into the car.

The back seat was empty, so I sat there, scooting over to make room for Clark. Four other women sat in the long side seat, and they all looked curiously at me. I looked back.

Clark climbed in and closed the door. "Hello, ladies."

"You're an asshole," the woman sitting closest to me snapped.

My jaw dropped and I looked at Clark. "She knows you?"

That got a massive eye roll. "Hell, no. And I find it insulting that you think she would just because she called me an asshole."

I raised my eyebrows in disbelief. "Really?"

"Point taken," he muttered.

"Simone said you were going to protect us," the second woman said. "If what you've done to that little thing's face is any indication, I don't want your kind of *protection*."

All four of the women were staring daggers at Clark, and I got it.

"Oh no, he didn't do this to me," I hurriedly said. "It was someone else. He's dead now."

"He's dead now?" This was from a striking black woman seated toward the front.

"Yeah. I, um, killed him."

There was a low whistle. "Holy shit, girl. Don't piss you off, amirite?"

They all laughed and the woman nearest me introduced herself. "I'm Celine. This is Rosie, Jen, and Arya."

"I'm Ch . . . erry," I said, thinking I shouldn't give my real name after just confessing to killing someone. "It's nice to meet you." I turned toward Clark, but he had his phone to his ear.

"You can leave me out of the female bonding," he said with a wave of his hand. "Be my guest."

I rolled my eyes. "You'll have to excuse him," I said to the women. "He's a smart-ass."

"He can be as much of a smart-ass as he wants, Cherry," Rosie said. "So long as he can keep us alive."

She sounded serious, taking me off guard. "Is that a real danger in this . . . line of work?" I was proud of that euphemism.

"Always," Celine said. "Especially these kinds of customers. But the money is really good, and we watch each other's backs."

Celine scrutinized my face. "Do you have any makeup on at all?" I shook my head. "Jen, do you have some concealer on you? Your skin tone is fair enough to match hers."

Jen dug in her purse, produced the concealer, and passed it to Celine.

"Close your eyes and hold still," she said. She was gentle with the makeup, and it didn't take long. "There you go. Much better."

They were all very pretty women. Celine was a blonde while Rosie was a redhead. Jen was a light brunette with ash blonde highlights. And they were all wearing beautiful cocktail dresses.

I turned to Clark in dismay. He was just sliding his phone into his pocket. "Why didn't you tell me to leave my dress on? That would've looked better than this." I motioned to my outfit.

His lips twisted, a wicked glint in his eyes. "And miss the show I got? I don't think so."

Sheesh. I didn't know if I should feel like an idiot, or if it was supposed to be a compliment. I decided both were valid.

"You look fine," Rosie said. "The clothes won't be on long anyway."

I swallowed hard. Clark's hand found mine on the seat between us, squeezing reassurance into me.

The Ritz-Carlton was only a couple of miles away, but it took twenty minutes to get there. The leather seat was cold against the backs of my thighs. I sat still, deliberately keeping myself from fidgeting. I could do this. It was just like a cosplay, except instead of Princess Leia or Harley Quinn, I was Vivian from *Pretty Woman*. And I would hardly need to do anything . . . except somehow stop Clark from killing a man in cold blood.

I kept my knees together when swinging my legs from the car onto the asphalt. Clark took my elbow to help me from the seat, then assisted the other women as well. They all towered over me, statuesque and wearing sky-high heels.

Clark kept hold of me as we walked into the building, where a doorman even more fancily dressed opened the door for us. I was twisted around looking at the fancy man, so when I glanced back, I stumbled.

"Wow."

I'd never seen a hotel like this before. *Elaborate* and *luxurious* only scratched the surface. Marble floors, polished wood, overflowing bouquets of flowers everywhere. Everyone I saw was dressed to the hilt, and I wanted to cower in a corner to hide my bare legs. The jacket was long enough to make it appear I had nothing on underneath. I saw more than one judgy glance come my way, though nothing but admiring looks were directed at Celine, Rosie, Jen, and Arya.

"Chin up," Clark muttered, guiding me toward the elevator, which had an actual person inside operating the controls.

"Floor, sir?" the elevator operator asked Clark.

"Twenty-second."

The elevator ride was too short but felt like an eternity. I was starting to sweat underneath the leather jacket. Clark caught my eye. He gave me a small nod and squeezed my elbow in reassurance. The other women seemed to be a little tense as well, no one speaking on the way up.

The top floor was quiet, the heavy carpet swallowing our footsteps as the elevator doors slid closed. Four men were clustered around a double door about thirty feet away.

The men saw us approaching and squared off against us. Each of them was twice the size of me and were toting the kinds of weapons that were illegal to carry in Manhattan.

One stepped forward to meet us. He looked us over, then addressed Clark in a thick Russian accent.

"You are late."

Clark shrugged. "Traffic."

The man grunted. "Follow me."

He led us past the other guards and into the suite. Clark was in the lead, and I brought up the rear. I kept my eyes straight ahead as we passed the men with guns. One of them had a severe body-odor problem.

Inside, the suite was palatial and luxurious, with panoramic views of the city. I barely glanced at the windows though, my attention drawn to two more guards in the room along with two suit-clad men, relaxing on opposite sofas. One I recognized as Alexeev. The other was a stranger.

"Finally," Andrei said, getting to his feet. He wasn't very tall, perhaps about five foot ten, but he was stocky and muscular. "We've been kept waiting a long time." His criticism was directed at Clark, whose face was a blank, cold mask.

"It's a good thing my ladies are worth waiting for," Clark said, smiling thinly.

Andrei turned to the other man. "Thomas, you are my guest. Please. Take first pick. However many you would like."

Thomas was taller than Andrei, and considerably younger. I pegged him for early forties. His suit was expensive and tailored, his hair dark with just a touch of silver at his temples. He reminded me of Pierce Brosnan in his *Thomas Crown* days.

He looked over the women one by one. They each looked completely at ease, giving him seductive smiles and posing. My palms were sweating and my heart was racing. When his eyes landed on me, I dropped my gaze to the floor. I desperately wanted to fidget but was too terrified.

It'll be okay. Clark's here. It'll be okay . . . I kept repeating inside my head.

I heard him walking toward us, and my heart leaped into my throat when he paused in front of me.

"What's your name?" he asked.

"Ch-Cherry," I stammered, still looking at the floor. I could barely hear over the pounding of my heart in my ears.

He put a finger underneath my chin, tipping my head up until I had to look him in the eyes. They were the gray of a stormy sky. He tipped his head to the side, considering, then one corner of his mouth lifted.

"I'll have this one," he said to Andrei.

"Just one?" Andrei sounded surprised.

Thomas looked over his shoulder and smiled. "Our tastes run differently, my friend."

Andrei laughed heartily. "The more for me. Come, ladies. Join me."

Rosie, Arya, Celine, and Jen all followed Andrei to a door that I knew led to a bedroom. Celine cast me a sympathetic look over her shoulder. Then the door closed.

Clark still stood in the center of the room, his hands in fists at his sides. The two guards remained as well.

"This way, please," Thomas said, ever so politely. He put his hand on the small of my back and led me into another bedroom. The door closed behind me and we were alone.

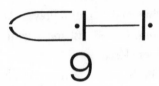

9

"You don't look like you do this very often," Thomas said, loosening his tie.

I hovered near the door, my mouth dry as cotton.

"Um, yeah. It's my first time." The first rule of lying: stick as much to the truth as possible.

He paused in folding his suit jacket, raising an eyebrow. "Ever? That must have cost Andrei a fortune."

My cheeks grew hot. "Not that. I mean, like this."

"Ah. For money, you mean."

I didn't hear anything beyond the door. Shouldn't Clark have disarmed those guards by now? How long would it take to kill Andrei? Would he come rescue me first, or after? If Thomas suddenly realized I wasn't a real prostitute, would he guess what was happening?

"H-how do you know Andrei?" I asked. Maybe this guy was just as bad, possibly worse.

"Take off the jacket," he said, ignoring my question. He was unbuttoning his cuffs and folding back the sleeves.

I took a step away, my back hitting the door. Thomas smiled.

"I knew I'd chosen correctly. I do enjoy having to work for it. You seldom get that with prostitutes."

That didn't sound good. At all.

"Take off the jacket," he said, "or I'll take it off for you."

"Okay, okay," I said hastily. "Just, um, you know. A little nervous." If Clark didn't get in here soon . . . Wait a second. I squinted at him. He looked . . . familiar. *Screw it.* I dug out my glasses and put them on.

"I like the glasses. They're a nice touch. We'll leave them on."

"I know you," I said, my eyes widening. Thomas froze. "You're Thomas Driscoll."

He froze in the middle of folding back his cuff. "How the hell—"

"The CEO of Psy-Gen Enterprises," I continued excitedly. Psy-Gen was on the cutting edge of robotic technology. "I've been wanting to meet you for a while." I thrust out my hand. He took it automatically, his mouth hanging open, and I pumped a hearty handshake. "Humanoid robots are the way of the future."

He regained his composure, his face flushing red as he snatched his hand away.

"Why is it that, with all the technology at your fingertips and genius engineers, the first thing robots are wanted for is sex?" I'd never understood that.

"Another judgmental layman, I see," he said. "You Puritans think it's so awful to have sex robots, well, let me tell you something. If sex robots were available—lifelike or even better than the real thing—don't you realize the demand for human sex trafficking would bottom out? All those millions of women and children forced into the sex slave industry would no longer be needed. Robots would fulfill physical needs and desires, no matter how perverse, and no one gets hurt."

"So you're doing it as a purely philanthropic gesture," I said. "Like I'm supposed to believe that? It's all about the money. It always is all about the money." Thoughts of my mom flashed through my mind, and I didn't have to fake the bitterness in my voice.

"I'm saying that not all new technological advances are the harbingers of *Terminator*," he tossed back. "And of course it will be lucrative.

Extremely. It should be, as much money as has gone into development. The millions have to be recouped somehow."

"What about using them for elderly companions?" I asked. "They can provide companionship while also providing health care and performing domestic chores."

"That's down the road," he said. "Sex is more lucrative. There's only so much money we can devote to a behavior that won't be. You think old people are going to pay for a robot like that? That they'd even be able to? Some might be able to afford it, but most can't. And there's no way the insurance industry will cough up that kind of money."

"But the software is more useful and can be tweaked for a variety of uses," I argued. "Sex robots can fund programming of other types of robotics."

His eyes narrowed. "How the hell do you know what software is adaptable?"

I crossed my arms over my chest. "Because I was the lead project manager when you outsourced to Cysnet. And programming how to tell if someone is experiencing disorientation due to the onset of a stroke is a hell of a lot harder than coding a blow job."

Thomas looked as though I'd slapped him with a wet trout. "You're joking," he said.

"Nope. Did they ever work out the problem with the teeth?"

He sat down heavily on the bed, still staring at me in shock. "Not yet."

I rolled my eyes. "It figures. Amateurs."

"Why are you here? Doing"—he motioned to my outfit—"this?"

"Long story. You know, I had an idea for the teeth problem, but they wouldn't listen to me. Jerry was in charge of that software, and there was no way some *girl* was going to tell him how to do his job. Idiot." Jerry had been a real dick. No pun intended.

"The elderly-care robots work perfectly. The software is genius. Everyone says so. There's just no way to sell them. We've got to get the sex robots working or we're going to go bankrupt."

"Is that why you're with Andrei?" I asked. "Looking for investors."

He nodded, grimacing. "You gotta take money where you can get it. The timeline's already had to be extended three times. We've *got* to have a working product before the end of the year." He eyed me speculatively. "So you're really a programmer. And you wrote that software. But you don't code anymore."

I shrugged, improvising. "I'm writing a book now. This is research."

"How about you postpone your . . . research and come work for me?"

I shook my head. "It's an intriguing idea, trying to program sexual behavior into a robot, but . . . ew. I don't want to."

"Think about it," he said, looking desperate. "I'll start your salary at five hundred thousand, and you'll get company shares. If we're the first to come to market with this, we'll make more money than Amazon. You'll be able to retire in five years."

"Sorry. I don't want to go to work every day trying to solve problems like how to make them 'fight more.'" I gave him a look to emphasize my point.

He only looked slightly abashed. "Just take a look at this code," he said, pulling out his phone. "My chief engineer sent it to me. There's a flaw somewhere that's causing it to behave erratically when it simulates orgasm. If you could just take a look . . ."

Okay, yeah, gross, but still. I hated turning away from a puzzle, which was exactly what coding was. Five minutes later, we were sitting side by side on the bed, and I was pointing out the lines of code that were causing the problem.

". . . loops back on itself and causes a programming conflict—" I was explaining when the door was suddenly flung open.

Clark stood there, gun in hand.

"Get away from her, you fucking asshole," he growled, his eyes a cold fury.

I jumped to my feet. "No, wait, it's okay. This is Thomas Driscoll, the CEO of Psy-Gen Enterprises."

"I don't care if he's the fucking king of England. He's one twitch away from having a third eye."

Thomas raised his hands, his face pale. "I don't want any trouble. I'm just here doing . . . research. Yeah."

Clark rolled his eyes. "That's a new one. Never heard it called that before. Does your wife buy that excuse?"

"He's not married," I said absently. "Look." I held up Thomas's phone. "I was helping him with this code for his sexbots."

Clark frowned. "Sexbots?"

"Yeah, that's what his company makes. Or, is *trying* to make."

Clark frowned at Thomas, his dark brows drawn together. "And you're here doing 'research'?" His lips twisted in disgust. "Dude."

Thomas turned red and his lips thinned, but he said nothing, his gaze still warily watching the gun in Clark's grip.

"Here you go," I said, handing the phone back to Thomas. "It wasn't hard, really. It just took a woman to see the problem with a female sexbot simulating orgasm in the code. Perhaps you should put a few more women on your team."

"So typical," I said in an undertone to Clark.

"Get my jacket and get behind me," he said. I obeyed while he spoke to Thomas. "Okay, here's the deal, bot-boy. You never saw her. You never saw me. You call the cops before ninety minutes has passed? It's going to be all over the news tomorrow that you were here and what you were doing. Stay in this room. I suggest drinking a lot of alcohol to account for not hearing anything. Passing out would be even better. Failure to comply with *any* of these instructions will result in pain and possibly dismemberment. To you. Just in case that wasn't clear."

Thomas's throat visibly moved as he swallowed. "Yeah. I got it."

Clark's smile was thin. "Awesome." He gave me a push toward the door.

"Wait a second," I said, doubling back. Taking Thomas's phone, I quickly dialed my own cell, then hung up. "Just in case," I said, handing it back. "I may want you to return the favor sometime." I scooted out the door.

"I'd suggest locking this," Clark said to Thomas, tapping the doorknob with the muzzle of the gun, then closed the door.

The guards were out cold and in prone positions facedown on the floor, their arms and legs zip-tied. I didn't ask Clark how he'd done it. He was already heading for the other bedroom. I followed hot on his heels, then ran into his back when he abruptly stopped.

"Stay here," he said.

"No."

"I'm not your employee anymore," he insisted. "Do what I say."

"I don't want you to kill him."

His face was a cold, hard mask. "Then you're destined for disappointment."

Clark didn't throw open the door the way he had mine, but just opened it normally. The sight that greeted us was one I knew I'd never be able to scrub from my mind. The four women, in various states of undress, were in the middle of performing sex acts on each other and on the paunchy white guy who looked much less powerful and dangerous without his expensive suit and armed guards.

"Ladies, leave us," Clark said. All of them immediately stopped what they were doing, grabbed their clothes, and filed out. They were calm and unhurried, as though this was not an unexpected occurrence in their profession.

Andrei was sputtering from his position on the bed. "What is the meaning of this? The girls are not harmed, and I purchased the entire night."

"This is about an old vendetta," Clark said. "And a man you probably don't remember. But he meant something to me."

"Ach, Christ," Andrei sneered. "Here for revenge, are you? Go ahead. Shoot. You will not make it out alive." He leaned against the headboard, his arms crossed over his chest, seemingly unperturbed by his nakedness.

"You underestimate me."

"And you underestimate me," Andrei shot back. "I am no amateur, boy. As soon as my heart stops beating, all the men in the hallway will come in here, guns blazing. You will all be cut to ribbons."

That sounded pretty foolproof to me. "Let's call the cops," I urged Clark. "They can arrest him for prostitution, and that'll give them authority to search this place. Let them do their jobs."

"You tortured my friend," Clark said. "You didn't even give him the mercy of a quick death."

"Mercy is for the weak."

"China, step outside with the other girls," Clark said to me.

I swallowed. My hands were shaking. "Please don't make me do that."

"I have to kill him slow. You don't need to watch."

"Please—"

"Stop begging for this asshole's life," he snapped, cutting me off. "Do what I say. Go with the other girls."

I still hesitated, and he cut his gaze to mine.

In that split second, Andrei lunged from the bed, latched onto my wrist, and yanked me in front of him as a shield. His arm latched around my throat.

Well, crap.

"Walk out while I will still let you," he said to Clark, dragging me backward with him. There was a terrace off this bedroom, and he took us through the doorway. I stumbled over the threshold and choked as Andrei held me up by the neck.

Clark followed, weapon still pointing at Andrei, his eyes calculating.

"Give me the gun," Andrei said, "or I'll toss her over." He shoved me into the railing and lifted me up off my feet.

I screamed, the vision of Fifth Avenue looming twenty-two stories below me. I grabbed hold of the railing as I dangled, bent at the waist over the side. Andrei had a hold of my belt, cutting me in half.

"If you drop her, I'll kill you."

"I'll count to five and then I'm letting go."

"All right, all right!" I could hear Clark's urgent voice over the wind, whipping my hair.

I had a grip on the railing, but if he forcibly tossed me over, it would rotate my shoulders in their sockets, and I'd be forced to let go. If Clark gave up his weapon, Andrei would shoot him and probably me, too.

I let one precious grip go on the railing and tugged at the buckle on my belt. As soon as it was off, I squirmed over the railing to the outside, hanging on for dear life. My legs were dangling in midair, and Andrei was left holding my belt.

A shot rang out, then another. Andrei collapsed. In a flash, Clark was leaning over the side. He gripped my arms and pulled.

I was shaking with fear and cold when my feet touched the concrete terrace. Clark grabbed me by my upper arms and shook me.

"Are you out of your fucking mind? *This* was why I didn't want you to come! Do you have any fucking idea what it would do to me to see you die?" He stopped yelling, his chest heaving. His eyes were wild, fear and fury in equal measure in his voice. "I've already seen it almost happen too many times."

Tears were leaking from my eyes, and I trembled in his grip. "You're h-hurting me," I stammered, the chill wind making my teeth begin to chatter.

Much cursing followed as he pulled me inside. I spared one glance at Andrei, whose eyes were flat and glassy in a death stare.

"God *damn* it!" Clark exploded, slamming his fist into a mirror on the wall. I jumped about a foot, still shaking from head to toe. Splintered glass fell to the floor.

I sucked in a breath at the blood on his hand. "Clark . . ." Okay, no time for a nervous breakdown. Blood was dripping. I ran to the bathroom and wet a hand towel.

"Give me your hand," I said to Clark.

He held it up and I wanted to start crying again. Shards of glass stuck out of his skin. I picked them out as best I could, wincing as I did. He didn't flinch, but just watched my face.

"That was . . . completely illogical," I said. "Deliberately injuring yourself in an act of anger or frustration accomplishes nothing."

"Maybe it makes me feel better."

"That doesn't make any sense."

"At least it's not my gun hand."

"Oh yes, *that* makes it all better." I wrapped his hand in the towel. "You're going to need stitches."

I went to step back, but Clark's hand on my shoulder stopped me. I felt the press of his mouth on top of my head in a silent kiss. I squeezed my eyes shut, then it was over.

"Let's go," he said flatly.

Contrary to what Andrei said, no gunmen came storming into the suite. The other women were gone, and we hurried for the door. Thomas's door was still firmly closed. When Clark opened the door to the hallway, only one guard remained. The one who'd led us into the suite.

"All clear?" Clark asked.

The guard glanced at his watch. "For at least another two minutes. I would hurry, if I were you."

Clark nodded. "Tell Josef I said thanks."

"Absolutely."

In the elevator, Clark wrapped his coat around me, and I slid my arms into the sleeves. We didn't stop on the bottom floor, but the second instead. His arm was around my back, moving me quickly along the hallway to the stairs. I barely processed everything that flew by before we were on the street. Clark issued a sharp whistle, and a cab pulled over.

"Waldorf," he told the driver, once we were settled.

"Wait," I said. "Why are you taking me there? That's not your hotel."

"No, it's not."

"We still have to go see my mom's handler tomorrow."

"And we will. But you're staying with Coop."

Panic rushed through me. "You're mad at me. Is this your way of punishing me? By sending me away?"

His gaze slanted to mine. Passing cars' headlights illuminated his face in flashes, but his eyes remained in the dark.

"I'm not mad at you. I'm mad at myself. I shouldn't have let you come. It's only one of the many bad decisions I make around you."

This didn't sound like it was going anywhere good. "What do you mean?"

"It means, I let our . . . friendship . . . cloud my judgment. I should've locked you in the hotel room and went on my own."

"But you didn't kill him in cold blood," I said. "I view that as a win."

I couldn't see his eyes, but I could feel them. Swallowing, I glanced away.

"You were seconds from falling to a rather spectacular death, and you view it as a *win*?" His voice could've cut glass.

Okay, he was right on that point. I'd screwed up. Spectacularly. No matter which way I tried to spin it, I was just a liability in Clark's world. Even when I just wanted to help.

I fidgeted in the seat, the pleather upholstery sticking to my ass and thighs. "I was just saying . . ." My voice was small and trailed away. I felt very small. Diminished. I hated being a screwup. I hated even more that Clark was seeing me as such when he'd always said how smart I was. Not looking so smart at the moment, now, was I.

After a few seconds, I cleared my throat and leaned forward over the seat. "Please take us to the nearest hospital. My friend cut his hand and needs stitches."

"Okay," the driver said.

"I don't need you to hold my hand while I get stitches. I don't even need stitches, just some Betadine and Band-Aids."

I grimaced. "Maybe you should just do the stitches yourself while you drink whiskey and bite down on some leather?"

One half of his mouth lifted. "As if I'd need to bite down on leather. Please."

I studied his expression and turned his words over in my head. He'd made a joke. "Does that mean you're not mad at me anymore?"

His smile faded and he sighed, reaching out to stroke my cheek. "I was never mad at you. Just myself."

I let it go at that. He wasn't arguing about going to the hospital, *and* he was touching me. Sometimes it's better to just stop talking.

Clark made irritated and impatient noises in the ER, but I ignored him. He was getting stitches. I had a suspicion that I was probably the reason he'd slammed his fist into that mirror, though I didn't understand why he'd do that. Yelling at me if he was upset was preferable to hurting himself.

Jackson texted while we were in the waiting room. Where are you? Are you coming back?

Yes. Just got sidetracked. I'll be back soon. Don't wait up.

After a moment's hesitation, I added ♥.

I got the read receipt, but he didn't reply. I hid a sigh. I really didn't need Jackson mad, now that Clark had gotten over his temper outburst.

After Clark had glanced at his watch for the millionth time, we were called back. He refused anesthesia, which caused me to berate him and then try to cajole him, but he was having none of it.

"I was just kidding," I pleaded. "Really, I'll still think you're a badass if you take the anesthesia."

"Can she be forced to wait outside?" he asked the doctor.

"Okay, okay," I hurriedly said, before they made me leave. I grabbed on to his right hand and squeezed, watching as the doctor began stitching. I flinched every time the needle pierced his skin.

"If you break my right hand, we're going to be in a world of hurt," Clark deadpanned.

"Oh. Sorry." I loosened my death grip.

Thirty minutes later, we were finally leaving. I'd managed to convince Clark to take some pain medication, but he refused anything that would make him sleepy.

It was late and I was starving, but too exhausted to think about eating, or to put up a fight when Clark took me to the Waldorf and deposited me in front of Jackson's suite. He rapped on the door and we waited. Despite the hour, it swung open almost immediately.

Jackson took in everything at a glance: my bedraggled attire, covered by Clark's leather jacket, smeared makeup from crying, Clark's bandaged hand.

I held my breath, expecting him to explode, but he did something surprising. Stepping forward, he folded me into his arms.

"Thank God you're okay," he murmured. "I've been worried sick."

Guilt hit hard, and I deserved it. I couldn't keep juggling two men who not only brought on near-death experiences, but worried over me. Clark had had a meltdown earlier because of me. The hand thing had been my fault. The emotions between Clark and me, and Jackson and me, were driving both of them to the breaking point. And my tangled feelings were doing the one thing that I should have seen sooner: they were interfering with my logic. I never should have gone with Clark tonight, but I hadn't been able to trust him to go alone—as I would have done just months ago at Vigilance. But I'd felt differently about him then, as just a rather obnoxious—albeit gorgeous—employee.

I gently extricated myself from Jackson's arms. "I know you probably want to talk, but I'm so tired. Can we just crash and talk in the morning?"

"We?" Clark asked. "I'm not staying. I'm just the delivery boy."

I turned to him and looked up, meeting his gaze. "Please, Clark. For me."

His jaw tightened into bands of steel as he studied my eyes, and I knew he desperately wanted to refuse. I should've felt bad for manipulating him, but hopefully it would be for the last time.

Finally, he gave a curt nod. "But I'm not sleeping in the middle."

No one, not even he, smiled at his deadpan joke.

"There's a couch," I said.

Jackson didn't object, or say anything, as we followed him inside the suite. It was spacious, and there was indeed a long, comfy couch.

"I need a shower," I said, leaving them both behind and heading for the bedroom. My things were there, along with a spacious bathroom. I stripped as I walked, leaving the shoes and Clark's jacket in my wake, tossed my glasses onto the counter, and stepped into the shower.

The water was freezing cold at first, but I didn't care. It warmed up quickly enough.

It was one of those rainfall showerheads, and I stood under it for a long time, thinking. I had a decision to make, and I didn't want to. It would hurt. Not only me, but the men I loved.

The men I loved.

In the solitary bathroom, I could face the truth. I loved Jackson . . . and Clark. They had each done so much for me, including risking their lives. How could I *not* love them? They had kissed me, made love to me, and taken care of me when I couldn't take care of myself. My problems became theirs—not out of necessity—but because that's who they were. Clark had tried to hide that part of himself, but somehow, I'd been able to draw it out.

But even after everything, I was only *in* love with one of them.

It was a long time before I got out of the shower. My stomach was in knots and my heart ached. Jackson glanced up when I stepped out of the bathroom. He was sitting on the edge of the bed, waiting for me. He still wore slacks and a dress shirt, despite the hour.

I had a towel wrapped around me, and I'd left my glasses in the bathroom. My hair was wet and finger-combed.

"That's twice in as many days I almost died," I said quietly.

His eyes darkened and his lips thinned, but he didn't say anything. I knew he wasn't happy that I'd been in danger with Clark. He'd warned me before.

"I want to forget everything for a while," I said. "My mom, her death, Danvers's betrayal. Everywhere that I hurt." Inside and out.

"What can I do?" he asked, his voice rough.

I dropped my towel and climbed into the bed. "Hold me?"

He took off his shoes and slid into the bed, tugging the covers up over us both. His arm wrapped around my middle and pulled me into him, spoon-style. I slotted my fingers through his and held his hand in both of mine, close to my heart.

I closed my eyes and savored the feel of his body against mine. Sex was chemistry and passion, and sometimes didn't even require names to be exchanged. But holding and being held, asleep and vulnerable, that wasn't something done with a stranger. It was intimacy on another level, and I desperately wished I didn't have to give it up.

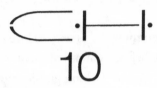

10

New Orleans. It was the last time I'd see Mark.

It had been four months. An eternity since Maui. And yet, I felt like we'd known each other all our lives. I could tell what he was feeling by the tone of his voice. Similarly, he knew me, knew what made me laugh or cry.

Inevitably, he'd be time zones ahead of me, yet would stay up until the early hours of the morning, drinking whiskey or gin on the nights he couldn't stand missing me, when only alcohol dulled the pain. I'd hide from the boys when they got home from school, setting out a snack to keep them occupied, while Mark's voice was in my ear. Missing him was a constant, acute pain.

I found out I was pregnant a week before we met in New Orleans. There was no doubt in my mind that the baby was his. Frank and I hadn't had sex in months, though I was quick to rectify that once I knew.

He was staying at the Ritz. Room 704. I'll never forget. I showed up at his door close to midnight, my heart pounding in anticipation of seeing him again. He'd yanked open the door and in another second, I was in his arms, his mouth on mine, and every day I'd spent waiting for this moment faded away.

I didn't tell him that night. I couldn't. We were so happy. We stayed up most of the night, making love, drinking champagne, and talking. It was heaven.

We spent the next day touring the St. Louis Cemetery. Perhaps not romantic, but it was the cool weather of late fall and the tourists had departed. We walked hand in hand and he'd stop every so often, just to pull me close and kiss me. The world faded away when he kissed me. I couldn't bring myself to spoil it.

It wasn't until the next day that I realized—I couldn't tell him. If I did, he'd never let me go. He had no children, had never been married. But he'd spoken of them, sort of wistfully. They were something he felt was beyond his reach. If he knew I was carrying his child, he'd move hell and earth to keep me with him, and then what would happen to the boys?

I had to say goodbye. Forever. And I couldn't tell him about the life we'd created. Together.

We had dinner at Ophelia's. It was our last night together. I was overly quiet. He was almost manic in his desperation to be upbeat. We drank too much and barely touched our food.

The walk back to the hotel was somber. I was barely holding it together. We walked with our arms around each other, not wanting a moment to pass without touching. He asked if I wanted a cocktail, but I said no, I just wanted him.

We made love slowly, drawing it out as long as possible. Tears leaked from my eyes as I held him, feeling him inside me. There's nothing more heartbreaking than finding your soul mate, and realizing you can't spend the rest of your life with them.

My flight was in the morning. We didn't sleep. I hadn't said anything, but he knew me so well, he realized something was wrong. I finally gave voice to the dread sometime in the middle of the night.

"We can't keep doing this," I said. "I can't keep doing this. It's killing me. We have to end it."

There was silence, and when he finally spoke, the pain in his voice made me want to cry.

"You're leaving me. Forever."

"Yes." I could barely force the word out. "You know it's what must be done. We can't keep on like this."

"Why not?" Anger and fear. "Don't you love me?"

I rolled on top of him, my heart beating against his, and looked into his beautiful gray eyes. "You're my life. My everything. But my children need me. Every time we part, it gets harder. Until one day, I won't leave at all. And I'll regret it."

His fingers combed through my hair, and he didn't speak. His eyes were bright. Too bright. I hated to think I'd made my strong man — my dream man — cry.

"I'd do anything for you," he said at last. "I'd go anywhere. Give up anything. Just say the word. I'll come live in Bumblefuck, Iowa, if it means I can still see you. Just don't end this. Don't end us."

Tears dripped down my face onto his chest. He carefully brushed my wet cheeks, wiping away the tears.

"Please don't make this harder than it is," I whispered. "It's killing me."

He didn't speak then, just made love to me, both of us knowing it was the last time.

I left while he slept, exhausted. I took the coward's way out, unable to say the word to him: goodbye. It was excruciating. A hundred times I wanted to turn back, fly back into his arms, and run away with him and our baby. Only by putting one foot in front of the other, one step at a time, was I able to board the plane that took me away from him forever.

I never heard from him again. My baby girl was born—the girl I'd waited so long for—and she had his eyes. I lived for her. She was living proof that what Mark and I had was real. He'd loved me, and I him.

I don't regret anything, though I know that I let happiness pass me by. Responsibility and a mother's love for her children take precedence over personal happiness. I was . . . content. And China. Dear China. Named for the place I met the man I'd never forget. She was how I could keep going.

So many wonderful memories. I cherish them. I relive them. What Mark and I had was beautiful and rare. It doesn't come twice in a lifetime. I'm *grateful I was lucky enough to find it, however briefly. As Tennyson said, "'tis better to have loved and lost than never to have loved at all." And we did. We loved.*

◆ ◆ ◆

The next morning, I dressed on autopilot, packing my backpack and suitcase. Jackson wasn't in bed when I woke up, and I didn't go looking for him. I was compartmentalizing. Some things had to be done, and it wasn't going to be pleasant. Emotions had to take a back seat, even if it killed me.

When I came out of the bedroom, Jackson was sitting at the table on his laptop while Clark was just exiting the other bathroom. He must've taken a shower. His hair was still damp and he was barefoot. He wore jeans, but his shirt was unbuttoned. I swallowed and forced my eyes elsewhere.

"Can we talk?" I asked them. "All of us?"

Both men assumed their best poker faces and took chairs opposite where I sat on the couch. I took a moment to study them, memorizing their faces and postures. Clark was sitting in his customary sprawl, his knees spread and an elbow resting on the chair's arm. The shirt had fallen open, revealing his chest and chiseled abs. I tried not to stare.

Jackson was in his relaxed-but-in-charge state, one ankle resting on the opposite knee, sitting upright with his arms resting on the chair. He was impeccably dressed in slacks and a shirt, the creases still fresh from the laundry-service ironing.

I took a breath, though I felt as if I needed a drink instead. "I can't do this anymore. With either of you."

Silence.

Jackson frowned. "What are you talking about?"

"It's too much," I said, struggling to explain. "I can't be responsible for hurting either of you anymore. I can't . . . I just can't do it."

"I've tried to tell you—" Jackson began, but I interrupted.

"I know, that it's your decision and it's all on you if things don't work out," I said. "But that's a lie to both of us. And this . . . quest I'm on, to find out what happened to my mom . . . it's dangerous. If something happens to me, I don't want either of you around to see it."

Jackson said nothing. Clark was stone-faced.

I blundered on. "I'm going to find out if my mom was murdered or if her death was an accident. If she was murdered, it had to be for the money. And if Danvers did it"—I took a deep breath—"then I'm going to avenge my mother."

"No fucking way." Clark finally spoke, his voice hard. "You're not going to try to hunt down Danvers and kill him. Did you not just give me shit last night about killing Andrei 'in cold blood'?" He used air quotes for that last part.

"Who the hell is Andrei?" Jackson said. "And you dragged China with you to kill him? After what she's been through?"

"Her face didn't get that way when she was with me," Clark retorted. "In case you forgot."

"China," Jackson said in his best let's-be-reasonable tone, "we already know this information is dangerous. It's extremely unwise for you to continue pursuing this, especially alone. Think it through logically. Your emotions are overly influencing your decision."

That stung—probably because it was true—but I didn't want to think about that. So I went into Defense Mode. "I don't care. It's my decision."

"Did I or did I not let you come with me last night because you insisted I needed backup?" Clark asked.

My face flushed, but I remained resolved. "And look how that turned out," I said. "You even told me yourself it was a bad idea. I'm not going to make the same mistake twice."

"Oh, so *now* you decide to listen to me. Your timing is fuck all, Mack."

It hurt to hear *Mack* instead of *baby*. Maybe he meant to hurt me. Maybe not. I couldn't blame him if he did. I'd certainly hurt him enough.

"Logically, you both know that this can't end well. Someone wins, someone loses. It all ends now."

"So we all lose."

Clark's flat words made me flinch.

Jackson uncrossed his legs and leaned forward, bracing his elbows on his knees. "China, I know you're upset, but I care about you . . . and so does Clark."

That last part took longer for him to say, and I had that sense of regret—again—that I'd been careless in my relationships with them. I'd made a decision I hadn't wanted to make, but I knew it would come to this.

"I know," I said. "But I'm saying goodbye. To both of you."

Jackson just looked at me. Clark, likewise, said nothing.

My gut was churning like I was going to vomit, and I had to swallow and take a long, slow breath. I knew how persistent my men were, and I guess that's how I'd come to view them. *Mine.* But the world didn't work like that. I needed to convince them absolutely that it was over, to make them move on. Though it was going to feel like cutting off my arm.

"You're both incredibly special to me," I continued, trying to keep my voice as steady as possible. "But it's too hard. I thought I wanted to marry Jackson, then hurt him when I wanted to see what Clark and I could have. Then I hurt Clark when I said I only wanted to be Friends with Benefits."

Jackson's brows flew upward. "Seriously?" he blurted. "You actually said that?"

I threw my hands up in exasperation. "See what I mean? Even Jackson knows that was a Bad Thing. It took me hurting you," I looked at Clark, "to figure it out. It's obvious I'm not meant to be in a relationship. I don't know what I'm doing. I don't know how I'm feeling or supposed to feel. I just hurt people." I got to my feet and slung my backpack onto my shoulder. "So . . . this is goodbye."

Unable to bear looking at them, I turned and headed for the door, suitcase in tow. My glasses were on, but everything was blurry.

"China, wait!"

Jackson's voice stopped me. I turned around. Both men were standing. Both had an expression on their faces that ripped through me. I knew I'd never be able to forget it.

"I know you're hurting about your mom," he said. "You're afraid you might follow in her footsteps. That the one you choose might betray you. But doing this—going alone to try to kill your father—that's not how to solve this. I know you know that."

That arrow struck too close to home, so I ignored it. I was excellent at doing that.

I forced myself to speak past the lump in my throat. "I'm going to go off the grid for a while, so don't try to find me."

"You, of all people, can't go off the grid," Clark said. "And why would you want to?"

"Because to find Danvers, I'll need to be bait. And to do that, I'll need to see him coming." I paused. "And nowhere that either of you can find me." I turned the doorknob before I lost the will to do so. "Goodbye."

I went out the door and they didn't follow. I wasn't sure if what I felt was relief . . . or disappointment.

◆ ◆ ◆

The Shangri-La Home for Convalescence was a sprawling building surrounded by carefully tended gardens and lawns. The sidewalks were in good repair without uneven slabs or cracks. There weren't a lot of flowers, and I guessed probably because of bees. But the shrubbery was well tended, some even pruned into artful shapes.

I checked in at the front desk and asked for a William Adams.

"And you are?" the receptionist asked.

"He was my mom's boss," I explained, "years ago. She's passed, but wanted me to find him and give him a memento of hers." Total BS, but I'd gotten better at fibbing lately. Perhaps it was the company I kept.

"You know he's quite ill," she said. "He may not remember your mother."

I nodded. "I'd still like to see him."

"Have a seat."

The reception area was pretty and well decorated, with nice carpet and leather furniture. Realistic-looking potted plants and greenery made it feel less like a medical facility and more like a residence. Yet there was an aroma that always lingered in old folks' homes, and it made me sad. Getting old had to suck, even more so if you couldn't care for yourself and had no family who could—or would—be there for you.

An African American man dressed in an all-white uniform of slacks and short-sleeve shirt walked up to me. He was bald, wore thin-framed glasses, and had a discreet name tag that said *Harry*. "You're here to see Bill?" he asked.

"I am. Is he . . ." I didn't know how to politely ask if "Bill" was cognizant enough to talk to me.

"You're in luck," Harry said with a smile. "He's having a good day. Follow me."

Harry led me out a back exit to the grounds. The sun was shining and it was a clear, beautiful spring day. The air smelled of freshly mowed grass, and birds were singing. For someone whose total exposure to the outdoors was when I had to collect Amazon boxes off my doorstep, it was deeply disconcerting. I glanced warily up at the bright sun. *Should've worn sunblock.*

An elderly man was sitting on a bench next to a small pond. Ducks waddled around him, and as we grew closer, I saw he was feeding them—tossing down a handful of bread crumbs now and then. They were loud quackers, voicing their impatience if he was too slow. It should have been a serene scene, but their agitation and jockeying for better positions with each other just made it irritating.

"Bill, did you sneak out some bread again?" Harry chastised goodnaturedly. "Those ducks are spoiled."

Bill glanced up and I saw recognition in his eyes. He smiled. "The ducks need me," he said. "It's good to be needed."

"I guess even ducks need to be spoiled sometimes," Harry replied. "Bill, I've got a visitor for you today."

Bill's smile faded immediately as he glanced at me.

"Now don't worry," Harry continued. "You don't know her. Never met her before, she says. Her name's China." He motioned me forward.

I pushed my glasses up my nose and did my smile. "Hi, Bill. Can I sit with you for a little while?"

Bill hesitated, then nodded. "Best now. I get worse as the day wears on."

Harry shooed away the ducks, who reluctantly waddled into the pond amid a great grumbling of quacks, then he headed back to the building.

"What's a young woman like you want with an old man like me?" Bill asked.

I judged him to be in his early seventies, with deep lines in his forehead and around his eyes. He still had most of his hair, though it was white, and he wore a fleece tracksuit that fit too loosely on his thin frame.

"I'm here because you used to work with my mom," I said. "In the late nineties."

Bill watched the ducks swimming. "Did I now?"

"You were her handler," I continued. "Her name was Kimberly. She went by her maiden name of Duncan."

Bill's gnarled hands were resting on his thighs. They curled into fists at the mention of my mother's name.

"I'm trying to find out more information about her last job," I continued. "She died shortly thereafter in a car accident. But I've had reason to believe lately that it might not have been an accident."

"You think your mother was murdered," he said.

"I do," I admitted. "She left me . . . information. About her last job. The one with Fortress Securities."

Bill finally looked at me. "I'm sorry to have to tell you that yes, you're correct. Your mother was murdered." He looked unbearably sad.

Even though I'd known that hoping otherwise was futile, it still was a blow to have the information confirmed. I swallowed, my throat dry. "But why? And who?"

"An agent went rogue," he said. "Someone we trusted. Your mom and he were to arrange to kidnap the Chinese operative and fake his death. We wanted to negotiate protecting him and offering him immunity as well as asylum in exchange for working with us to offset what he'd done."

"But that wasn't what happened. The Chinese agent disappeared, then there was Kim's . . . accident."

My stomach was in knots. "Who did it?" I prompted.

Bill's gaze turned to the pond again. "His name was Danvers. Mark Danvers. He was a trained operative, and they'd worked together before, a job in China." He paused, glancing at me. "That's your name, isn't it? China?"

I nodded.

"How odd," he mused. "Anyway"—he sighed—"they were supposed to work together, but he turned. He had a well-placed asset inside the PRC that he'd had for years." He paused, adding, "People's Republic of China," in case I didn't know what he meant. "Very valuable asset, especially as the lease on Hong Kong was ending. So many wanted asylum before it was handed back to the Chinese.

"That asset was compromised shortly thereafter," he continued. "Damn shame. We finally found Chen, too. Dead. He'd been tortured beforehand. We thought it was for the backdoor information. And Danvers . . . well, he was in the wind. Has been ever since, as far as I know. Losing his asset must've just sent him off the deep end. Who the hell knows why he did what he did?"

I sat very still, the impact of all he'd said rolling through me like a tidal wave. My very worst suspicions were confirmed. My mom had trusted Danvers, but rather than help her eliminate the threat, he'd seen a golden opportunity to make a lot of money. All he'd had to do was kill Chen . . . then kill my mother—his former lover and the mother of his child.

My stomach rolled and bile rose in my throat. How could my mother have been so naive? Had she really been that blinded by love that she could look Danvers in the eyes and not see that he was planning to kill her? Her journal painted such a completely different picture of him, it was almost impossible for me to reconcile her words with his actions. It made zero sense. Unless he was just that cold and calculating of an actor to pull off a betrayal of that magnitude.

Bill went quiet for a long time, which was fine with me. I was dealing with emotions I'd never felt to this degree before. Rage, bitterness, fear, hopelessness.

Grief.

How much of me was my mother's daughter? And how much Danvers's? I couldn't trust myself or love. My father had loved my mother. She'd loved him, too, in a way. But she'd fallen *in* love with Danvers, who'd used that love against her. Had played her. How could I be sure I wouldn't use Jackson's or Clark's love against them? I'd been right to leave. It was safer, better, this way.

Bill looked at me, his gaze far away. "You look like her," he said. "Kimberly."

"Thank you. Do you have any idea how I could find Danvers?" It was a long shot, but I had to ask.

"Why would you want to?" he asked, frowning. "He's dangerous. Perhaps even dead by now."

I hoped not. "He's my father."

His face blanched in shock, and I thought maybe I'd said too much. In the next moment, that was confirmed. His eyes lacked focus as he looked at me.

"Kim? Is that you?" Before I could respond, he grabbed my arm. For an old guy, he was surprisingly strong. "You have to run. You're in danger."

"I'm not Kim," I said, trying to soothe him. "I'm her daughter. It's okay." It was as though I were speaking to a wall.

"You have to go!" He was getting increasingly agitated. "They're coming. For both of us!"

"No one's coming," I said. He was bruising my arm. "It's okay. We're safe, Bill."

The use of his name seemed to penetrate his panic, and he fell silent. He looked back at the pond, and I gently pulled out of his now-lax grip.

We watched the pond for a while. I found I was reluctant to leave. Bill was the only person besides Danvers who'd known my mom's other life. Even if his mind wasn't what it used to be, there was a chance he might be able to tell me more about her.

After a while, he turned and saw me, reacting with some surprise. "Who are you?" he asked.

I thought of Clark having to endure the same question from his own mother, over and over again, and my heart hurt for him. "I'm China," I said. "Kimberly Duncan's daughter. Do you remember her?"

His face cleared. "Ah, yes, Kim. Such a nice girl. So smart."

"Do you know why she joined the CIA?" I asked.

"Joined?" he asked. "Oh, she didn't apply. They recruited her. IQ level off the charts. Got her straight out of college. She was a linguist, you know. Could pick up languages the way most people learn a favorite song."

I hadn't known that. Mom had never spoken to me about being especially smart or above average in anything. But I'd been young.

"Like most, it didn't take her long to become disillusioned. The idea of sacrificing for your country can be more appealing than having to deal with the politics and bureaucracy that keep you from doing your job.

"She met a nice man, a farmer, who fell head over heels for her. She was fond of him, too. She told me he was safe. A good man. A simple man. She could have a family and a quiet life, in Nebraska of all places."

Fond. Mom had been fond of Dad. That was safest, wasn't it? To love someone less than they loved you? Because then they couldn't hurt you. Not like Danvers. She'd fallen hard for him, and she'd paid the ultimate price for that love.

"But once they get their hooks in you, it's almost impossible to get out. She knew Chinese, you see. Standard and Mandarin. Could speak it like a native. And that was too valuable in an asset not to tempt her back a few times. Of course, one of those times was one too many . . ."

He gazed at the water again, sadness marking his features. Then he seemed to shake himself from his reverie. "And you're her daughter?"

"I am."

He patted my knee. "So good of you to come. Tell Kim I said hello."

I didn't want to upset him again by reminding him that she was dead, so I just smiled and rose. "It was nice talking to you."

Bill smiled faintly and waved, the recognition in his eyes fading. I looked around and saw Harry not far away, helping another patient make her way slowly to a grouping of chairs where another elderly woman waited. He glanced up and I waved, indicating I was leaving. He nodded in acknowledgment.

I walked back to my rental car, deep in thought. I'd been working on a plan for luring Danvers out of wherever he was hiding. But I needed a base of operations and some equipment.

As I drove, I stopped at an ATM and withdrew as much cash as it would let me from my accounts. Then I did that at four more ATMs until I had a decent amount to live on for a few months.

The nearest computer store had the rest of what was on my list. I bought a new laptop and two firewalls, plus three routers, cabling, and some extras, then I was back on the road. I returned the rental car, then took an Uber to a used-car lot, where I paid $2,000 in cash for a ten-year-old Toyota Corolla standard, with no bells or whistles.

Digging in my backpack, I pulled out my travel pack of Clorox Wipes and proceeded to wipe down the interior of the car.

"What're you doing?" the salesman asked. He was middle-aged, with thinning hair and what Mia would call a "molest-ache."

"I have no idea how many people have driven this car, and I certainly don't want their germs," I said, carefully cleaning the steering wheel.

The salesman grumbled something and walked away. I didn't pay any attention. Now I had everything I needed to disappear for a while.

I had no illusions that Danvers would kill me if he could, especially once he found out I knew his secrets. I'd learned from my mother's blindness. Love and trust were powerful weapons that went hand in hand. Give them to the wrong person, and you may not live to regret it.

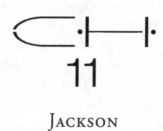

11

JACKSON

The door closed, yet Jackson stood there dumbly, waiting for it to reopen. She couldn't be gone, not like this. He'd fought too hard, waited too long, given so much . . .

"What the fuck are you waiting for? She's gone."

Clark's cold words shook Jackson from his trance. He rounded on him, rage flaring in his veins.

"This is all your fault," he snarled. "You can't offer her *anything*. All you want to do is take and take and take."

"Fuck you," Clark shot back. "You treat her like some kind of experiment in a zoo. Something to watch and study and build a cage around."

"And you treat her like your own personal savior."

"At least it's personal."

Jackson roared in anger and lunged for Clark, who leaped deftly out of the way. A fist hammered into his kidney, and Jackson buckled, rolling away from Clark before getting to his feet.

His eyes were misted red with rage and pain, and he charged again, ignoring the hits to his jaw and abdomen as he tackled Clark to the ground. They crashed into a delicate coffee table, which shattered on the impact of their bodies.

Jackson straddled Clark and began pummeling him, taking out all his frustration and anger on Clark's face.

Blood flew, then Jackson was hit with a massive blow on the side of the head. Clark had a hold of one of the coffee-table legs. Jackson fell off Clark, dazed. His eyesight was seeing triple as he tried to regain his feet.

"You asshole," Clark ground out. "Your need for commitment drove her away. In one breath you say you understand her, and in the next, you're shoving her into a fucking corner."

He flew at Jackson, who'd only just stood, and they grappled. Clark got Jackson into a choke hold. Jackson's fingers pried at the arm at his throat, but couldn't get loose. Reaching behind him, he shoved his thumbs into Clark's eye sockets. Clark grunted and abruptly let go.

"Are you fucking kidding me, douchebag?"

"You tell me, asshole."

They continued pummeling each other, the blows getting weaker as they tired, the beating taking a toll on both of them. A punch to the gut, an elbow in the ribs. The room was slowly turning, the floor and the wall interchangeable as they each tried to keep going.

Finally, they squared off, unsteady on their feet and breathing heavily. The coffee table was in shatters. The furniture had been shoved aside. Decorative vases littered the floor, along with their sad dried floral arrangements.

Jackson snickered.

Clark glared. "What the hell is so funny?"

"You have a flower in your hair, Miss Daisy."

Clark ground out a curse as he ran his fingers through his hair. Jackson collapsed on the sofa, still laughing. God, he was so fucking tired. He rested his head back against the couch and closed his eyes. He heard Clark sink into the armchair opposite him.

"I'm too old for this shit," Clark said.

"What? Fighting over a woman?"

"Fighting, period. It's gonna hurt like hell tomorrow."

"Getting old sucks."

"Speak for yourself, old man."

They both sat there, saying nothing, just breathing. Finally, Jackson broke the silence.

"Now what?" He didn't have to explain. Clark would know what he meant.

"I'm not about to let her try to trap and kill Danvers, if that's what you mean," Clark said.

"I didn't think you would. My point is, what's the plan?"

"She'll be mad if we follow her."

"So we don't let her know we're following," Jackson said with a shrug. "If she goes off the grid, that means cash only, maybe Bitcoin. She'll ditch the cell and get a new laptop."

Clark thought for a moment. "She won't stick around here. Neither will she go home. She'll go somewhere else."

"No one knows where Danvers is. Where would she choose to go?"

They both were quiet, thinking. Then Clark asked, "This is all about her mother. Where was she from?"

Jackson pulled up some files on his phone. "Louisiana. Ponchatoula. It's about an hour outside New Orleans."

"Then she'd go there. Despite wanting to go off the grid, she'll want something familiar."

"I don't think she's ever been to New Orleans."

"No, but she'll still feel a tie there. She can't help it. Familiarity—even so distant—is what she gravitates to."

Clark was right. Jackson knew it. They fell into silence.

"She loves me, you know," Jackson said at last. "Despite what you think. We're good together. And you know I'm better for her than you are." Clark said nothing, so Jackson kept going. "You're the guy who promises danger and adventure, but in the end, you only bring heartache. She deserves better than that."

"And you think you're it." It wasn't a question. His voice was flat and his face expressionless.

"I know I am. She almost died trying to clear your name. How many more ghosts from your past are going to show up at some point? What other motivation do you need than watching her slowly bleed to death? Sheer luck saved her in time. Next time—"

"There won't be a next time," Clark cut him off.

"And you're positive of that. Sure enough to stake her life on it?"

Clark's eyes looked empty. "I mean, *there won't be a next time*," he said, carefully emphasizing each word. "There's only one ending to this story, and I suggest we stop measuring our dicks if we're going to stay one step ahead of her."

Irritation flared, but Jackson kept hold of his temper. "Do you have contacts in New Orleans? It would help if we can have eyes on her when she gets to town."

"Yeah. Chances are she'll take a bus. It's the most anonymous way, and she's been reading those Jack Reacher books lately."

Great. Only *he* would have a genius girlfriend who thought she could be Jack Reacher when she broke out in hives if the clock on her microwave didn't match the clock on the DVR.

He sighed. "Okay, then. I'm going to start tracking down Danvers."

"How the hell do you propose to do that?"

"He's no tech guru. He'll have a digital footprint somewhere. And I've got some of the best network sniffers and hackers on my payroll. We find him first, before China does."

"And then what? You're going to kill him?" Clark's sneering derision set Jackson's teeth on edge.

"Turning him over to the FBI should be adequate," he said. "He's committed fraud, murder, and I'm sure a laundry list of other crimes."

"Some of which I'm sure he did at the behest of the CIA."

"So what's your point?"

"You're going to deprive China of her chance for closure, that's my point."

"And you want to let her *kill* her father so she has 'closure'? You're out of your mind. Do you have any idea what that'll do to her? I don't care if he's a worthless piece of shit. China isn't the kind of person that can kill someone in cold blood and walk away."

"Then she needs to decide that for herself, not have you do it for her."

They glared at each other. Finally, Jackson heaved himself up. "I'm going to get to work. I suggest you do the same before she gets too far ahead of you." He looked steadily at Clark. "Can I trust you to work with me on this? Or are you going to somehow twist the situation to your advantage?"

A wince, so small and quick he might have imagined it, flew across Clark's features. "I'll keep you updated," he said, rising from the chair. "She's what matters. Not us."

"At least we can agree on that," Jackson said. "I'll let you show yourself out." He didn't wait to watch him leave, but went back into the bedroom he'd shared with China and shut the door.

He could still smell her in the air. Not perfume, never that. Just the faint odor of antigerm gel that she was constantly using. Romantic? No. But it brought her to mind immediately, that sharp scent.

He'd lain awake last night, holding her as she slept. He'd been very aware that it might be the last time. Despite what he said to Clark, he was not at all sure that he'd win China's heart in the end. For someone who craved and needed routine and structure, she had an affinity for Clark that Jackson couldn't understand. What was it about Clark that drew her? Maybe it was something he himself could emulate?

Or was it the age-old attraction of a woman needing to fix a broken man? Because Clark was broken. Even a fool could see it. Jackson couldn't compete with that.

He shoved his fingers through his hair in frustration. So a well-adapted grown man with his shit very much together held less appeal than a man in severe need of therapy, with a penchant for killing people? It wasn't fair.

Of course, life wasn't fair, was it, he thought as he threw his things together. You did the best with the hand you were dealt. A smart, geeky kid works hard and grows up to be a billionaire tech titan. Hires a trainer to put meat and muscle on his bones and a stylist to add the clothes. Gets the right haircut and Lasik surgery . . . and later the geek is a man 99.9 percent of women would give their right arm for. Except the one he wanted.

In his office the next morning, Jackson stared morosely out the glass walls to the line of cubicles. The one China had occupied now had another resident. Steve, maybe? Or Dave? He couldn't recall. He just knew he could no longer look out and see her ponytail lightly bouncing as she typed along to whatever rock band was blasting in her ears.

His desk phone beeped and his assistant's voice emerged from the speaker.

"Sir, Mr. Dunlop is on line two."

"Thank you." Jackson picked up the phone. He'd e-mailed his attorney earlier to call him. "Good morning, Richard."

"Mr. Cooper, good morning. What can I do for you today?"

That was one thing he liked about Richard. He didn't waste time with chitchat. "I need to modify my will. Can you come by the office this afternoon?"

There was silence for a moment—he must've taken Richard by surprise—then he recovered. "Of course. Would two o'clock work?"

"That's fine. I'll see you then." He hung up the phone.

Clark's job was to find China, but Jackson's was to find Danvers before China did. Which was why he sent out an e-mail to two people on his staff: the VP of network security and his IT director. Ten minutes later, they were taking seats in his office.

"I have a special project I need done," Jackson began. "Someone we need to track down, without him knowing."

Willard—the security guy—perked up. He was the most paranoid person Jackson had ever known, which made him excellent at his job. He also held fantasies of being some kind of James Bond–like covert agent near and dear to his heart. To that end, he was clean-shaven and well dressed, though about fifty pounds more than MI6 Double-O fitness requirements.

"Sounds serious," he said. "What'd he do?"

"Doesn't matter. I just need him found, as well as any information we can dig up on him."

"What's the timeline?" Drew—IT—asked. He was the Abbott to Willard's Costello—tall, rail thin, with wire-frame glasses, and zero sense of humor.

"Yesterday." Both of them looked taken aback at that, but Jackson continued. "His name is Mark Danvers. He was military and CIA. I have a copy of his file. It hasn't been updated in years, but it'll be a start."

Drew and Willard were both taking notes—Drew on his tablet and Willard with pen and paper—as Jackson spoke. They discussed having two teams of five members each that they would oversee. Names were thrown around until all ten people had been decided on, including two experts in cryptography.

"I won't micromanage," Jackson said. "You can coordinate and plan the best strategy with your teams. Report to me immediately if you find anything, otherwise I want weekly updates."

They departed and Jackson was again left alone with his thoughts. He wanted to *do* more, do *something*, but he knew that the best he had were working on it. Instead, he got on the phone to his realtor. There was something he could do, if the future turned out as he hoped it would.

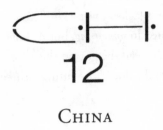

12

CHINA

I unlocked the door to the apartment and stepped inside. I still hadn't grown accustomed to the heat. This place was an Airbnb monthly rental that I'd paid for via Bitcoin and that was located in one of the less-than-savory parts of New Orleans. July was a crappy time for the air conditioning to go out. I'd been suspicious of its wheezing when I'd moved in more than a month ago, and I'd been right. It was on its last legs, and those legs had given out in the middle of the night.

Muttering under my breath, I pulled out my cell. I had a voice mail from a missed call.

"Sorry can't make it today to fix your unit. We're all backed up. Someone will be out tomorrow."

Fabulous.

I set the groceries I'd picked up on the counter, my mood going from bad to worse. In my head, I added *Suffering through no AC in New Orleans during summer* to my list of Reasons I Hated Mark Danvers. It was a long list. Recent additions had been *Having to tell Mia she couldn't stay with me this summer* and *Weeks since I'd spoken to Grams.* The last one was incremental and was already at ten.

Organizing and sorting the groceries didn't take long. My dietary needs were simple. Red Bull, Fig Newtons, some frozen meals (including frozen pizza and Chinese, since I couldn't order takeout), and Pop-Tarts.

Incorporating a new routine for breakfast had been a difficult decision. There were so many breakfast items available. In the end, I'd decided on Pop-Tarts because a) they were portable, and b) they had enough flavors for me to vary day to day and still have a routine. The week began with a semblance of health (strawberry, blueberry), and ended without any pretense (chocolate chip cookie dough, hot fudge sundae). The inner-cynicism made me smile, when there was precious little to smile about at the moment.

So far, my search had yielded few results. I'd spent weeks scouring the deep web for traces of the account with the money stolen all those years ago and what might have happened to it. Once the money had been received by that account, it all disappeared into a dozen different accounts around the world, then a dozen more, until it was removed so far from the source that it was a needle in a haystack to find. I'd written a program to automate the money-laundering trace, but it was combing through years of data and took time.

I'd also decided to infiltrate airline databases because obviously he would have flown over the years, but there were a lot of Mark Danverses in the world. When I'd finally found the right one, the most recent address on file had been a fake one. Google Street View had shown me it was an empty lot in downtown Detroit.

Ha. Good one, Dad.

But I wasn't going to give up. He was out there somewhere, and hopefully, still in the United States.

I ate frozen pizza for dinner, glumly watching the latest *Game of Thrones* episode on my computer. I couldn't even muster much enthusiasm when the dragons started kicking some ass, and I'd been waiting *years* for that.

As I did nearly every night, I took out the police report I'd finally received. It had shown me how he'd done it.

According to an eyewitness, my mom had been driving behind a semitruck. The weather was bad, with low visibility from the sleet and snow. Another car attempted to pass my mom and apparently lost control just long enough to run into us with enough force to push our pickup sideways.

Mom had overcompensated in her steering, trying to stay on the road, and the ice had done the rest. We'd been sent careening into the guardrail, spun a 360, and caught the back edge of that semi. It jackknifed, twisting in the middle of the road. The trailer hit our pickup and sent it tumbling down the embankment into the median.

When it stopped, the pickup was lying on the driver's side. Good Samaritans passing by stopped to help and were able to get me free. Unfortunately, the pickup's underbelly was rusted, and the crash had caused the gas tank to leak. Flames gave enough warning but not enough time to get my mom out of the vehicle.

The automobile that had initiated the chain of events didn't stop, and its driver was never found. My mom was the only fatality.

I didn't remember any of that. I wasn't a therapist, but blocking out the horrific death of my mother in an accident I survived seemed pretty normal. I was sure I probably had survivor's guilt, too, if I were to be clinical about it. Killing Danvers wasn't just about avenging my mom but putting my own ghosts to rest as well.

I checked my trace program—it was still going—and sighed with impatience. My mind wandered and it was just so damn hot. Even with the windows open, the heat was oppressive. I took my third shower of the day, leaving my hair wet, and put on a tiny pair of bikini panties and a thin camisole. I'd had to do some clothes shopping when I'd arrived, and no one seemed to have *Star Wars*–themed pajamas here. I'd made do with some plain clothes that were serviceable but not any fun. I hadn't been able to muster up much more than indifference to not having my normal clothes, which was very unlike me.

There was a quiet ding from my computer. The program had finished.

I sat down to take a look. The laundering had gone through more than a dozen countries over the years, a myriad of shell companies and banks, before finally returning to one account in Luxembourg. I stared at the blinking account number and the sum of money it contained.

Time for Act I of *The Wrath of China*.

I had an account ready on Grand Cayman, and with a few keystrokes, the money began siphoning from Luxembourg to the Cayman Islands. I watched the numbers, feeling a measure of satisfaction that I was depriving Danvers of his money. But it wasn't enough. It wouldn't be enough until he'd paid in blood.

When it was done, I closed my laptop and climbed into bed. I lay on top of the covers in the dark, staring at the ceiling. I could hear traffic outside and people talking, laughing, having a good time. Sometimes, like tonight, I didn't think I'd ever laugh again.

The look on Jackson's face when I'd left . . . and Clark's. I missed them. Three inadequate words for the hole left in my life. But it had to be done. I was no more capable of having a normal romantic relationship than my biological father was. Jackson and Clark would move on, and, in time, they'd forget about me—that odd girl who'd disrupted their lives with her fandom T-shirts, her obsessive routines, and her tendency to take things literally.

I loved them both, just in different ways. I didn't regret being with them—as in the biblical sense. After all, wasn't sex the ultimate expression of love for someone? The act had been cheapened by society into something selfish, but I didn't view it that way. Even my Friends with Benefits attempt with Clark had still been born out of love for him, though I hadn't wanted to face it at the time.

My eyes were leaking again, but I didn't bother brushing away the tears that rolled into my hair. This was the only time of day I allowed myself to remember and to mourn. It hurt inside, a persistent ache that wouldn't ease. All I wanted to do was sleep, to keep the pain at bay, but sleep turned on me. Dreams turned to nightmares that left me shaken and more tired in the morning than if I hadn't slept at all.

Right before sleep claimed me, I realized I had no idea what day of the week it was. And I didn't care.

A pounding on the door startled me awake. I shoved my tousled hair back from my face and grabbed my glasses, then reached for the handgun I kept loaded on my bedside table. I'd bought it weeks ago and had even taken a class on how to shoot. I didn't like it, but I resolutely kept going to the gun range to practice. Danvers would have no problem using a gun, and I couldn't afford to be squeamish when the time came.

The pounding came again, and I hurried toward the door, gun in hand. It didn't have a peephole, so I called through the door.

"Who is it?"

A man answered. "It's your friendly neighborhood Spiderman," he said.

The voice was familiar. I made sure the chain on the door was set before opening the door a crack.

"Oh," I said. "It's you." Relief mixed with disappointment as I swung open the door.

Kade Dennon stood there in jeans and a T-shirt, arms crossed over his chest. He gave me a once-over, his gaze sticking on the gun. "Expecting trouble?"

"I was hoping you were the repairman."

"Did he overcharge you?"

I sensed sarcasm by the lifting of one dark brow. "He hasn't come yet."

I sighed and headed toward the couch, then realized I didn't have pants on and changed course for the bedroom. I heard him come in and close the door as I grabbed a pair of shorts and tugged them on. When I came back out from the bedroom, he'd made himself comfortable on my couch.

"It's fucking hot in here," he complained. "What's with the AC?"

"It's broken, hence my hoping you were the repairman." I flopped down on a chair, finger-combing my hair into a ponytail. He was watching me, an odd look on his face. "What?" I asked. I knew I didn't look put together, but he'd yanked me out of bed at—I glanced at my watch—six thirty in the morning.

One side of his mouth lifted in a sort of smile. "Nothing. Just some déjà vu."

I frowned. It wasn't like we'd spent a lot of time together, so how could he have déjà vu? *Oh well. Whatever.*

"How'd you find me?" I asked, since that was the most important question.

"Because you've been digging the same places I have," he said, "trying to flush out Danvers."

"You told me he killed my mom. I found proof. I want to find him."

"And do what with him?"

I shrugged, noncommittal. "Maybe I need a 'father-daughter' moment."

His lips twisted. "I like your style."

I glanced down at my clothes, confused. "What do my clothes have to do with it?"

Kade rolled his eyes. "Never mind."

"Wait," I said, making a connection. "You said we've both been digging in the same places? What are you talking about? Vigilance? Have they been tracking my deep web searches?"

"*They* haven't," he said. "*I* have. I'm not just a pretty face, you know."

"You?" I stared in disbelief. "You." Then I laughed. I couldn't help it. He had the gall to look offended.

"What the hell?" he said, holding his arms out, palms up. "You think I'm joking?"

I tried to quell my laughter. "It's just, I've been around hackers and IT geeks all my life. *None* of them look like you."

"Hey, do I judge you by your looks?"

Okay, he had a point. I was a pint-size grown-up Punky Brewster, but my brain ran in ones and zeros.

I cleared my throat, swallowing the last of my giggles. "True. My apologies. You were saying?"

His eyes narrowed and he leaned forward. "Remember that Asian kid who hacked your firewall and your Iron Man and ended up helping you out?"

Yes, I remembered. It had scared the crap out of me when he'd taken over my Iron Man Mark IV replica suit.

"How did you know about that?" I'd only told Clark.

Kade relaxed back against the couch, looking smug. "Meet your Asian hacker."

I waited.

His smugness evaporated into irritation. "Me, China. It was me." He muttered something unflattering to my intelligence under his breath.

"Oh." Was he serious? "Oh!" He *was* serious. The gorgeous Kade Dennon—sexy even with a touch of gray at his temples—was a hacker genius. Who knew? "Well . . . that's . . . cool."

"I know, right?" He rolled his eyes again. "My point is, China, that you and I need to team up."

"Why?"

"You know, two minds are better than one. Birds of a feather flock together. The enemy of my enemy is my friend. I love it when a plan comes together."

One of those wasn't an idiom. I opened my mouth to point that out, but he interrupted.

"Anyway, my point is that we'll have better luck finding him because," he leaned forward, bracing his elbows on his knees, "you're not looking deep enough."

"What do you mean? I've dug through every database and then some. He's a ghost." My frustration leaked into my voice.

"And you're innocent and naive. I'm familiar with the type." His dry tone made me wonder, but he kept going before I could ask questions. "You need to go into the dark web. You can lure him in."

"Lure him how?" It had been the same thing I'd been thinking of doing, once I found out where he lurked.

"You're his kid," Kade said with a shrug. "Take his money away. He's going to want it back. And his dear progeny will have it. Use your imagination."

I felt the need to put my head between my knees and take deep breaths, but pushed it aside. "And you think that'll work?"

"Yep. Curiosity killed the cat, you know."

I got that idiom. Danvers equals the cat. "And how am I supposed to lure him in close enough to kill him?" I asked.

His smile was cold. "You're the puzzle guru. Leave him a puzzle to follow, and stay one step ahead of him until he's right where you want him."

"Why are you helping me?" It was weird, him taking such a personal interest in it.

For a long moment, I didn't think he'd answer me. Then he spoke.

"Because I *was* Danvers."

That made no sense. I waited to see if he'd continue and explain. I didn't have to wait long.

"The government likes their assassins," Kade said. "They handpick them, train the humanity out of them, teach them the most effective ways to kill, point them at the target, and set them loose. Danvers is one. I was one."

Looking at him, it wasn't hard to imagine that he'd been trained as an assassin. That was actually easier to believe than the hacker part, but I didn't think it would be an appropriate thing to mention. "Was?"

"I changed careers a while back," he said. "Ironically enough and such a fucking cliché, but I met someone. And she made me want more. She offered me more. And she accepted who I was."

Hmm. Interesting. Still, "That doesn't explain why you want to hunt Danvers down."

Kade's blue eyes iced over. "Danvers committed heresy. The unforgivable sin. He had the love of a good woman who was devoted to him. Got her pregnant with his child. Then not only abandoned her, but killed her. You deserve a shot at vengeance. And he deserves to die."

"He didn't abandon her," I correct him. "She ended it."

"Doesn't change the fact that he killed her."

Okay, then.

"Jackson doesn't agree," I said. "He thinks I'm acting out of emotion and not logic. That I'm afraid I'll end up like my mom."

Kade settled back. "What about your other boy toy? Clark. What does he think?"

I shrugged, pulling my knees to my chest and bracing my feet on the seat. "He thinks like you do, I guess."

"Where are your sidekicks anyway? Did you ditch them?" I nodded. "Why?"

"Because it was too hard. Too painful. Somehow, things got complicated and I made bad decisions. I hurt them both, and choosing one over the other just seems . . . wrong."

"So you try to fix a bad decision by making another bad decision?"

I stiffened at his tone, which sounded judgy. "I'm doing the best I can. They don't make instruction manuals for relationships." Or I totally would have bought it, read it cover to cover, and highlighted the most pertinent parts. "Besides, what do you know about it?"

"Oh, you'd be surprised."

"Can we get back to Danvers, please?"

"Fine. I take it you've already set up a secure network and a different computer for your work?"

"Yes. Local network, and two DMZs. I've enhanced the firewalls between them myself."

"Good. You'll need to download Tor on the laptop to access the dark web."

"Yes, I'm aware." Now it was my turn to roll my eyes. "Just because I don't frequent the cesspool that is the dark web doesn't mean I don't know how to access it."

Tor was the acronym for The Onion Router, the original name of the project used to create the software. It kept the user anonymous, sending Internet traffic through relays to access content, with each relay adding or removing a layer to the onion. Like playing a game of Telephone, where one person starts with a whisper to someone else, which gets repeated—only instead of the *message* getting mutated going from person to person like in the game, with Tor, no one would know who'd started it.

"You'll need this." He handed me a piece of paper. "It's the CIA server with the database you'll need. Hack it, and the key to the dark web's underbelly is in there. You just have to find the right key."

Now *that* was information guarded like Fort Knox. Few people even knew that since the dark web had become every would-be hacker's playground as a tourist, the real bad guys had gone even deeper. Even to access the sites, you now had to have a 64-bit encryption key. And the keys were held by third parties, so as to keep vendor and customer anonymity.

The problem was finding a third party to connect the two. I knew a lot of hackers, but there was no way I'd associate with anyone who actually had that kind of information. Lucky for me, Kade had just handed me the location of the virtual lockbox where the CIA kept the keys they knew about.

Kade rose from the sofa. "Good luck." He was almost out the door before he glanced back at me. "And by the way, you should call him."

"Who?"

"You know who," he said. "The one you're in love with. Because the other one will move on, but him . . . you're his one and only."

I didn't want to believe him, because then I'd hope. And if I hoped, then I'd have to face that maybe I'd made a mistake. A mistake that was possibly irreparable.

He stared at me for a moment, then left, closing the door behind him. I didn't move from the chair for a long time.

Loading Tor on my laptop wasn't the only precaution I took—any newbie browsing Wikipedia knew to load Tor—so when I felt I was as secure as I was going to get, I logged on.

Digging through the dark web was akin to sifting through a dumpster. Occasionally there'd be something humorous or innocuous, but the dark web was dark for a reason. I especially avoided servers offering images. The worst you could think of—and so many things more horrible and reprehensible than your imagination could conjure—was photographed and on display. It made me sick for humanity.

The CIA server was well concealed and well protected. It took me more than three hours to hack into, and I had to go through two firewalls to do it, all while concealing my hack attempts.

The database was one that held the names, and most important, the curve and the keys used by the websites for encrypted access. It didn't surprise me that those using the most advanced kind were those the CIA kept track of inside the deeper dark web.

Mathematicians (and the government) are always searching for better methods of encryption. Currently the most advanced way—and the method for the websites forced from the dark web to go even darker— was using elliptic curve cryptology. The mathematics were complicated, but like any code, it starts with a single number. A single random number to begin the coding process. There were rumors and reports that the current random-number generator for an elliptic curve encryption could have been built with a back door, meaning that any key could be reproduced by someone with the right secret starting number.

I didn't doubt for a second that somewhere buried in the NSA was the code for that back door.

Once I found the database, my fingers flew over the keyboard, sending the commands to download. Despite my care, chances were higher than likely that my intrusion had been detected. Even now I was being chased by techs on the opposite side as they hunted me down through my layers of anonymous routing through the Internet. Some hackers lived for the thrill of just avoiding detection. That "thrill" made me nauseous.

As soon as the file was downloaded, I severed the connection, pulling the network cable for good measure, and blowing out a deep breath. I was still sweating, and it wasn't just because of being without AC. Being logged in to a supersecret and more-classified-than-classified CIA server for longer than a few minutes was anxiety-inducing. I no longer had my Vigilance Get-Out-Of-Jail-Free card. Men in black would just show up at my door, and I'd disappear, never to be heard from again.

I sat back in my chair, closed my eyes, and took a moment to breathe. My heart was racing as though I'd been running from the cops, which I had been—figuratively.

Once I'd calmed down, I got another Red Bull from the fridge and sat down to go through the database, querying the different tables to pull a comprehensive report of who was in it and what they did for the CIA when the CIA didn't want anyone to know what it was doing.

The database wasn't as large as I thought it'd be (*"That's what she said"*—Clark's voice inside my head.) And the list of those who were willing to kill for a paycheck was even smaller. Of those, Danvers was at the top, and it wasn't alphabetical.

I looked at the information for several minutes. This was it. The ticket to finding him. And yet . . . for some reason, I hesitated.

Not for the first time did I think about what Jackson had said. *Should I be doing this?* Maybe this was the wrong course of action for my life. Vengeance never ended well in the movies. Unless you were a superhero.

I decided to sleep on it. I had the information. It could wait another twelve hours. Because once I moved forward, there would be no going back from this point.

Powering off my computer, I got ready for bed. I made my tea and ate two Fig Newtons, then climbed into the lumpy bed. I missed my bed. I missed my apartment. I missed my things.

I missed Jackson and Clark.

I looked at my cell, sitting on the floor next to the bed. I'd had it turned off for weeks. Even though the geolocator on it was disabled, I hadn't wanted to take chances.

Don't lie to yourself. You didn't turn it off so no one would track you. You turned it off so you wouldn't hear the silence of them not *calling.*

It was ridiculous. I had left. Of course neither one would be calling. Switching it on would only be more painful, as my text messages would be empty, as would my voice mail. I wasn't some lovestruck teenager mooning over her ex-boyfriend(s) and listening to Taylor Swift songs (though I *had* preordered her next album and listened to the new single five times).

All this was going through my head as I picked up my phone and pressed the power button. Kade's words were echoing inside my head. *"You should call him."*

And say what? I wondered. *I know I left and said we were over, but hey, I miss you and I'm in love with you and that scares me to death. Want to meet for a drink?*

Yeah. That oughta go over like a lead balloon. Why would he risk it? I'd hurt him before, chances were I'd do it again.

I desperately wanted to call Bonnie, Mia, and Grams. Any of them. All of them. My life was unrecognizable to me. I'd taken one of those online tests yesterday, and it determined I was severely depressed. Of course, the test had been via Buzzfeed, but still.

As I'd predicted, there were no messages and no texts. I'd told people not to try to reach me, that I'd be out of touch for a while, so it wasn't as though it was a surprise. But the feeling of isolation—one that I'd craved and cultivated for many years—was now unwelcome. I'd changed. And at the moment, I wished I could change back.

It was cold outside, the snow coming down in swirls of white. She shivered despite the fact that she was inside and wearing her winter coat. A group of students moved past her, pushing open the doors and letting in a gust of frigid wind. One smiled at her as she passed by, which seemed odd. They weren't friends. All the students were at least eight years older than she was, and none had spent any time speaking to her over the weekend.

Should she smile back? Maybe it was a social thing, like Mom said people did. If she did smile, would the girl stop and talk to her? She wouldn't know what to say if she did. What if the girl asked questions and she said the wrong thing? But what if the girl was trying to be nice and she didn't smile back, would the girl think she was being a snob?

By the time she'd decided to half smile (just in case the girl was looking at her by mistake), the girl's friend walking beside her said in a loud whisper, "See? I told you. She's weird." Then they were gone, out the door after the rest of them.

The door clanged shut, echoing in the now-empty foyer of the university building.

China stood, feeling as brittle as the icicles on the edge of the roof outside.

A pickup truck pulled up outside, its headlights cutting through the falling precipitation. China recognized it and hurried out into the winter storm. She climbed up into the warm cab, the sight of her mom behind the wheel making the icicle inside her melt.

"Hey, honey," her mom said, reaching over and hugging her. "Did you have fun?"

"It wasn't supposed to be fun," China corrected her. "But I learned a lot. I knew all the answers to the professor's questions. I even fixed an answer he'd gotten wrong." She'd been very proud of that. After all, it wasn't every day that an eight-year-old got to correct a tenured mathematics professor at the University of Nebraska.

Her mom sighed, then smiled. "Of course you did, sweetheart. I'm so proud of you." She squeezed her one more time. "Put your seat belt on. The roads are bad."

China obediently clicked the belt and settled back into the seat. She was short, and not just for her age, so she was barely tall enough to see over the dashboard and out the windshield.

The snow was so thick, all she could see was a curtain of white, angrily pummeling the truck as her mom drove onto the highway. The other cars were moving slowly, too, though there weren't many of them. China was nervous, but she trusted her mom. They'd get home safe because Mom would make sure of it. She always took care of her "baby girl."

"Did you make any friends?" her mom asked.

"No." That answer was always the same.

"You will someday," Mom said, smiling.

"I don't need friends."

"Well, you might not need them, but they're nice to have. And one day, you'll meet someone who's your best friend and completely understands you. Then you'll fall in looooove—"

"Mom!" China blushed, but was grinning. She pushed her glasses up her nose. "That's gross."

Mom just laughed, the sound warm and comforting. It made China laugh, too, though she didn't see what was funny. Boys were gross. Her two brothers were proof of that, always making fart jokes, and burping, and missing the toilet.

It was slow going and China didn't talk more. Idle chitchat wasn't her thing, and she knew her mom needed to concentrate on the road. She'd gotten behind a semitruck now, which seemed to make it easier to see the road, since she only had to follow the taillights.

The warm cab and thrum of the engine lulled China into a doze. She hadn't gotten much sleep in the dormitory over the weekend. Although she'd had a room to herself because of her age, the other students had been up late partying and being generally loud. She'd told herself she couldn't sleep because they were being rude, not because she felt left out.

You'd think she'd be used to feeling left out by now. The "weird" girl.

Something loud jolted her awake and she bumped her head on the window. She'd slumped against the door in her sleep. She was jerked hard against the seat belt again and came fully awake.

The pickup was swerving, her mom frantically working the steering wheel. China's heart jumped into her throat.

The semi swerved, then started a slow rotation. China watched in horror as the cab came into view. Everything seemed to be in slow motion as it came closer and closer, dwarfing the pickup.

China screamed at the impact, which sent the pickup sliding across the icy road. Darkness loomed outside her window, and she screamed again.

"Mom! Mommy!" She hadn't said Mommy *in years, but fear terrorized her. As the truck teetered, she held her breath. A hand clamped around her arm, and she looked left. Her mom's eyes were wide and terrified. Then they pitched over the side of the embankment.*

China screamed for her mom over and over. She lost control of her bladder, and her pants grew soaked. She was sobbing uncontrollably as the pickup tumbled over on her side, smashing in her door and breaking her window.

Then they were upside down. She didn't have the breath to scream anymore. The seat belt was cutting into her abdomen and chest. But she could feel her mom's grip, tight on her arm.

Another turning of the sky in an ear-splitting crunch of metal and glass, fracturing apart. Then . . . everything stopped.

China was suspended in the air, held in place by the seat belt. She struggled to breathe.

"It's okay, sweetheart. You'll be okay."

Mom's voice. China frantically looked to the side. Mom was squished against her door, the steering wheel mangled and pressed down into her thigh. Her face was bleeding, but her eyes were calm.

"Are you okay?" she asked.

China managed a shaky nod. "I-I think so."

Her mom smiled. "Good. Just stay calm, okay? Someone saw, I'm sure. Help will be along any minute. Can you unbuckle your belt?"

China reached down and tried to press the buckle, but her hands were shaking. She shook her head, looking fearfully at her mother.

"It's okay. Just keep trying."

Her mom reached, but was too far away and pinned to be able to get to China's seat belt. China grew alarmed at this, but her mom just smiled and kept repeating, "It's okay. Just keep trying. It'll all be okay."

Snow crunched and China looked out her window, but she only saw sky. Snow was still falling through the broken glass and into the cab. Suddenly, the truck creaked as someone climbed up. Then a man's face appeared at her window.

Her mom gasped audibly. "Mark? Is that you?"

"Hello, Kimmie."

"Oh, thank God. Mark, help us. China's okay, I think, but my leg is fractured. Possibly my elbow, too. I can't reach her seat belt—"

"I'm not here to rescue you, Kimmie. I'm here to finish the job."

China's wide gaze swung from her mom, to the man, then back. Her mom's face was bloodless, her mouth slightly agape as she stared, unblinking, at the man.

"What are you talking about?" she said at last.

"Did you think I wouldn't find out? That I was too blind to see?" His voice was full of contempt.

"Mark, I don't know what you're talking about." Her mom's voice shook for the first time, and China began to be scared again.

"Of course you don't. Sticking with it till the end, are you? The Company would be so proud."

Her mom's face was white with pain, and tears began rolling down China's cheeks.

"Please, I'll do whatever you want," she begged the man she'd called Mark. "Just get China out. She's a child. She's—"

"She's collateral damage," Mark interrupted. "Her death is on your head. The wages of sin." He cast a quick glance at China, then was gone, dropped out of sight.

China's mom let out a sound, the kind that made the hair stand up on the back of China's neck. It was a sound that she sometimes heard on the farm, when a coyote would corner prey. An animal, grievously wounded, voicing their fear and anger at whoever could hear. To her horror, China's mom began to sob.

"Mom, please! Don't cry!" Never in her life had she seen her mom cry. "Mommy!"

Her shriek seemed to get through, because her mom abruptly stopped crying. Her head jerked up and she pulled at the dashboard, trying to see outside. There was a noise from beyond the cab, and a strange smell. Like . . . when Dad fueled up the combine.

"Oh God," her mom murmured.

Suddenly she was clawing the seat, trying to pull her way out from behind the wheel to get to China.

"China! I need you to undo your seat belt."

"But, Mom, I—"

"Don't you dare tell me you can't!" Her mom was yelling at her. She never yelled at China. "Undo it! Now, China!"

Her hands fumbled at the clasp, her fingers numb from the cold. The button was so hard to press, the seat belt straining. She gritted her teeth and pushed . . .

It gave, and she tumbled, falling across the seat into her mother's arms.

"Mom!" China grabbed her and held on, her arms tight around her mother's neck. She could smell faint traces of her mom's perfume, the kind she always wore. Sometimes when her mom was out of town, China would sneak into her parents' bedroom and steal away her mom's pillow, just so she could have that smell near her while she slept.

Instinctively, she knew this would be the last time she'd smell that unique scent.

China was sobbing into her mom's neck, and she could hear her mother's voice in her ear.

"It's okay. Some things are meant to be, my baby girl."

"That man—"

"Don't you worry about that man. Forget him." Her mom pried her off her neck to make China look in her eyes. "Promise me. Promise me you'll forget all about him."

"I p-p-promise." Her nose was running, she was still crying, and her pants were wet with urine, but she didn't want to move. She was too scared to move.

"Hey!"

A voice from outside.

"Hey! Anyone in there?"

"Yes! Here! Help us!" Her mom's shout startled China.

Two men suddenly appeared at the passenger window, the pickup dipping again as they climbed up.

"You two okay?" one of them said.

"She's okay, get her out," her mom said. Her voice was firm, demanding. The men immediately scrambled to get access to China through the window.

"Come on," one of them said, hooking his finger into the back of China's jeans. "We need to get you two out, pronto."

The sky was brighter now, and as China was pulled back, she could see flames licking underneath the hood. She was far from stupid, and she immediately knew what this meant.

"Mom! It's on fire!" She scrambled back as the man helped pull her through the window. He tried to drop her onto the ground, but she pulled out of his grasp, scooting to the side. "Get my mom out!"

He knocked out the rest of the glass in the window and climbed inside. China watched as he braced himself above her mom and started working on her seat belt. It came undone and China breathed a sigh of relief. Then he started working her mom out from underneath the mangled dash.

A scream splintered the cold air, and China shivered. Her cheeks were cold, but her tears were hot tracks as she watched her mother's face grimace in pain. A broken leg. A broken elbow. Pinned under the steering wheel of a 1990 Chevy pickup.

There was a burst of flame, and China jumped back, staring in horror as the flames moved to the windshield. She could see the man in the cab hesitate, the flames reflected in the glasses he wore.

"Get my mom out!" she cried. "Get her out!"

He looked back at her mom, and they seemed to exchange an unspoken understanding. She nodded, and he began backing out of the cab.

"What're you doing?" China screamed. "Get my mom! You can't just leave her there!"

He was out of the cab now, and China shoved him out of the way. If he wouldn't rescue her mom, then she would. She started climbing back in . . . and was abruptly caught by an arm around her waist. She started kicking.

"Let go of me! Let me go! I've gotta get my mom!"

The arm was like iron, slowly pulling her loose as China fought and screamed.

"No! Let me go! I want to stay! Let me go!"

China was mindlessly fighting, her hands gripping the edge of the window. The broken glass cut into her fingers, making them slippery with blood.

"China."

She froze at her mom's voice. Her gaze lifted to her mother's blue eyes, bright with tears. Incredibly, her mom smiled.

"I love you, baby girl. Make me proud."

She kissed her fingers and blew . . . then China was yanked from the truck, tucked underneath the man's arm as he ran up the embankment.

"No! No! Mommy! Don't leave her! Don't leave her! Please! Don't—"

An explosion ripped through the night, engulfing the pickup in flames. China screamed and screamed and screamed . . .

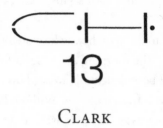

13

CLARK

The day after his fight with Jackson—which Clark knew he'd totally won—he was in New Orleans, a shitty place, in Clark's opinion. Drunks everywhere. Tourists everywhere. It smelled like stale beer and vomit.

And that was just the airport.

He checked in at the Ritz—because why the hell not?—and made a phone call.

"Slattery, what the hell are you doing?"

"Good to talk to you, too, Alessio."

"You are asking for trouble," Alessio growled, his Italian accent thick despite years on American soil. "Mama will not allow you to leave the city if she finds out you are here."

"I know. I want to bargain with her."

"What are you talking about? What bargain?"

"I want a meeting. Tonight. Can you help me?"

Alessio sighed. "All right. It is, as they say, your funeral. I will be in touch."

Clark stripped off his shirt and lay flat on the bed, staring up at the ceiling. He folded his arms behind his head. Each day China had been gone had felt like an eternity.

How had it come to this? For supposedly such a heartless badass, a little girl with a ponytail and glasses forever sliding down her nose had been what brought him to his knees. Clark Slattery had fallen in love.

It eased his mind to dwell on her, so he closed his eyes and brought her image into focus. The morning after they'd first made love was a favorite. Her hair had been deliciously tousled over her pale shoulders, her lips pink and swollen from his kisses. Without being hidden behind the clear lenses of her glasses, her eyes were a clear blue and focused intently on his face.

For someone who maintained that she had difficulty reading others, she had little trouble reading him, it seemed. Except his selfishness. That was something she was blind to. Considering she was the most unselfish person he'd ever known, it wasn't surprising that what she didn't possess in her own soul, she also couldn't see in others.

And he had been selfish. He could see it now, though he hadn't been able to before. Now that he'd decided on his course, he could be honest. China made him feel like he'd finally won something. That all the shit he'd done and been through had been worth it. From starting out as one of the "good guys," to turning into one of the worst kind, and finally into one of moral ambivalence. He wanted to believe that since he'd known her, he'd found the right path again. One his mother would have been proud of. China had done that. She'd made him want to be a better man, someone worthy of winning her. The one thing he hadn't considered was whether or not he could make her happy.

China was young. She had her whole life ahead of her. Clark felt as though he was twice his age.

He'd seen a lot of men in battle—some behaved courageously. Others did not. It was always so easy to talk big about how you'd do things . . . until suddenly bullets were flying, and the guy next to you gets ripped in half by a grenade. That's when shit got real. China had gone through more shit than some soldiers he'd known. She was brave and smart, and she didn't let anyone push her around. Not even him.

Clark had been with a lot of women, most of whose names he hadn't bothered to learn. His mother died. His brother died, then ended up worse than dead—he ended up a murderous lunatic. People he'd been charged with protecting had died under his watch. Everything he touched was tinged with death. And he was tired. Just so damn tired.

There was only one thing he could do—and he did it well. That was delivering death to someone's door. So that is what he would do.

His cell buzzed. He put it to his ear without looking at the screen. "Yeah."

"She will meet with you, tonight, midnight. The usual place. Do not be late."

"Got it." He ended the call.

The "usual place" was the second floor above a tavern off Bourbon Street. The walls and floors had to be reinforced, Clark thought, because the noise from the reveling crowd in the bar diminished appreciably as he climbed the stairs. Not the smell though. Smoke and liquor, tinged with sweat and desperation. The smell lingered.

Men with guns greeted him, though "greet" was stretching it. Since he was expected, he was relieved of his weapons and taken into the parlor. Mama was waiting.

"Mama" was an age-indeterminate, heavyset black woman. She'd ruled her "family" with an iron fist for the better part of four decades. Her hair was thick and white as snow. You might be fooled into thinking she was the warm grandma type, with cookies in the oven and sweet tea in the fridge. But when you got close enough to look into her eyes, you'd realize your mistake.

Mama was harsh but fair when one of hers got outta line. She owned the majority of the brothels in New Orleans and sold illegal firearms on the side. A few had attempted to overthrow her over the years. None had lived to regret it.

Clark sat down on the hunter-green velvet chaise stuffed with horsehair. The furniture in the parlor was all antiques, and just as uncomfortable. Mama regarded him from her overstuffed chair, which looked a great deal more comfortable than his. The light was dim and reminded him of gas-lamp light, though the chandelier above their heads was electric.

When she spoke, Mama had a thick accent that was part Creole, part swamp, and part her own. Her voice was higher than you'd assume it would be.

"Clark," she said, "it's been a while. Why you comin' ta town? Ah warned you abou' that." She spoke softly, as though gently chastising him, rather than the death threat it actually was.

"Hi, Mama. I'm here because I need your help."

"Now why yous thinkin' ah be helpin' with some o' your business?"

Clark settled back against the chaise, resting one ankle on the opposite knee. "As a trade. You help me. Once my business is through, I'm yours."

Her sharp eyes narrowed. "Mama don' grant mercy twice, boy."

"I know."

There was silence for a moment, and Clark didn't look away from her penetrating gaze.

"Who is she?" Mama asked.

Clark's eyes widened fractionally. "Excuse me?"

Mama waved one meaty hand, calloused and rough from the years she spoke to no one about. "Mama's nobody's fool, boy. You only do sum'tin like this for love of a woman. Who is she?"

He hesitated. "Her name is China," he said. "She's in the city. I need to find her." He'd hoped he could leave his personal feelings aside and portray this as just another job. But Mama had seen through him immediately.

Clark reached into his jacket, slowly because he didn't want some trigger-happy lackey to use him for target practice. He withdrew a photo and handed it to Mama.

It was a shot of China, complete with ponytail and glasses, her eyes rolled heavenward. Seeing it sent a pang through him. He'd insisted on taking her picture one time while they were at her favorite Chinese place. The evening sunlight had been shining through the window, giving her an almost golden glow.

She'd been carefully cutting her beef-and-broccoli into bite sizes and pairing them off so she could have "one of each in every bite." She'd been left with a surplus of broccoli, which had stymied her until Clark had reached over with his chopsticks, grabbed the offending broccoli, and stuffed it in his mouth.

Her smile had made him feel as though that warm, golden glow of sunshine was bathing him instead of her, and he'd snapped a photo as she'd rolled her eyes in protest.

"She's not your usual type," Mama commented.

"She's different. Height about five two, weighs about one ten. She'll have arrived in the city in the last couple of weeks. She won't be in a hotel. Most likely a cheap Airbnb or VRBO. It's likely she'll have ordered consistently on Mondays from a pizza place, and Thursdays from a Chinese joint."

"Why is she runnin' from you?"

"She's not running from me," Clark corrected. "I just need to find her. Will you help or not?" His patience was at an end. There was a gnawing in his gut that wouldn't ease until he knew where China was.

Mama nodded. "Yas, I be helpin' you. But when your business is done . . . you're mine. We clear?"

It was amazing how easy it was to sign your soul over to the devil when it was for someone you loved. "Crystal," he replied.

She nodded in satisfaction, lifting her arm to beckon Dax—her right-hand man. "Then we shall begin."

◆ ◆ ◆

It didn't take long for Mama's Minions (Clark was particularly amused by his own cleverness with that one) to find China. An unsigned note was dropped off at his hotel after five days.

2480 NE Dauphine, #5

The knot in his gut loosened. They'd found her.

He waited until it was fully dark before going, which had cost him all he'd ever learned in the field about patience. He parked two streets away and made his way back. Dark jeans and a black T-shirt was enough for the shadows to envelop him. His weapon was tucked into the back of his jeans. Never leave home without it.

This was what he was used to. This was what he was good at. The hunt. His muscles were loose and ready, his senses taking in everything around. The dog barking a block down. The couple arguing in the driveway across the street. Sirens to the south and heading east.

The streetlights were laughable. The ones that worked were few and far between. The street was narrow, tiny alleys like capillaries running to a vein branched off between the buildings. Though the sun had gone down, the heat still lay like an oppressive, moist blanket. Taking a deep breath felt as though breathing through cotton.

Number five was lit from the inside. Clark saw movement and froze, his breath catching in his chest.

There she was, sitting in front of the artificial glow of a computer monitor. Her silky, thick hair pulled back in the ponytail that Clark was forever wanting to tug, as though the perpetual eight-year-old boy inside just couldn't resist the temptation.

The dull ache he'd felt since she'd walked out the door of that hotel room burst into a searing pain. And it scared him, which was even worse. Because if he was scared he'd lose her, then he'd fuck it up. She could get hurt. He had to face the fact that he'd already lost her. Jackson would be the last man standing, and that was okay. He could live with that.

Or not.

Ha. Morbid humor. A sure sign he was Not Right, as his mother would say. But you had to be Not Right to do this job. He'd stopped being normal a long time ago. For a while, he thought maybe he'd found his way back, in the arms of a girl who refused to eat fish because "they swim in their own waste," and for whom calling Harry Potter "kids' books" was a mortal sin.

Clark didn't know how long he crouched there, under the window, watching her. She didn't move from that spot. Occasionally, she'd take a drink of the Red Bull at her elbow, but her eyes were glued to the screen as she typed.

His knees grew cramped, but he stayed. Just being near her soothed him. She was probably—no, definitely—the last person since his mother who'd looked at him and seen something inside to love. There was a gift in that.

She rose after a while, arching her back and stretching. Clark's avid gaze traced the soft curve of her shoulder, to the swell of her breasts under the thin camisole she wore. She wasn't wearing pants, just a pair of tiny white-lace panties. They were the kind that cut up so high in the back, Clark wondered how it didn't drive her nuts. But at the moment, her curved ass lovingly traced by the white line of the panties made his cock twitch.

Yeah, this wasn't perverted or anything, he thought, and yet . . . He still watched as she bent and logged off the computer, his mouth going dry at the sight. He was hard as a rock inside his jeans, and it was only by sheer will that he didn't rub himself. There had to be a line somewhere, though he thought he'd probably already crossed it.

Watching her take down her ponytail and run her fingers through that thick, luscious hair was almost a religious experience. As usual, China had no idea how sexy she was. Her appeal was effortless, not based in any kind of artifice. She just . . . was.

Suddenly, her head came up, as if she'd heard something. Clark stopped breathing, but she wasn't looking his way. She was looking out the back.

Might as well make himself useful, other than being inches from jacking off outside her window, or worse, coming in his pants like a preteen boy.

Clark made his way soundlessly around the building, picking his way through the narrow alley until he emerged from the other side. He took a moment, letting his eyes adjust to the darkness that was thicker there.

A rustle in the darkness. Muted whispers. Movement by the back door.

Cold fury raged in his veins. *This was what you got, Mack, for choosing a shitty part of town.* He moved fast and silent. Two men at the back, one standing watch while the other worked at the lock on the door. The one keeping watch never saw him coming. A blow with the butt of his gun to the back of the head, and he went down like a rock.

His partner swung a startled gaze as Clark grabbed on to the iron railing of the back porch and vaulted over it, landing directly behind the would-be intruder.

"Whatcha doin' there, dickhead?"

Clark's cold smile froze the guy for a second, then he clumsily swung a knife. Clark evaded easily, the jab so slow he could've yawned first. In the next breath, he had the knife and it was pressed to the guy's neck, right under his ear.

"You have no idea how much I'd love to slit your throat," Clark hissed. "But it would leave a stain. So I'll give you and your buddy one shot to get out of here, and don't come back. If I see your face again, I'll cut it off and wear it for Mardi Gras. Understand?"

The guy's eyes were white with terror. "Yeah," he managed to gasp. "I got it."

Clark stepped back, and watched. They always tried to get a jab in, thinking they'd just been caught off guard. He wasn't wrong.

The douchebag turned like he was going to walk down the three concrete stairs, then jerked around, swinging a fist . . . and met Clark's full force with his nose. Cartilage crunched and blood spurted. He opened his mouth to yell . . . and found Clark's hand cutting off his air supply.

"Make so much as a whimper, you whiny piece of shit," he growled, "and I'll cut out your vocal cords."

A jerky nod, then Clark hurled him down the steps, hearing a grunt as the wind was knocked out of him. Then he gathered his partner, who was just now stirring in the bushes, and they beat a hasty retreat. Clark pocketed both his gun and the knife. He glanced back inside the windows.

Whatever China had heard, she'd dismissed. The lights were all off save for the sole one in the tiny kitchen above the stove. He could see the shadow of her body as she climbed into bed and pulled the covers up "just so," as she said. He wondered if she'd had her tea and Newtons, those fucking shitty cookies he kept buying even though she wasn't there to eat them anymore.

All was quiet. He stood outside the door, leaning forward and resting his forehead on the frame. His fingers lightly grazed the handle. So close . . .

But wishing and hoping were for fools, and he liked to think that trait wasn't a part of his résumé.

He climbed off the porch and rounded the house to where the air-conditioning unit was. It only took a moment to disable a vital part. He knew China, and she didn't like the heat. She'd call for a repairman, and that's when he'd get some listening devices and cameras in the house. She'd said she was going to lure in Danvers. That was just fine, because Clark would be waiting.

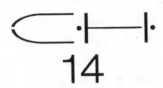

14

I sat straight up in bed, my throat raw from screaming from the nightmare. I was bathed in a cold sweat, and tears were leaking from my eyes.

Throwing back the sheet, I stood on shaking legs. In the bathroom, I splashed cold water on my face. Leaning against the sink, I tried to breathe. Every time I closed my eyes, I saw the fire that had consumed Mom.

Never before had I remembered the details of the accident, and now I knew why. I'd been a child—albeit precocious and smart—but still just a child. The last few moments with my mom, seeing the heartbreak and pain of betrayal on her face . . . it had been too much for me. I'd blocked everything.

I'd seen him. I'd heard him. He wasn't human. He'd looked right into her eyes, and into the eyes of her child, and coldly sentenced them to die.

Any hesitation I'd experienced last night was gone, burned away in the fire of my memories.

I showered on autopilot, my emotions pushed aside as I formulated my plan. I didn't just want to kill Danvers—I wanted to punish him, make him feel pain.

By the time I sat down at my computer with my Red Bull, I was ready to go. I hit a key on my keyboard to activate network traffic logging. My firewalls were logging, too, but it never hurt to have too much data.

I pulled up the website listed for Danvers in the database. I snorted in derision at what popped up on the screen. A pet-photography business. The screen was filled with fluffy kittens and puppies with lolling tongues and wagging tails. There were several galleries to view (I didn't bother), but if someone tried to book studio time, they were informed that the calendar was currently full and they were not accepting appointments.

The menu had a log-in for previous customers to enter their passcode to view their pets' photos. That's where I typed the key. I hit "Enter" and waited.

The kitten on the home page flashed, and the website morphed, like Umbridge's cats on her office wall, hissing and snarling when Harry entered. An empty box appeared in the middle of the screen with a blinking cursor.

Leave your message. Check back later for a response.

Okay, here went nothing.

I typed in a number. It was a long number. It was the exact amount—to the penny—that my mother's life had been worth to Danvers. The entire contents of his account that now resided in my Cayman account. Then I hit "Submit."

I wondered how long it would take to get a reply, but no sooner did the thought cross my mind than the screen blinked.

That's a lot of money.

My pulse sped up. It was him. **Blood money.**
The cursor blinked, then the reply. **Who is this?**

You left me and my mother to die seventeen years ago. The cursor blinked for several moments before there was a reply.

So this is your revenge? Stealing money?

Consider it back payment for child support.

What are you talking about? Who are you?

I'm your daughter.

The cursor blinked and I waited. This response took the longest.

You expect me to believe that?

Why would I lie? I already have your money.

She would have told me.

You didn't give her the chance.

So what do you want? It's a little late for going to the Daddy/Daughter dance.

I stared at the screen for a minute, confused. *Oh. Sarcasm.* I want to meet.

Why?

I hadn't expected that question. The answer seemed obvious to me. Because you're my biological father. Duh. I didn't add that I also wanted to kill him.

You still haven't told me your name.

China. China Mack.

The cursor blinked so long, I was afraid he wasn't going to answer.

Okay.

And he was gone. No other word about when or where.

Now that it was over, the adrenaline faded, leaving me feeling shaky. I'd just had a conversation with the man who'd killed my mom and left us for dead. The same man who'd inspired such love and devotion in her. I'd kill him, but first I had questions.

It didn't take long before notices started coming in from the alerts I'd set up on every airline in the country. He booked a flight from LAX to New Orleans within hours. I calculated that he'd be here by tomorrow night.

Now to prepare the welcoming committee.

It was early the next evening, and I was watching multiple video feeds on my computer. By now, I was sure Danvers had my full name, address, and photograph. He'd probably also dug up my entire education and employer history, right up until I'd gone to work at Vigilance. After that, the trail would go cold.

I had little faith that he'd knock before entering, and I wasn't disappointed. I could hear the door open—these old houses were creaky like that—though I didn't hear footsteps. I held my breath, waiting. A moment later, he stepped into the room.

He looked different from the old service photo that had been in his CIA file, but the description my mother had given was still apt. Gray eyes, square jaw, thick brown hair now touched with gray at the temples. He wasn't tall—topping out at perhaps five feet ten or eleven—but he was wide, his chest was deep, and every inch was muscle. Lines were etched around his eyes, as though he'd spent too many years squinting into the sun.

He'd aged well.

I waited, letting him speak first.

"You wanted to meet me. Here I am."

I remotely activated the program I'd written and watched the video feed on my laptop as the China-bot I'd left in my apartment turned around to face Danvers. She looked real and so like me, it sent a shiver down my back. Thomas had done an excellent job.

"Hello," the China-bot said pleasantly. "I am your welcoming committee. China couldn't be here, but she invites you to find her. She's having dinner at a restaurant I believe you know." China-bot tilted her head to the side. "I do hope you remember. Your last dinner with her mother was there."

Danvers was stone-faced, watching her.

"But first," she continued, "you have to survive me." She smiled sweetly and pushed her glasses up her nose (I'd added that little gesture). "I self-destruct in five . . . four . . ."

Danvers reacted instantly, making a running leap for the window. His arm hit the glass hard, shattering it as he flew through.

"One." China-bot's placid voice was a stark contrast to the violent explosion that followed, and my feed cut off. The blast would've taken out the bedroom of my tiny rental house, and there went my damage deposit.

I took a swig of my Red Bull and toggled my video feed. China-bot #2 was next on deck.

It took thirty minutes for Danvers to arrive at the restaurant, except it was no longer open. It had gone out of business a couple of years ago. The interior still had scattered tables and chairs, coated with dust.

The windows were boarded up, and the sign was faded. China-bot #2 was patiently waiting. An inaccurate assessment, given that robots were incapable of patience or impatience.

He was more careful this time, approaching the robot warily. I keyed up her program.

"You made it." China-bot #2 smiled. "Lucky you. Do you remember this place? Kim did. She remembered a lot. She wrote it down, too, and left it for me. It would be a tender, tragic love story, if it didn't include betrayal and murder."

"I gotta say, this is an odd way to meet my daughter," he said. "You going to try to kill me again?"

I typed, and China-bot spoke my words. "It's the least you deserve."

"I could just walk away."

"I still have your money."

"You think I give a shit?"

That made me pause. If he didn't want the money back, why was he here?

"Your robot malfunction?" he asked, his voice laced with sarcasm.

I decided to ignore the money comment. I had questions to ask. "I want to know why," China-bot said. "Why would you betray my mother? She loved you."

He laughed outright. "You honestly believe that?"

I was completely taken aback. "What are you talking about? Yes, of course I do."

"Well, she didn't. I didn't betray her. She betrayed me."

The idea was so absurd, it took me a moment to respond. "You're absolutely, utterly wrong. I've spoken to her handler. He told me how you tortured and killed Chen."

"Yeah. So? He deserved it."

His casual nonchalance chilled me to the bone.

"I remember, you know. I remember you walking away and leaving us to burn."

For the first time, I saw him flinch. "I didn't know that was going to happen."

"What did you think would happen? You ran us off the road. My mother burned to death."

"Stop." His voice was sharp. A loud staccato in the silence.

"Why? Is the thought of the mother of your child burning to death bothersome to you?"

He did something unusual then. In a move so fast I barely saw it, he'd dropped a knife into his palm and thrown it at China-bot.

It was a good throw and hit the robot right in the larynx. Or where the larynx would be if it was an actual person.

Well, I guess I knew who I'd gotten *that* particular skill from.

"It's not a person," China-bot said, though now she looked creepy because her lips weren't moving, and there was a knife sticking out of her neck. No blood.

Danvers turned and spied the tiny camera I'd set up close to the ceiling. He walked toward it until he filled my frame.

"I don't know how many robots you have waiting for me," he said, "but I'm done with this shit. Time to meet Daddy, China." Reaching up, he yanked the camera off the wall, and my picture went dark.

I wasn't going to panic. He had no idea where I was holed up. And even if he did, he wouldn't know which room. The Ritz didn't just give out their guests' room numbers.

Still, I was looking over my shoulder as I filled my bucket of ice. It had been an hour since the confrontation with Danvers. I'd checked his website, but he hadn't been back online. I was still contemplating how I was going to track him down again as I went back into my room. My Red Bulls needed ice.

I popped open another can and started pouring, glancing up into the mirror above the desk.

Danvers was right behind me.

I spun around, throwing my Red Bull can at him.

He batted it away with one hand. "Seriously?"

"How did you find me?"

"You're in room 704," he said. "You thought I'd remember the restaurant but not the room number?" He looked me up and down, taking in my jeans, my *I AIM TO MISBEHAVE* T-shirt, my glasses, and ponytail. I pushed my glasses up my nose and shifted my weight from one bare foot to the other. "So you're the real thing. The robots were taller."

"Because worrying about what you think is at the top of my list," I shot back.

"Feisty. I like it."

"Oh. Yay." I narrowed my eyes. "You just going to stand there and stare?"

He didn't answer. He was studying my face intently. I wanted to look away, but I made my gaze remain steady. I wasn't going to let him intimidate me.

"You look like her." His voice was rough.

I didn't answer.

"Why didn't she tell me?"

I didn't know if he was talking to himself or me. "She thought you wouldn't let her go, if you knew," I said. "She thought what you two had was real. She was desperately in love with you."

He started to shake his head.

"Yes," I insisted, horrified to realize my eyes were filling with tears, and my voice was getting louder. "She loved you and you *betrayed* her! You *murdered* her! She would have done anything for you. How could you do that?"

I flew at him, heedless of what a dumb idea it was, and hit him. I'd never hit anyone with my fist before, and the crack of my knuckles against his jaw sent searing pain through my hand. I ignored the searing pain and shoved him. He stumbled back a few steps.

"You will rot in hell," I seethed. "You were everything to her. I will never forget the look on her face when she realized you weren't going to help us. Do *you* remember? Do you?" My voice echoed around the room, and I was blinded by rage and pain. "*You're* the reason I don't have a mother!"

I attacked him again, slapping and punching any part of him that I could reach. Tears were dripping down my face. Every ounce of pain inside me sought to punish him, to hurt him back. Death was too easy. I wanted him to *hurt*.

He didn't fight back. Just stood there and took it. Until I ran out of steam. I collapsed onto the side of the bed, sobbing. I struggled to get control, sucking in gasping breaths until the tears subsided. The whole time, Danvers did nothing but stand there.

Finally, I could talk again. "How could you do it?" I asked. My voice was quiet after the shouting earlier. My throat was raw. "Just tell me." I didn't look at him. I stared at the floor.

"She wasn't who you thought she was," he said. "I don't know what she told you, but she played me. She made choices I never could have, and in the end, she paid the price. The life of a CIA agent isn't rainbows and unicorn farts."

I looked at him. "Whatever you *think* she did, you're wrong. I was young, but I knew my mother."

"Really? Well, let me tell you something. I had an asset in the PRC. A billionaire businessman who had a lot of officials on his payroll. You have no idea what I went through to protect that asset, the intelligence he gave us." His voice was tight as he spoke. "I had to send good men to their deaths. I had to look the other way. But then I found out that I wasn't the only one looking the other way."

"What do you mean?"

"My asset. He liked little boys and girls. You know what they have too much of in China? People. Lives are cheap. I found out an underground child-trafficking ring was supplying my asset, and that the traffickers were protected by the CIA. Because keeping the information flowing was worth more than the lives of hundreds of Chinese kids."

The bitterness and anger in his voice was unmistakable.

"What does any of that have to do with you killing my mom?"

"Chen's uncle ran the trafficking ring," he said. "Your mother knew about it and did nothing. The CIA did nothing. So I stepped in."

I shook my head. "No. No way. There is no way my mom would've done that. How do you know she knew about Chen's uncle?"

"She was *protecting* him. Of course she knew."

"*You* didn't," I retorted. "It's the CIA. Isn't it more likely that she was kept in the dark for the same reason you were? Did you even ask her?"

His silence said it all.

"So you killed her for nothing? You miserable bastard."

"I wasn't trying to kill her," he burst out. "I wanted to take her out of play so I could get to Chen. That was all." He paused and cleared his throat. "I didn't know the truck would explode. And people were coming. I thought she had help." His face was the color of paper.

"Well, I guess if you didn't *know*, that makes it all okay." Bitterness and sarcasm. I'd finally gotten the hang of the latter.

"I thought she'd played me," he continued. "A honey trap to confirm the identity of my asset. He was captured shortly after I told her who he was. He was tortured, then sent to a work camp."

"My mother never played you." I got up and dug into my backpack. I slapped the journal against his chest. "Here. Read it. *Then* tell me if you still think she was a fucking honey trap, you moron."

He stood there, staring at it in his hand as if it were some strange, alien object. Finally, he opened the pages.

I headed for my Red Bull, wishing I had something stronger. To realize that my mom had died for a misunderstanding—that her lover hadn't trusted that her feelings were real—was heartbreaking. Thinking himself betrayed, he'd behaved in kind. Like a reverse *Romeo and Juliet*.

It was just so damn sad. And made me so fucking angry.

I pounded my Red Bull while he read. At one point, he sat down. Well, his knees sort of buckled, and there was a chair behind him, so he ended up sitting. When he was finished, he closed the book and stared into space.

I didn't say anything, just gave him some time to process. Finally, I spoke. "She didn't play you."

"I knew when you told me your name," he said flatly. "I just didn't want to believe it."

"Yeah, she named me after where you two met."

His gaze swung to mine. "And she named you after me. My middle name. Mackenzie."

That was new information. I took another swig of my Red Bull, but it was empty.

"So now what do we do?" I asked.

"Weren't you going to kill me?"

I shrugged. "There's no point now. Your own insecurities killed her. Killing you would just be putting you out of your misery. Though don't think I'm not tempted." My anger was abating, an inch at a time. I'd read the journal, too. I couldn't kill him. Mom would never have wanted me to. She'd lived the life of a CIA agent. If she'd known why he'd done what he'd done, she probably would have understood.

"But it'd make you feel better."

I studied him. He was still pale, his face blank. But his eyes . . . his eyes were dead. Regret was a terrible thing, knowing you couldn't take back something you'd done. Living with his regret was more punishment than death would be.

"I don't think it would, actually," I said.

"Tell me about her. What was she like? As a mother?" There was an edge of desperate longing in the question that hurt to hear.

"She was an amazing mom," I answered. "She understood me, the way no one else did. I'm . . . different."

"I read your file. Asperger's?"

"Borderline. Mom was the one who helped me interpret and understand the world. They say that ninety-five percent of what you say is body language, and the remaining five percent are the actual words. I only understand that five percent. What other people take for granted in communicating is incredibly difficult for me to interpret. And half the time, I'm wrong. Over half, actually."

"But you're smart," he said. "I imagine you've taught yourself quite a bit over the years."

"I get along okay. Mom used to point out when I took things people said too literally. Humor and sarcasm are the hardest. She was funny. She made me laugh because I understood her humor." I paused, remembering. "She was proud of me, of how smart I was. She never made me feel as though I was the weird one. With her, I was normal. When she . . . was gone . . . I felt so alone."

Danvers was quiet for a while, thinking, I supposed. "This job . . . it turns you into the worst version of yourself. You become paranoid, sure that everyone is against you. You have to deal with the dregs of humanity, until you become so cynical and jaded . . . you end up betraying the very person who saved you."

He stood and walked to the window, his back to me as he looked out at the city. "When I met Kim, it felt as though God was finally smiling down on me. What else could explain a woman like her falling for someone like me? It was too good to be true, or so I believed at the time. How could anything—anyone—be so perfect? The times we had together were the happiest I'd ever been in my life. Happier than I'd ever even hoped to be."

His words were painful to hear. After reading the journal, I'd felt like I knew him through my mom's eyes. Now, listening to him speak of her, my anger melted away. I felt nothing but heartbreak at how something so beautiful had ended so tragically.

"I did beg her, you know," he continued, matter-of-fact. "I'd have done anything to be with her. When you find that kind of magic, losing it feels like ripping out your soul. Maybe that's why it was easier to believe that it had all been a lie, rather than facing the fact that she'd chosen someone else over me."

"She didn't choose someone else," I corrected him. "She chose her *children*. That's not the same thing. You loved who she was. If she'd abandoned her children, she wouldn't have been that person."

He turned to face me. "Logic has nothing to do with love. You can tell me she did the right thing—the moral thing—until you're blue in the face. It doesn't matter. The result was still the same. Someone else got her. Not me. Someone else got to have dinner with her every night, watch her eyes sparkle when she laughed. Sleep next to her in the same bed and kiss her in the morning. I was selfish. I didn't give a shit about her kids. I just wanted her."

It was enough to make my eyes start burning again. I blinked back the welling tears and cleared my throat. "I know my mom was happiest with you. For what it's worth, I wish things had turned out differently, too. And I have something for you to watch."

I keyed up Mom's video that I'd converted and stored on my laptop, then played it for Danvers. His eyes were glued to the screen, his gaze avid as he watched my mom speak. His jaw was clenched into tight bands, and his throat worked as he swallowed. I had the impression he wasn't a man who cried—ever—but was fighting that urge now.

When it was finished playing, I packed up the laptop and Mom's journal into my backpack. "Thank you," I said, "for coming. I needed an explanation. And closure. Perhaps you did, too."

"You haven't redeemed me," he said roughly. "If anything, you've condemned me."

"What do you mean?"

His gaze was stark. "Keep the money. I never spent a dime of it. Just didn't want it to end up in Chinese hands."

I blanched. "I don't want the money. What would I do with that much money?"

He shrugged. "I don't care. Consider it your inheritance. I can't bring Kim back, and I know you can never forgive me. But at least you can be comfortable. Travel the world if you want. Just stay out of North Korea, okay?"

Suddenly, I realized what he was *not* saying. "What are you going to do?"

"Atone."

Damn it. That's all I needed. Him killing himself. "No. That is *not* going to happen. You're the only parent I have left."

That took him aback and he didn't reply. Then my cell buzzed. I glanced at the screen.

"You're calling instead of breaking and entering? That's a switch."

"Smart-ass. I like it," Kade drawled. "And good work, by the way. We've got your twenty, and a team is headed your way to collect Danvers. We have a proposition for him."

I jumped to my feet. "What? What do you mean? You never said anything about that. I told you *I* was going to take care of it."

"Please," he scoffed. "Like you were going to kill your sperm donor in cold blood. I think the worst of people on a regular basis, and even I knew that wasn't going to happen."

"What are you going to do with him?"

"He has some things to answer for," Kade replied. "If he's smart, he'll take what I'm offering. If not, then he'll just disappear. See? Problem solved."

"But I don't want him to disappear." I rushed to the window and looked out, but saw nothing unusual. Well, it wasn't as if they were going to all wear matching neon shirts with CIA DEATH SQUAD printed on the front.

"Not your call, but I appreciate the input. Now just cooperate when they come to the door, and no one will get hurt. Should be about three minutes. Oh, and your buddies are there. Rooms 904 and 906. Adjoining. Ain't that sweet?" He ended the call.

I grabbed my backpack and shoved my feet into my Converses. "C'mon," I said. "We have to hurry."

Danvers didn't move.

I grabbed his arm and pulled. It was like trying to move granite. "C'mon!"

He shook his head. "You go. Or stay. It's me they want, not you."

"They can't have you." I was becoming frantic. The clock in my head said we'd lost more than a minute already, arguing.

"I'm not going." He was implacable. "He said he's offering something. Maybe I can still be useful. Maybe it'll be the last time I'll have to be useful."

I shoved my face into his. "You owe me," I gritted out. "So get your ass in gear. We've got to get out of here. I'm not ready to give you up yet. So chill on the whole martyr thing."

Life seemed to finally spark in his eyes. "Fine," he bit out. "What's our time?"

"With you screwing around, we're probably down to sixty seconds."

He growled out a curse. "They'll be covering the stairs and elevator. There's no way out."

What Kade had said came back to me in a flash. "Yes, there is. We go up."

"I said, they'll be covering the stairs."

"Out the window. I have a friend two floors directly above us. We just need to climb up."

"You say 'just,' I say, seven stories down to a splatter on the sidewalk."

"They're not getting you," I repeated, adamant. "So you can either watch me risk my life to get you to safety, or you can sit here on your ass and let them take you. Which is it gonna be?"

His eyes narrowed. "You're a lot like your mom."

"Thank you."

It took more precious seconds to open the window, then another to boost myself out. The railing wasn't a proper terrace, but purely for decoration. However, I could see that two floors above was an actual terrace. If I could just get there.

I stood, holding the window and trying to ignore the fact that concrete waited below. This wasn't safe. It was dangerous on the level of stupidity. I wasn't going to be able to make it, and they'd find me with my brain bashed in.

I started to hyperventilate, frozen with fear. Danvers poked his head out the window.

"Are you waiting for a rope? Because there isn't going to be one."

I gritted my teeth. It took a monumental effort of will, but I stretched up to grasp the lip of the concrete. I wasn't tall enough.

"Hold on," Danvers said. He put his hands on my butt and pushed.

I grabbed the lip and pulled, the muscles in my arms screaming. If I could just get a knee up, I could reach to the bottom of the next level's faux terrace.

Danvers was beside me, then ahead of me, making it look so damn easy. If I could have spared the breath, I'd have cussed.

He made it to the faux terrace and latched an arm through the grate, then reached down and easily swung me up next to him. I sucked in a deep breath, trying to calm my racing heart. The wind whipped my ponytail into my face. Danvers reached over and combed it out of the way. The look on his face was one I couldn't figure out. More than sad. Wistful, perhaps?

"One more," he said. "Let's go."

Yippee.

We repeated the procedure, this time without my nearly passing out from hyperventilating, and stood on the expansive terrace of some kind of suite. Of course it was a suite. Jackson wouldn't stay anywhere else.

Jackson.

Was he really in there? My heart leaped at the thought. It had been so long, and felt even longer. Would he be glad to see me? Why was he here, in New Orleans? Was it mere coincidence we were at the same hotel? Or had he known where I was and came here deliberately?

"What are we waiting for?" Danvers asked, yanking me out my thoughts. "Do you know these people or not?"

"No. I mean, yeah, I do." Taking a deep breath, I moved forward and knocked on the glass door. The curtain wasn't pulled, and I could see into the suite. I knocked again, louder.

Then I saw him.

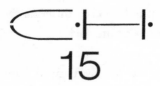

15

Clark took one look at the door and made a beeline for it, yanking it open and pulling me into his arms.

"Holy shit," he breathed. "Please tell me you did not do what I think you just did."

"Okay. I won't."

I hugged him hard. I'd missed him, missed his sarcastic sense of humor and cynical worldview. He was a lot like my dad—Danvers—come to think about it. Speaking of which . . .

I pulled away and turned. "Clark, this is Mark Danvers. Mark, this is—"

Clark slammed his fist into Mark's jaw.

"Oh my God! What are you doing?" I sprang between them, though it didn't look as though a fight was forthcoming. Mark was eyeing Clark warily, one hand rubbing his jaw. Clark was glaring at Mark with venom in his gaze, but didn't look like he was going to hit him again. "What the hell, Clark?"

"In case you've forgotten, he's the reason my brother was left behind in that hellhole for six years," Clark reminded me. He looked back at Mark. "Operation Gemini, remember?"

Mark nodded. "The information we got out of there helped us bring down Gaddafi. And helped the Israelis set Iran's nuke program back a decade."

"Good men lost their lives."

"Good men always do."

"Clark, who are you—" Jackson walked in the room. He stopped short when he saw me.

All the loneliness and despair I'd been fighting since I'd left rose up inside me. I'd been so stupid. My mom had been right. Some things only come along once in a lifetime, and I'd almost missed it. It might still be too late.

Jackson's expression had registered surprise, then relief. Now it was a politely blank mask. I was familiar with that mask. I often donned it as well. It was the I'm-really-not-hurting-I-swear mask.

I walked over to where he still stood, tipping my head back to look him in the eye. His gaze ran hungrily over my face before settling on my eyes.

"Is it too late?" I asked quietly. "Have I lost you?"

His Adam's apple bobbed as he swallowed, and when he spoke, his voice was rough with emotion. "You can never lose me."

He picked me up in his arms, and I wrapped mine around his neck, not minding the crushing hold he had on me. He buried his face in my neck, and I felt his chest hitch against mine.

"Don't leave me again," he whispered.

"I won't. I promise."

I would have gladly stayed like that forever, but then he spotted Danvers. Carefully setting me aside, he approached him. I braced myself to witness another punch, but he didn't.

"Do you remember me?" Jackson asked stiffly.

"Should I?"

"You held a gun to my head and made me blow the cover on those men."

Understanding dawned on Danvers. "Oh, you were that computer geek, right?"

"*Am* that computer geek," Jackson corrected.

"And China's with you? That sounds like a good match. And you're rich, right? I've seen you before, on magazine covers. The tech billionaire." He looked from Jackson to me, then back. "If you're asking permission to marry my daughter, permission granted. Take care of her the way she deserves. Get her out of this dangerous shit."

Before Jackson could respond, there was a sharp rap on the door. Before anyone could move, it was flung open.

A loud explosion. Blasting my eardrums and blinding me. Jackson dropped to the floor, covering my body with his. I strained to see, my vision still recovering. I could feel vibrations of feet on the floor. People were in the room.

The smoke cleared. Men with guns were taking my dad.

"No!" I pushed at Jackson, struggling to get up. "You can't take him!"

I was on my feet and rushed toward my dad, but Jackson caught me up in his arms. I fought him, yelling at the men.

"Stop! You don't have the authority to take him!"

They ignored me. Then through the uniformed men, I saw Kade. "You!" He glanced over, one dark eyebrow raised. "You lied to me."

He sauntered over. "I never lied to you. I ran across an opportunity for Danvers to redeem himself for his sins."

"What is it?"

"Well, his old buddies, the Chinese, are holding some Americans prisoner. A missionary and his family. Wife and three kids. Since they have a real ax to grind with your dad, we offered a trade."

"You can't do that," I said.

"Well, it's his decision, and if he has any soul left, he'll cooperate." He headed for the door.

"At least tell me where you're taking him so I can say goodbye," I called after him.

Kade turned around, considered, and said, "Alvin Callender Field. Oh-seven-hundred." His brow furrowed as he saw Jackson's arms wrapped around my waist. "So it's him, then, huh? I would've thought it'd go the other way." Then he was gone, along with the soldiers and Danvers.

"Oh my God. What am I going to do? I can't let him get sent to China." I glanced from Jackson to Clark.

"Don't look at me," Clark said. "I'm all for him getting sent to China. Or me killing him."

"No, you don't understand. He told me what happened." I explained everything he'd told me about his asset, Chen, and the child-trafficking ring. When I was finished, Jackson looked stunned. Clark, stricken.

"That's horrible," Jackson said, combing his fingers through my ponytail. "Are you okay?"

I shrugged and nodded. "It's awful, yes, but actually better than thinking he'd never loved her. I'm glad I know the truth. But I don't want to lose him now that I've found him. I know it sounds strange, but he's the only parent I have left."

"I'm not helping you save him." Clark's voice was hard. "He sent my brother to a fate worse than death, I don't give a shit about his reasons."

"I can't do it without you," I said.

"Then that's too bad."

I was angry. "After all you've done, *this* is where you draw the line? On helping my father? Your brother tried to kill me. Twice."

Clark flinched.

"China—" Jackson began.

"No." I cut him off. "This is between me and Clark."

"We'll negotiate," he persisted. "No one needs to get shot."

"I'm not talking about shooting anyone. But if we need to threaten force, Clark's our best bet." I couldn't let the love of my mother's life be taken and likely killed.

"What am I supposed to do? Take Danvers hostage?"

I looked at him.

"No." He shook his head. "I'm not doing this. I'm out, Mack." His gaze went from me to Jackson and back. "I'm out of all of it." He headed for the desk and began holstering his weapons that were sitting on the wood veneer.

"Give me a minute with him," I said to Jackson.

"Don't push it, China," he warned me. "I don't want you to regret it." But he still headed into the next room.

I watched Clark for a moment. "Is this your way of getting back at me?" I asked finally.

He finished checking the magazine for his weapon, rammed it home, and slid it into the back of his jeans. He tugged his shirt down over it and turned around. His eyes were as cold as I'd ever seen them.

"You're making this personal," he said.

"You did it first," I shot back. "It's personal why you won't help Danvers. Maybe it's not just because of the past, but also because of the present."

"Because you chose Jackson?" He shrugged. "It is what it is. Life goes on."

It was as though the Clark I'd known in my bed had disappeared, replaced by the man I'd first met months ago. It was physically painful to see him so withdrawn and guarded with me.

"I'm sorry," I said. "I'm so, so sorry. I love you, but I'm *in* love with Jackson. Being away from both of you made it clear to me who I can't live without. But I don't want to lose you. You're my friend. I—"

"Stop talking." His voice was sharp. I shut up. "Don't say anything else, Mack. In this case, more words only make it worse. Not better."

It was only with the greatest amount of self-control that I didn't take it all back. I hated seeing the Clark I knew be buried again. Would he remain there forever? Never again to see the light of day?

"For what it's worth," he said, "I don't blame you. I'm not a risk worth taking, trust me."

"That's not—"

"Shh." He reached out, one finger stroking my cheek. His eyes reminded me of Danvers's—full of pain. Leaning down, he slid my glasses off, then pressed his lips to mine.

It was a sweet kiss, even more heartbreaking for knowing it would be our last. He was leaving. I knew it.

When he lifted his head, tears were rolling down my cheeks. He looked pained.

"Please don't," he whispered. "That's not how I want to remember you."

I made a valiant effort, swiping my eyes with the back of my hands. I sniffed, an indelicate snort in the silence. But it made Clark's lips curve upward ever so slightly. He slid my glasses back on.

"Stay safe. Be happy. Don't take any shit from Coop."

I nodded, unable to speak. I watched him grab his leather jacket as he headed for the door. He paused and looked back once. I opened my mouth to beg him to come back, but it was too late. The door slammed shut behind him, and he was gone.

My knees gave out and I crumpled to the floor, sitting down hard on my ass. I stared at the door, expecting . . . I didn't know what. That he'd come back? Stroll in, flash a cocky grin, and say, "I got you good, Mack."

Jackson crouched down next to me. "Hey, babe." He gently grasped my chin and turned me toward him. Our eyes met. "It'll be okay. He'll be okay."

"How do you know?"

"Because I do." He took my hand and drew me to my feet.

"What are we going to do?" I asked. "I have money. All that money. Do you think they'd take it instead?"

"I don't know, but we'll try. Have you eaten anything today?"

I thought about it and glanced at my watch. It was after nine o'clock. "I can't remember." It hardly seemed like the same day, so much had happened. "I don't even know what day of the week it is."

"Now I *know* you've been living under a rock," he teased. "Why don't you go take a bath? I'll order room service. You need rest, too."

I was too tired—physically and emotionally—to argue. The bathtub was a porcelain, dual, old-fashioned, clawfoot slipper tub, and it was so deep, it took more than ten minutes to fill. But as I sank into the steaming water, I decided the wait had been worth it.

A few minutes later, there was a knock at the door, and Jackson came in. "Dinner's here," he said. "But it'll stay hot for a while." He backed out, but I called him.

"Care to join me?" I asked. "I've missed you."

He stripped and stepped into the tub. I turned around so I could lie between his legs and rest my back against his chest.

"How'd you two know where I was?" I asked.

"Clark's had people looking for you. He found you a few days ago. My people had found Danvers and saw when he caught a flight here."

I nodded. Neither development surprised me. It felt good to be in Jackson's arms again, and I took his arms and wrapped them around me. I could feel what the position was doing to him against my back. I closed my eyes, blocking out everything else except us. The feel of him, his strength surrounding me. He'd been steadfast, despite everything. He still loved me, and I'd nearly thrown it away.

"Thank you," I said.

"For what?" His voice in my ear sent a shiver through me.

"For waiting. For not giving up on me."

In response, he held me tighter. I appreciated that despite his obvious arousal, he wasn't trying to move things along. Social convention probably said that this would be a tasteless time to be intimate with someone.

I never was one for following social convention, even in the situations where I could decipher what it was.

I turned in his arms, careful of where I put my knees, and straddled his thighs. His cock lay between my legs, hard and ready. He was watching my eyes, taking a moment to brush back stray tendrils of damp hair loosened from my ponytail.

"I love you," I said.

His smile was brilliant. "What a coincidence, because I love you, too."

I positioned myself over him and slid down, letting his length slowly fill me. Our gazes were locked. When he was fully inside, I let out a gasp.

It didn't take long. We'd been apart for too many weeks for our first time back together to last longer than a few minutes. But I wasn't complaining.

Afterward, I rested, curled on his lap. The water was growing cold. Before I knew it, Jackson had stood and lifted me with him. I clung to his neck, curling as close as I could, the cold air giving me goose bumps.

Not just towels, but bath sheets. Jackson wrapped one around me and deposited me on the bed. I admired the view as he went to get himself a towel, then he set the room-service tray on the bed and climbed in with me.

I was ravenous. "What did you order?"

"A few different things," he said. "I wasn't sure where you were in your schedule."

Pizza, Chinese, pancakes, and roasted chicken. Dessert was Fig Newtons and a pot of hot tea. My eyes watered at his thoughtfulness.

"Thank you," I managed, leaning over to kiss him. His jaw was slightly roughened with whiskers, and I lingered over the kiss. It had been too long.

"How are you doing?" he asked, once we'd demolished a significant portion of the food.

I shrugged. "I'm okay. Better now." I sent him a small smile. "I want to go in the morning and see if there's anything I can do. I'm . . . sad . . . that Clark is gone. But I know it was probably for the best. Three's a crowd, right?"

"Yeah," he said. "But that doesn't mean you don't feel the loss."

I couldn't look at him, but he lightly gripped my chin and turned my gaze his way.

"I understand," he said. "I get it. You don't have to pretend it doesn't hurt."

I had to blink several times, but I nodded. "Thank you."

When we were finished eating, Jackson set the alarm and we curled up together under the sheets. I felt at peace—at home—for the first time since I'd had to leave my apartment. It occurred to me before I drifted off that the comfort of normalcy and familiarity wasn't just about being with my things, but being with my someone.

The sun was up, and it was already hot enough to make me sweat as we drove to the military airbase. It wasn't far, and when Jackson gave our names at the gate, we received an escort to a distant hangar by the farthest runway.

Kade was there when we parked and got out of the car.

"Where's the Reject?" he asked.

I gave him a withering look. "Clark had to leave. And don't call him that."

His lips twisted. "I expected you to go for the bad boy. Look at you, defying the cliché."

"I don't want to talk about it. Now where's my father?"

"He's inside. This way."

We started following him toward the hangar.

"I didn't realize US policy now consisted of trading our citizens to hostile countries to be killed," Jackson said, his tone one of casual inquiry.

"Danvers is an enemy of the state," Kade replied. "If he stays, he'll be tried for treason. Might as well get some use out of him."

Jackson nudged me and I stopped the retort on the tip of my tongue.

Inside the hangar, there were only a handful of people. The armed soldiers were gone, and only a few nondescript men in suits remained. Danvers was sitting alone, arms handcuffed behind his back. Kade led us to him.

"We're fresh out of Kleenex," Kade said, "so don't get weepy."

"You're really an asshole, you know that?" I snapped.

"So I've been told." He walked away.

"He's not wrong," Danvers said. "I stole that money so it wouldn't end up in Chinese hands. I defied orders."

"I don't care. I'm not letting you be taken into Chinese custody."

"It's okay," he said. "Just let it go. The family I'm being traded for deserves to come back. I'll take what's coming to me."

"We're going to offer the money," Jackson said. "In exchange."

"Hell, no," Danvers said. "You're going to undo what I did? I don't think so. Don't offer them a dime of that money."

"But—" I began.

"I mean it." It was the hard voice of authority.

I pressed my lips together. I felt powerless. I'd just found my father, and they were going to take him from me.

"I can't do this," I muttered, spinning on my heel and rushing away. I couldn't say goodbye. Spying Kade, I aimed for him.

"Please. Don't do this," I said once I'd reached him. He was sipping black coffee from a Styrofoam cup. "I want to offer them something else."

"What have you got?" he asked, raising one eyebrow.

I took a deep breath. "Me."

"Excuse me?"

"I'm the one responsible for blowing up their installation in the South China Sea. They'd want me, more than Danvers, I'm guessing. What do you say?"

"You'd do that? Offer to take his place? This man you just met. The man responsible for the death of your mother. Just so we're clear."

"Yes. My mother was in love with him. She wouldn't want him to die like that."

"She wouldn't want *you* to die like that," Kade retorted. "Nice try and a laudable effort, but no. I'm not handing you over to the fucking Chinese." He glanced at his watch. "Showtime."

He motioned to the only guard, who got Danvers up and moving. Jackson joined me and took my hand. I clutched it like a lifeline.

A small private jet sat outside. Two Chinese men emerged, followed by the family. The father was carrying the smallest child, who couldn't have been more than two. The mother looked wan and exhausted as she led the other two children by the hand. One was clutching a well-loved rabbit. When they reached the ground, one of the men stepped forward to meet Kade. Two of Kade's men in suits went forward and quickly escorted the family into the hangar.

"You have our package?" the man asked, his voice accented.

"Right behind me." Kade motioned to the guard next to Danvers.

The guard had his weapon out—a pistol—and gave Danvers a push. Something about the guard drew my eye. He seemed familiar . . .

Suddenly, Danvers was no longer handcuffed. He knocked the guard to the ground and grabbed his gun. A shot rang out and Jackson tackled me. I saw the Chinese delegation hit the deck, too.

More shots, but I couldn't see what was going on. I was terrified. Who was shooting?

It was over in seconds. Jackson gradually eased up. The Chinese had brought weapons. The two men were on the ground, and one of them didn't look like he'd be getting up soon, if ever again. There was a gun still in his hand.

On our side, two were down. The guard . . . and Danvers.

I got to him just as Kade did. "What a clusterfuck," Kade growled. "Where'd they get you?"

"Arm. Just a flesh wound. Hurts like hell."

"The plane is gassed up and ready. Don't let the door hit you on the ass. And I don't want to see your face again. If not for your daughter, I'd waste your ass. Lucky for you, she's served her country well. She's the reason—the only reason—I'm letting you go."

"Understood." Danvers got to his feet. He was holding his left arm awkwardly, but other than that, he seemed unharmed.

"What's going on?" I asked.

"An escape," he said. "The guard undid my handcuffs and told me to take advantage. So I did."

"Are you going to be okay? You're bleeding."

"I'll be fine. But I've gotta go. I'll be in touch." He gave me a quick kiss on the forehead, then was hurrying toward the plane. I watched as he climbed the stairs, which lifted and closed after him.

I stared, openmouthed. The Chinese had pulled their weapons when Danvers had pulled his escape maneuver. They'd shot and wounded him, but not badly. But he in turn had shot and mortally wounded them. What about the guard?

"China."

I turned at Jackson's voice. There was something wrong with how he'd said my name . . .

He was kneeling next to the guard, who was still lying on the ground. The guard's hat had fallen off, his camo uniform making him ubiquitous on a base full of identically clad men. But as I grew closer, I realized why he'd seemed familiar.

"Clark!"

I ran, dropping to my knees next to him. There was blood on his uniform. Jackson was pressing his hands against a wound in his chest. Clark's eyes were closed.

I barely heard the plane behind me taxi away. All I could see was Clark's blood.

"Oh my God, oh my God," I kept repeating, over and over. In the distance, I heard sirens.

"Press here," Jackson directed, grabbing my hand and placing it over another wound in his chest. The uniform was so bulky, I couldn't tell exactly where he'd been hit. "Harder."

My hands shook, but I obeyed, pressing down on the blood pulsing from his body with every heartbeat. Clark was going to die. No one could bleed this much and *not* die.

"Mack . . ."

The word was barely audible. I jerked my head up. Clark's eyes were barely open, but he was looking at me.

"You weren't supposed to be here," I said, my voice a strained whisper.

"Couldn't do it," he managed. "Couldn't tell you no after all. How 'bout that?"

"I was wrong," I babbled, choking back tears. "I should never have asked that of you."

"'s not your fault." His eyes drifted closed again.

I was sobbing so hard, everything was a blur. Somehow, he lifted his hand and rested it on my back.

"C'mere," he breathed.

Obediently, I bent closer so I could hear him.

"I . . . love you, Mack. It was worth it. Remember."

Panic clawed at me. This was my nightmare come to horrifying life. Clark's blood on my hands, literally and figuratively. Him dying in my arms while I was helpless.

"Please don't die. Please. You can't die."

But he didn't respond. His eyes were closed again.

Then the paramedics were there, and Kade was directing them to Clark. Jackson and I were unceremoniously shoved out of the way. In minutes, they had him in the back of the ambulance, and it was speeding away.

I whirled and latched onto Jackson. "We have to go with him. He can't be alone."

The look on his face held both sadness and pity. He didn't answer.

"No!" I yelled. "No! He is *not* dead. Not Clark." I was sobbing again, so hard, I couldn't breathe. My hands were wet, and Clark's blood, it was all over me and Jackson.

"Get her out of here," Kade said harshly.

"No! We can't leave him. Please," I begged Jackson. "Please, let's go to him." I wasn't making sense even to me, but I couldn't leave.

"We have to go," he said.

I fought him, but I was crying and couldn't get away. Finally, he picked me up, cradling me to his chest and shushing me. He walked with me to our sedan. By then, I'd quieted. I was numb. Shock, I realized. Jackson put me in the car and got behind the wheel.

I couldn't face what had just happened. I curled into my seat and closed my eyes. I wanted to sleep. In sleep, I wouldn't have to think about it, wouldn't have to feel the sticky blood on my hands.

I woke lying on a bed. I sat straight up, panic coursing through me.

"It's okay. You're okay."

Jackson. He moved from a chair to sit on the side of the bed. We were back in the hotel room. I looked around, confused. It was still light outside, the bright sunlight of midday blazing in the sky.

"It's okay," Jackson said, gently pushing me back onto the bed. His face was grim, the lines around his mouth and eyes deeper.

I was naked but wrapped in a thick robe with the RITZ CARLTON embroidered on the left chest. My hair had been brushed out, too.

Looking up at him, I suddenly remembered all that had happened. I felt the tears coming, so I turned my face into the pillow. Jackson gathered me up in his arms, shifting me onto his lap. I curled against him, wetting his shirt like a crybaby.

"Have you heard anything?" I sniffed.

"He's in surgery. That's the last I heard."

"And Danvers?"

"His plane went down somewhere over Tahoe."

I sucked in a breath. "Is he—?"

"I don't know. He may have bailed. They're searching for the wreckage now." Jackson held me tighter. "Don't give up hope."

I closed my now-dry eyes. I was all cried out. My emotions were numb.

"You were right," I whispered. "I pushed Clark. And look what happened."

"It's not your fault. He's a grown man. It was his decision."

"No, I told him he was just trying to get back at me. He wouldn't be fighting for his life if I had just accepted his decision."

The hotel phone rang and Jackson answered it.

"Yes . . . I see." His gaze moved to mine. "Yes, I'll tell her. Thanks for letting us know." He cradled the receiver and turned to me. He took my hands in his. I suddenly went cold all over.

"Which—" I began.

"Sweetheart, I'm so sorry. Clark . . ."

I yanked my hands from his and covered my face. This couldn't be happening. Just a few hours ago, I'd been hugging Clark. Now . . . he was gone. It wasn't possible.

But if anyone knew how quickly death could snatch a loved one, it was me.

I lay down on the bed and rolled away from Jackson. I was so tired. I stared at the wall as he lay down next to me and pulled the covers up over us. He didn't try to talk to me. He just slung an arm over my waist and pulled me close.

We lay there for a long time until, at last, I fell into a troubled sleep.

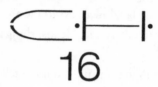

16

It was an unusually cool August day when Clark Slattery was laid to rest in Arlington National Cemetery. I wore a sleeveless black dress and black flats, my hair in its usual ponytail. Jackson was next to me in a black suit. We both wore sunglasses to shield our eyes from the brightness outside.

We weren't the only attendees. Those from Vigilance who'd known him were also there, as well as a few people who showed he'd had an . . . eclectic . . . set of acquaintances.

The flag-draped coffin sent a chill through me. I jumped with each shot of the gun salute. The playing of "Taps" made tears roll down my cheeks, the sound made even more lonely and haunting drifting over the hills and trees of Arlington. My consolation was that Clark wouldn't be alone—he was surrounded by those who'd come before.

The flag was folded the requisite thirteen times, and to my surprise, the officer presented it to me.

"He wanted you to have it, ma'am," he said. "And these." He deposited Clark's dog tags on top of the flag. "Our country thanks you for your sacrifice."

I couldn't speak past the lump in my throat, so I just nodded. I'd wanted to see Clark one more time, but his coffin had been closed, per his wishes. I wasn't sure I wanted my last view of Clark to be of his empty shell anyway.

Then it was over, and it had been a blur of pain and sadness and tears. Several people from Vigilance murmured words of condolences and shook my hand. Jackson stood by my side the whole time, speaking when I couldn't and being the strength I so desperately needed. He seemed to know when my knees grew weak, sliding an arm around my back to lend support until it passed.

Finally, it was just the coffin and us. The sky had clouded over. Rain was coming. But I couldn't go, not yet.

"Can I have a moment?" I asked him.

"Of course." He kissed me lightly and I handed him the flag. "I'll wait in the car," he said.

I watched him walk away, then turned toward the ebony coffin.

"Goodbyes," I said. "I've never been good at them. Most I've had to say have come too soon." I placed a hand on the cool, smooth surface. "I wasn't ready to say goodbye to you. You were my friend. My *best* friend. The only normal friend I've ever had who understood me." I paused. "And of course, the sex was amazing." I smiled, thinking of how Clark would've preened at that, though he'd pretend not to. My smile faded.

"I'm sorry for hurting you. That I couldn't give you what you needed. I thought maybe I could, but then I realized, that wasn't fair to you or me. You deserved someone who was in love with you, not someone who stayed just because you needed them. I just wish you could've found your happy ever after before—" My throat filled and I couldn't go on.

"I hope that you're happy, and at peace, where you are now."

Leaning over, I pressed my lips to the coffin lid, about where I imagined his face would be. When I stepped back, I slid off my glasses and placed them carefully on the lid, and draped his dog tags around my neck.

"Goodbye, Clark."

A steady drizzle had started now, and I picked my way carefully to the car, everything a bit blurry, so I was glad it wasn't far. By the time I'd settled inside, the drizzle had become a gentle pour. No thunder or lightning, just the falling water. I couldn't help but think it was a cleansing rain, washing away the past.

As we drove out of the cemetery, passing endless rows of white stones, the sun filtered through the clouds.

"Look," Jackson said, pointing.

There was a rainbow, the brightest I'd ever seen, up ahead. I glanced at Jackson.

"You know I don't believe in superstition," I said. "Rainbows are just refracted light under the right meteorological circumstance. It doesn't portend anything."

He just smiled. "Of course not. It couldn't possibly be anything else."

I narrowed my eyes, his gentle teasing not going unnoticed, then I looked back at the rainbow. It *was* very pretty. And nicely timed. It made my heart lift just looking at it.

Something I'm sure Clark would have known.

◆　◆　◆

"Attending your own funeral? And I thought *I* was a narcissist."

Clark glanced over at Kade, standing nearby with a black umbrella. "It's not often someone gets the opportunity." He motioned to the umbrella. "Did you happen to bring another one of those?"

"Nah. Besides, it'd detract from the moment if you weren't standing in the rain, looking at your own coffin."

Clark rolled his eyes. "So I'm officially dead, then?"

"Yep. Complete with a death certificate." He eyed Clark. "It was your choice, you know."

"I know. It's the right thing. I just hate hurting her."

"Think of it as closure. Now she can ride off into the sunset with her white knight and won't have to worry about that heart she broke one time."

Clark knew he was right, but still. It had been harder than he thought it would be, watching her cry over him. When she'd put the dog tags on, his own throat had closed up, and he'd had to blink a few times.

"Once you're done with physical therapy and are given a clean bill of health, we'll talk about your new career," Kade said. He handed him a card. "Call me when you're ready."

Clark pocketed the card, not seeing as Kade melted away into the gathering rain. He was watching China as she got into the black sedan. He knew it would be the last time he'd ever let himself see her. If she ever found out he *wasn't* dead, it would throw her whole life into chaos—and she'd probably kill him herself for putting her through this.

Clark wasn't a praying man, but he closed his eyes and thought a few things that he hoped would come true. Perhaps that was a poor man's prayer. He hoped she was happy with Jackson. He hoped she found peace and acceptance in her life with him. He hoped she had lots of little Chinas, just like her. He hoped nothing bad ever again caused her tears and pain. He hoped all of these things as hard as he could.

When he opened his eyes, the rain was letting up slightly, and everyone had gone. Even the sedan was out of sight. As he stepped from behind the tree, something caught his eye.

A rainbow, beautiful and bright, painted the sky in front of him. He paused, taking a moment to appreciate its perfection, and he wondered if maybe, just maybe, his prayer had been heard.

He walked to the empty coffin. Picking up the wet glasses China had left, he carefully folded them and slipped them inside his jacket pocket. Turning, he headed in the opposite direction of the rainbow, into the clouds and oncoming storm.

Epilogue

"This itches," I complained. "And I can't see."

"It's a *veil*," Mia said with exasperation. "It's not supposed to be comfortable."

The lace got in my mouth and I blew air, spitting it out. "It's really irritating."

"Too bad." Mia was implacable. "And stop licking your lips. Your lipstick is going to come off."

Okay, so I'd heard of bridezillas. But what did you call the niece of the bride who was cracking the whip on a smoky eye, nude lipstick, and an updo that was crafted so beautifully—and hairsprayed so heavily—that I was afraid to stand too near an open flame?

"Honey, have a mint julep."

I'd lost track of how many mint juleps Grams had drunk, but this time, I accepted her offer. Twenty minutes until showtime.

I took a swig of the amber liquid, and promptly coughed for ten straight seconds.

"Grams! Now her eyes are watering! I have to redo her makeup." Mia's indignant outburst was followed by a removal of the hated veil and a careful reapplication of some kind of makeup on my eyes that involved no less than three different brushes.

The veil was reapplied and fussed with until Mia was satisfied.

"Okay! You can look now."

I got up from the chair, once again grateful that I'd held the line on not wearing heels. Instead, I had a white pair of Converses that Mia had glammed up with lace and glitter. I thought they'd look ridiculous when she'd told me what she was going to do, but instead they'd turned out rather pretty.

I held my breath as I walked to the full-length mirror, hoping Mia's magic had worked to transform me into a beautiful bride. When I saw my reflection, my breath came out in a rush.

"Wow," I breathed.

I looked . . . perfect. My dark hair was a stark contrast to the white of my dress and veil. The dress itself was simple. Sleeveless with a sweetheart neckline, it showed my shoulders, arms, and a classy amount of cleavage. I was suddenly glad that Mia had insisted on taking me tanning for the past two weeks (despite my quoting statistics to her about the correlation between skin cancer and tanning beds).

The dress was formfitting satin with tiny jewels nestled among the folds of fabric wrapped around me, so when the light hit, I sparkled. An attached train of yards of delicate lace stretched behind me, matching my veil. In my hair, Mia had woven more jewels similar to the ones on my gown. The dog tags I wore that were hidden inside my neckline didn't exactly go with the dress, but no one had said a word about my taking them off.

"Oh, honey," Grams said with a teary smile, "you look just beautiful."

"That's not the mint juleps talking, is it?" I teased.

She laughed. "Your man is going to be speechless." She sidled a bit closer. "Now I know you're probably nervous about tonight. I just want you to remember that the first time may twinge a bit, and depending on his size, it may look like he isn't gonna fit. But I can assure you—"

"Stop!" Mia and I spoke at the same time.

"Um, I'm good, Grams," I said, my cheeks burning. "You know, there's books and . . . stuff." Now wasn't the time to tell her that the white dress was due to custom rather than a testament to the state of my hymen.

"I just want you to be prepared," she said. "On my wedding night, your granddad ended up chasing me around the room with that thing because I was positive that it couldn't be done." She winked at me. "Your granddad was generously endowed, you know."

"Nope. No. Didn't know that. Didn't need to either, Grams."

"I'm just saying, I was a lucky woman."

Mia was choking back her laughter at my dismay. She was no help at all.

"And don't even think of letting him anywhere near the back door. One time—"

"Where's Bonnie?" I blurted out, desperate to stop Grams's reminiscing.

There was a knock on the door. Mia opened it a crack and peered through—she'd been adamant about the groom not seeing the bride— and opened it enough for Bonnie to slip inside.

She saw me and squealed. "Oh my God, you look amazing!"

"Thank you, but *get dressed*! The wedding is in ten minutes!" She was my bridesmaid, Mia my maid of honor. Mia was already wearing her gown, a dress similar in style to mine, but with a skirt ending below the knee. Her color was scarlet. Bonnie's was a deep blue. Each color suited them the best.

Grams was walking me down the aisle, and she wore a champagne-colored skirt and blouse with a matching jacket. The jacket had fancy embroidery that she said her friend Marjorie had added to "jazz it up."

"I'm hurrying," Bonnie said. "I had to check on the hors d'oeuvres. I'm not sure those chicken kebabs were a good idea."

I winced. Bonnie had insisted on catering the reception, despite her lack of experience and, well, culinary skill. Jackson had agreed, but had quietly hired other chefs disguised as waitstaff and kitchen help to fix whatever Bonnie messed up. Of course, she didn't know this, and I wasn't about to tell her. Instead, I pasted on my smile.

"I'm sure they'll be great."

Another knock on the door, and this time it was the wedding planner, though it was difficult to see him past the massive arrangement of white roses he was carrying.

"A delivery for the bride," he said.

Grams and Mia managed between the two of them to set the arrangement on a table. I counted the roses. Two dozen.

"Here's the card," Mia said.

I opened it and read.

One for every year I've missed.

I'm sorry I can't make the wedding, but I'll be in touch. Maybe we can meet sometime. If you'd want that.

—Mark

Danvers. He'd survived. They'd searched the wreckage when they were finally able to get to it, but it had been in a heavily wooded area. There wasn't a body, but it had been assumed that wildlife had taken care of that. But they'd been wrong. Somehow, in the middle of nowhere, he'd made it out.

I smiled. Yes. Yes, I'd like to get to know my father, would like to know the man my mom had loved so much.

Ten minutes later, we were all as ready as we were going to be. Bonnie and Mia helped with my train as we walked down the narrow hallway of the tiny chapel the wedding planner had found in Upstate New York. The church only held fifty people, but that was okay. Not many were invited to the actual wedding. Those "five hundred closest friends" would be at the reception we were having later tonight.

I could hear the pianist playing behind the closed vestibule doors, and I took a deep breath.

"Grams," Mia said sharply. She motioned to the glass Grams was still carrying.

"Oh yes," she said. Glancing around, Grams emptied the rest of her mint julep into a nearby potted plant. "There we go. Here, honey." She handed the glass to the wedding planner, who must've seen it all, because he took it without batting an eye.

"Good luck," Bonnie said. "You're beautiful." She kissed me lightly on the cheek. The planner handed her a bouquet and sent her down the aisle, carefully keeping me out of sight.

Mia was next. "I love you, Aunt Chi," she whispered.

"I love you, too." I hugged her, even though the planner started fussing over my train.

Her eyes misted. "Don't make me cry! I'll look like a raccoon." She received her flowers, and down the aisle she went.

Grams looked at me. "You sure about this, honey? With all that money you got now, we can turn around and skip town if you want. Head to Vegas. We could be hitting the slot machines by dinner."

"Grams, you know the odds of winning at slots are—"

"I do know, but that doesn't mean I don't like pressing those buttons."

I grinned. "Yes, Grams. I'm sure. Jackson's the one."

It had been a whirlwind two months, but the October wedding was perfect. Today was a beautifully crisp fall day, and the trees surrounding the tiny chapel were all shades of gold, red, and orange. The white church nestled among them looked like something from a Thomas Kincaid painting. And my husband-to-be was waiting for me at the altar.

The planner smiled as he handed me my bouquet. "It's time."

I took Gram's arm and a deep breath, then nodded.

He opened the doors, and I saw the rows filled with people. Anxiety suddenly hit as they all stood, everyone staring at me. I froze.

Then, like a beacon, there was Jackson. He stood in the center at the end of the aisle, and the look on his face was one I could only describe as adoration. Everyone else melted away, and my anxiety, too. I smiled. He smiled back. And I took my first step.

They threw the traditional rice for us as we left the chapel, though we got into a nontraditional helicopter. Chartered limousines would take the guests to the reception, but Jackson had said he wanted to give me my wedding gift first.

"But I didn't get you anything," I'd said. "I didn't realize it was customary for the bride and groom to exchange gifts." None of the books or magazines I'd read had mentioned this.

"It's kind of for both of us," he'd said, then had refused to discuss it further.

Now I watched out the window, trying to figure out where in the world we were going. Everything looked so much different from up here. It wasn't until the pilot had set us down on an expansive lawn that I realized where we were.

"Why are we stopping to see Harrison Cummings?" I asked as he helped me down from the chopper. The last time we'd been here, I'd thrown up in the guest bathroom.

"I wanted to give you your present," he said, taking my hand and leading me across the lawn.

I still didn't understand, not until we stood on the front step of the massive Tudor mansion and he dangled a set of keys in front of me. My eyes widened.

"Really?"

He nodded, grinning. "You said it was your dream home, right?"

"Yes, but . . . how?"

"I made him an offer he couldn't refuse," he said, mimicking *The Godfather*. "All the furniture, too. Though we can always redecorate, if you want."

"No! I love it just the way it is."

"Then unlock the door so I can carry you across the threshold, Mrs. Cooper."

And that's just what we did.

ACKNOWLEDGMENTS

This book has been the most difficult I've ever written, since it was during the most heartbreaking time of my life. I sincerely hope the book has lived up to your, the reader's, expectations for this series. I've enjoyed introducing you to China, Jackson, and Clark and their adventures. I hope you've enjoyed the journey, too. (P.S. Look for Clark in his own series in 2018.)

So many wonderful people helped me in the writing of this book. From plotting sessions, to encouraging phone calls, to telling me that no, I really don't suck.

Thank you to my Snow Angels for encouraging me, checking on me, and generally just making me feel I had a purpose to get out of bed each day and open up my laptop to write. I love you all.

Many thanks to Mary Burton and Melinda Leigh for helping with plotting and character motivation. Mary, you're simply amazing. Thank you for boiling it down to one question. And Melinda . . . I'm sorry I couldn't kill him! You're tougher than I am. I'm guessing it's the Jersey thing.

To my unfailing and faithful friends who listened to me whine and cry and throw pity parties. For sending me wine and notes of love and encouragement. I simply could not have finished this book—or gotten through the past six months—without you. Tracy Brogan, Marina

Adair, Nancy Naigle, Cathy Bybee, Momma Vey, Leslie Thompson, Jen May, Lisa Rockers, Raydeen Graffam, and Jill Sanders. Thank you, Mary, for a very well-timed trip to Florence. Getting away was so good for me. I appreciate your generosity so much.

Thank you, Jessica Poore, for not only crash-reading this manuscript for me, but for all you've done over the years I've been with Montlake. You put your heart into your job, into your authors, and it shows. I love you dearly.

Maria Gomez, thank you for being the absolute best (and patient) editor any author could wish for. It's been an absolute pleasure to work with you over the course of eleven novels and three series. Your laugh is pure joy. And you should give a class on how to critique without ruffling authors' fragile feathers. I always come away from a critique with you feeling more energized and excited about all the stuff I need to change. A rare talent, indeed!

Melody . . . what am I going to do without you?! You have been the woman behind my curtain, making everything I write so much better. I dreaded getting those edits, but I always knew the pain was worth the final product. Thank you for your patience as I've struggled with this manuscript. I know it's good when you tell me it is.

For my wonderful daughters, who've listened to me whine and moan about this manuscript, put up with me being awake at all hours trying to finish, and eventually stopped asking me, "How many more words, Mom?" after the fourth or fifth glare. I love you both to the moon and back.

My agent, Kevan Lyon—thank you for running interference, for being my cheerleader, for your patience and your advice. Thanks for being the sympathetic ear when I needed to cry and going to bat for me when I needed just a little more time. And a little more. And a little more. I'm lucky indeed to have you on my team.

Thank you to Montlake Romance and the APub family. It's been a pleasure to work with all of you over the years. I've said it before and I'll say it again, Montlake changed my life, and I'm so glad it did. Fifteen books we've done together, and I'm proud of each and every one. I hope you are, too.

Last, thank you to M. G. So much of my sadness is in this book—tragedy and heartbreak—but beautiful moments, too. Focus on the beauty, for it remains, even when it's beyond reach. Or, as you might say, "And yet, life goes on." And, oh yes, one more thing: table.

AUTHOR BIO

Photo © 2014 Karen Lynn

Tiffany Snow is the author of *Follow Me*, *Break Me*, and *Find Me* in the Corrupted Hearts Series; she is also the author of the Tangled Ivy Trilogy and the Kathleen Turner Series. Tiffany has been reading romance novels since she was too young to be reading romance novels. Born and raised in Saint Louis, she attended the University of Missouri in Columbia, earning degrees in history and social studies. Later she worked as an information-technology instructor and consultant. At last, she now has her dream job: writing novels full-time. Mother to two wonderful daughters, Tiffany makes her home in Kansas City, Missouri. Visit her website, www.tiffany-snow.com, to keep up with her latest projects.